MIDNIGHT CRAVINGS

Eve sat up and climbed out of bed. A few steps and she found herself in the hallway . . . outside Linc's door.

Now what?

She was going to knock, that's what. And then she was going to go inside. And then she was going to tell him that she couldn't stop thinking about him . . .

"Can't sleep?"

She whirled around to find Linc standing in the doorway that led to the kitchen. The sight of him wearing nothing but a pair of snug, faded jeans stalled her heart for a long moment.

"Hungry?" he asked.

"In the worst way."

ALSO BY KIMBERLY RAYE

Sometimes Naughty, Sometimes Nice
Kiss Me Once, Kiss Me Twice

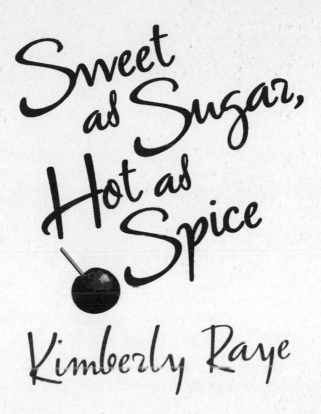

Sweet as Sugar, Hot as Spice

Kimberly Raye

WARNER
FOREVER

NEW YORK   BOSTON

ISBN 0-7394-5706-3

Warner Forever is a registered trademark of Warner Books.

Cover art and design by Shasti O'Leary Soudant
Book design by Giorgetta Bell McRee

Warner Books

Time Warner Book Group
1271 Avenue of the Americas
New York, NY 10020

Printed in the United States of America

For James and Estella Adams,
Thanks for being such wonderful parents.
I love you both with all of my heart!

Sweet as Sugar, Hot as Spice

Acknowledgments

I would like to acknowledge the people in my life who helped keep me sane during the writing of this book. A great writer and an even better friend, Nina Bangs, for answering her telephone every time I needed to angst and whine and angst and complain and . . . did I say angst? My agent, Natasha Kern, for knowing so much more than I ever could about the crazy business of publishing. My husband, Curt Groff, for being such a whiz with computers and an all-around sexy guy. And my editor, Melanie Murray, for her continued faith in the Farrel sisters and their over-the-top mother. Thanks from deep in the heart!

Chapter 1

She was totally screwed.

The truth struck Eve Farrel as she stood beneath the blazing spotlights near center stage and listened to her youngest sister vow to "love, honor, and cherish . . ."

This revelation had nothing to do with the fact that she was wearing a floor-length, yellow tulle dress and matching satin pumps in front of both a live audience and several million dedicated *Get Sexed Up!* home viewers. It had everything to do with her mother, the show's host, and, like Eve, an unwilling witness to the ceremony being broadcast in the name of ratings.

Jacqueline Farrel sat in the front row and stared at Eve as if she were the last pair of Anne Klein slingbacks at a Macy's half-off sale.

Make that a very bright, peppy, vibrant, *yellow* pair of slingbacks.

Okay, so maybe the getup had just a little to do with the sick feeling in the pit of Eve's stomach. She didn't do bright or peppy. Rather, she lived in black, from her thigh-high patent-leather boots and her favorite tight, skimpy leather miniskirt, to the thick layer of eyeliner usually rimming her eyes. Black said bold, bad, *wild*.

Even more, her mother hated black.

Which was why it had become Eve's signature color at the age of fourteen when she'd dyed her platinum hair Clairol's Raven No. 102—just an hour before the family's annual Christmas picture. Jacqueline had turned the same shade of red caused by her severe allergic reaction to shellfish. Then she'd rushed off in a huff to rethink her decision to have children in the first place, unintentionally giving her daughter some much-needed space.

Eve had been shocking her mother ever since.

Up until last year, that is, when her older sister, Skye, had one-upped Eve by doing the unthinkable—she'd waltzed down the aisle with the hottest NASCAR driver to ever do a Pep Boys commercial. Now her younger sister, Xandra, was smiling and exchanging platinum wedding bands with her significant other on national television.

Xandra had planned to hold the ceremony at a hotel in Houston, but then the producers of *Get Sexed Up!* had approached her with an offer she couldn't refuse. The "Smart Dating" segment they had recently aired, which featured Jacqueline giving dating advice to single women, had been so successful that several of the participants had not only nabbed a boyfriend, but were on their way to the altar. The producers had asked Xandra and her fiancé, Beau, to take part in the show's Valentine's Day special—a reality multiple wedding, complete with an in-studio ceremony and a complimentary reception at the posh Beverly Hills Hotel. Xandra had agreed because it would guarantee her mother's presence on the most important day in her life.

Jacqueline Farrel was the show's host, after all. Contractually, she *had* to attend, even if it went against her entire philosophy—namely that marriage was the worst evil, second only to a terminal illness. Lasting relationships weren't built on a flimsy piece of paper but a solid foundation of shared interests, mutual respect, and great sex—her infamous Holy Commitment Trinity. Despite great effort, however, she'd obviously failed to enlighten two of her three offspring. But all hope was not lost. She still had one single daughter left to save the Farrel name and serve as a shining example to Womanists everywhere. She had Eve.

And Eve had a migraine the size of Paris Hilton's ego.

She was screwed, all right.

The floor tilted just enough to make her sway. Sweat beaded on her upper lip. Her hands went damp, and she had to readjust her grip on the heavy bridesmaid's bouquet.

Geez, it was hot. And stuffy. And bright.

She blinked away the tiny black dots dancing in front of her eyes and swallowed against a rising wave of nausea.

"Are you all right?" The whispered question came from the woman who stood just to Eve's left. Skye Farrel-MacAllister was the matron of honor and the expectant mother of twins.

"I'm fine." Eve swallowed again as reality weighed down on her: Skye, her older sister and the one everyone had expected to follow in Jacqueline's footsteps, was happily *married,* of all things, *and* having twin boys. Not so long ago, Skye hadn't been able to keep a boyfriend long enough to add his name to her electric bill, much less start a family.

"You don't look fine," Skye said beneath her breath as the exchange of rings finished and the minister declared, "What God hath joined together . . ."

Skye caught Eve's trembling hand in a gesture that looked like an older sibling's sign of affection, and not the subtle but crystal-clear *Screw this up now, and I'll kick your ass* warning it truly was. Obviously, Skye put nothing past rowdy, rebellious Eve, who'd long ago developed a reputation for acting on impulse.

But this wasn't an impromptu road trip to Mexico. Or a mud-wrestling match at a local sports bar. Or karaoke night at her favorite club.

This was her baby sister's wedding, and she was going to behave herself. Which meant she *wasn't* bolting for the nearest exit.

"You look like you're going to throw up," Skye added.

Big Brother had nothing on Big Sister.

"I'm fine." Eve swallowed and cleared her throat. "Really." She drew a deep breath and gave her older sister a reassuring squeeze before disengaging her fingers.

Pulling her shoulders back, she clutched her monstrous bouquet of yellow roses, buttercups, and daffodils stem-wrapped in ribbon and sweetheart lace. Lace that matched the trim on her dress. Which matched the color of the bunting draped around the set. Which matched the giant satin bows marking each row of chairs. Which matched the hue of the daisy petals sprinkled down every aisle.

". . . Marriage is a joyous union that marks the beginning of a new life together . . . ," the minister's voice droned on.

A drop of sweat tickled its way down Eve's right temple. The razor burn under her arms prickled.

". . . by the power vested in me . . ."

She blew out a deep breath and inhaled again. Her nostrils burned with the sickeningly sweet scent of flowers coupled with the half gallon of perfume the wedding coordinator had spritzed her with prior to the walk down the studio aisle. Her stomach pitched and rolled.

". . . I pronounce you man and wife . . ."

Get it together, Eve told herself. *Now.*

She hadn't made a huge name for herself in the erotic video market by upchucking every time a difficult situation arose.

She was *Eve Farrel,* for heaven's sake.

The ballsy, headstrong producer and owner of Sugar & Spice Sinema, the fastest-growing production company in L.A. and the only one that specialized in how-to sex videos for couples. Her life was one crisis after another. She worked with temperamental actors and actresses. She endured the endless pressure caused by tight production schedules and small budgets. She dealt with know-it-all cameramen and clueless production assistants and snotty set caterers who couldn't tell a blueberry bagel from a cinnamon-raisin.

". . . And now let us seal this blessed union with a kiss . . ."

She was *not* going to throw up, despite the hot lights and the horrible dress and the overwhelming smell and her mother's adoring stare.

Rather, she was going to paste a smile on her face and make it through the few minutes it would take to waltz back up the aisle. Then she was going to head for the reception like the headstrong, confident, capable woman she was. And then she was going to do what any headstrong, confident, capable woman would do in her present situation.

She was going to drink.

Heavily.

Three hours later, after an endless stream of pictures, a question-and-answer session with several local radio shows, and an interview for *Entertainment Tonight*—they weren't about to miss out on the biggest reality event of the year—Eve finally walked into the Crystal Ballroom of the Beverly Hills Hotel.

The reception was already in full swing, the room packed with guests. The live band belted out Kool & the Gang's classic "Celebration" for a dance floor overflowing with people. Uniformed waiters squeezed this way and that, carrying silver serving trays laden with everything from cold shrimp to hot meatballs to champagne. Long, tapered white candles sat in polished gold candelabra and flickered from the center of each round banquet table. The tables themselves, draped in crisp white linen, were lavishly set with gold-etched china and sparkling crystal. Large sprays of yellow flowers filled every nook and cranny. Several sets of French doors opened out into a garden filled with more tables and flowers and people.

The place was bursting at the seams.

Thankfully.

While Eve would have given her right eye—her throbbing eye, thanks to the headache from hell—for some peace and quiet, chaos was preferable at the moment. The more people, the easier it would be to steer clear of her mother.

Or so she hoped.

She retrieved a frozen margarita from the bar, bypassed the seats reserved for the wedding party, and headed for a table in the farthest corner of the ballroom.

Eve had just downed half the icy drink and slid off her shoes when a six-foot-plus, sometimes green-eyed, sometimes blue-eyed woman—depending on her contact supply—collapsed into the seat next to her.

"I am *so* glad you invited me," Trina Carlington declared in the breathless, excited voice she used for the "Call now to meet sexy singles in your area, and you could hook up with me" late-night radio spots she recorded for a local Top 40 station in her spare time. She spent the rest of her time as chief marketing director for Sugar & Spice Sinema. Trina could sell *anything*.

A former *Playboy* playmate, she'd played it smart by banking her money and using it to put herself through school. She'd since earned a degree from Stanford University, interned with the prestigious Bart & Baxter ad agency, and could boast an impressive list of measurements, thanks to L.A.'s leading plastic surgeons. She currently wore a slinky, strappy red dress that clung to her shapely body and made even Eve—who had more than her own share of curves, thanks to Mother Nature—slightly envious.

"Weddings aren't usually my thing." Trina pulled out a mirrored tube from her gold Fendi bag and retouched her flaming red lipstick. "I always end up dancing with somebody's dorky cousin or drooling uncle." She licked her lips. "But I've already done the macarena with the vice president of a major network, the electric slide with one of the producers from the *Today* show, and the twist with some rich guy who's staying in the hotel's penthouse suite and decided to crash the reception because he's in the mood for wedding cake."

Besides being smart and beautiful, Trina taught dance lessons to underprivileged kids at the YMCA.

"Have I ever told you how much I hate you?" Eve asked.

"At least once a day. Now"—she nailed Eve with a stare—"why are you sitting here when you should be dancing and having fun?"

"I *should* be dancing, shouldn't I?" Doing a little bump and grind with the most chauvinistic guy in the place always sent her mother into a tailspin, which was why Eve had done so at every family function she'd been forced to attend over the past decade. "I would be if I thought it would do a bit of good. But it's not going to work this time. This is serious." Eve scooted her chair even farther into the shadows of a huge potted palm that sat next to the table. The giant plant effectively hid her from the sight of the woman seated across the sea of wedding guests, near a silver fountain flowing with champagne punch.

"What are you talking about?"

"Marriage and the fact that it's the eighth deadly sin as far as my mother is concerned. Everything else pales in comparison." Dread rolled through her. "Which means I'm actually the good daughter now. *Me.* Can you imagine that?" She shook her head. "I've never been the good daughter. I *can't* be the good daughter. Then I'll have to put up with more than one visit a week from my mother, and I can barely handle *that.*"

"She's a busy woman. I doubt she'll have the time to

torture you more than she already does."

Eve watched as Jacqueline Farrel downed her fourth glass of punch and glanced around for the umpteenth time, as if searching for someone. Her gaze paused on the potted palm.

Eve ducked and grabbed her friend's arm. "My mother didn't see you come over here, did she?"

"You're way too paranoid."

"If only." Eve took another sip of her tart drink. Warmth exploded in the pit of her stomach, but it did little to calm her pounding heart, particularly since her mother's gaze had yet to waver. "She saw you, didn't she?"

"How would I know?" Trina shook her head. "I have much more interesting people to watch than your mother." She smiled and her eyes sparkled. "I just love men in tuxedos."

"Only because a tuxedo means well-dressed, which usually means a hefty bank account."

"Exactly." Trina beamed. "Check out those hot bodies over there."

Eve's gaze shifted to the four tuxedo-clad men who stood several feet away near the bar. They were talking and laughing, seemingly oblivious to the cameras that clicked around them and captured each of their expressions on film.

"They must be television bigwigs or actors or something," Trina said.

"NASCAR drivers." At Trina's questioning look, Eve added, "Since Clint was attending the wedding with Skye—thankfully Valentine's Day fell on a Monday this year—the show's producers decided to tape a 'Hot New

Men of NASCAR' interview for their brother channel—Spike TV."

"Clint's been racing forever. He's not exactly a NASCAR virgin."

"No, but three out of the four drivers for his team are. He must have invited them to tag along to the reception."

"I've never been into NASCAR—Sunday is my day to catch up on all the reality shows I tape during the week—but I'll have to start watching." Trina's eyes gleamed as she pointed a red-tipped nail. "I'd definitely trade the last three *Bachelor*s for that one cutie right over there."

Eve's gaze zeroed in on the blond hunk who stood near a giant hammer-shaped ice sculpture (made in honor of her new brother-in-law, who was the founder and owner of Hire-a-Hunk Construction). Linc "Shooter" Adams—so named for his style of laying low during the first half of a race, then *shooting* into the lead during the final stretch—looked mouthwatering in a black tuxedo. He had his arms draped around two different women—a brunette on one side and a strawberry blonde on the other—while he smiled and flirted with a very attentive female reporter who was holding a microphone in front of him.

"It's all good, sunshine."

The deep, rich southern drawl echoed in Eve's memory and awareness skittered up her spine. She frowned. "I might trade in that football-playing *Bachelor*—he *did* pick the wrong woman—but the rest of those drivers are definitely preferable to Linc Adams."

Trina and Eve watched as the reporter laughed at something Linc said and leaned in even closer. Eve's frown deepened. "He is every Womanist's worst nightmare."

Which was why, when Skye had offered to fix Eve up with him last year, she had actually agreed to it. She'd needed to do something to win back the Rebellious Daughter title she'd held for so many years. Big mistake.

"He's a chauvinist?" Trina asked.

Eve nodded. "He's the one who guzzled beer out of a bra cup at the Victoria's Secret party after last year's spring fashion show."

"That was *him*? I saw that on E!" Trina's eyes narrowed as she sized up Linc. "But he looked a little . . . different."

"He doesn't usually dress this well. When he's not racing, he lives in board shorts and T-shirts and a very inebriated grin."

Eve's thoughts rushed back to the Sonoma race she'd attended the day of their blind date. The first car designed and manufactured by the MacAllister Magic Race Team had been introduced that day. But Eve hadn't felt nearly as much excitement at seeing her brother-in-law's groundbreaking car as she had when she'd glimpsed his new driver. She'd been dreading the fix-up date following the race, but when Linc had climbed from behind the wheel and smiled at Eve, she'd started to think that she might actually *enjoy* the date.

He'd had a really great smile and he'd looked nice enough. While she'd heard the rumor that Linc was a wild player-type interested only in sex, she'd thought maybe it was just that—a rumor. He *was* a competitive athlete, after all. Competitive athletes had to have drive. Determination. Talent. *Substance.*

That's what she'd told herself. But when the race had ended, Eve's fantasy of stimulating conversation and a meeting of the minds had melted away.

Linc had shed his racing suit, pulled on a worn, ripped pair of shorts and a T-shirt that read I BRAKE FOR BEER, BABES, AND AMMO, and proceeded to flirt with every female within hearing range during their dinner date. Eve wasn't sure why it had bothered her so much. She knew his type all too well. She *was* his type.

Or rather, she had been.

While she still looked every bit the wild, sexy, do-any-and-everything woman, she'd changed inside. Turning thirty (she was now thirty-three) had hit her hard and forced her to reevaluate her priorities. Having fun had its place, but it didn't pay the bills or fill her with a sense of accomplishment. Sugar & Spice Sinema did that, and so she'd started to focus on furthering her career as a producer.

No more wasting time on meaningless affairs with equally meaningless guys. She'd decided that the next man she devoted her attention to would be that perfect someone with whom she could build a life and have a family. The next man would be the real thing. The man of her dreams. Her Mr. Kaboom.

And so she'd promptly told off Linc in a voice that made most men tremble. But he'd simply smiled at her and murmured in that deep, rich southern drawl, *"It's all good, sunshine."*

She, in turn, had traded his celestial reference for one with more anatomical accuracy. She'd tossed a breadstick at him for lack of anything better, and walked away.

She'd kept her nose to the grindstone ever since. A choice that was now paying off. Just last month she'd been commissioned by HBO to produce twelve segments detailing the evolution of sex in American culture.

This was it: the big time. Her chance to garner major exposure as a serious filmmaker. Provided she could keep her focus over the next nine months, until the project's completion.

"I can't remember," Trina's voice pushed into her thoughts. "What sort of bra did he drink out of?"

"What?" Eve's attention shifted back to her friend and the familiar predatory light in her eyes.

"What sort of bra?" she asked again.

"What difference does it make?"

"I'm wearing a Very Sexy Body Bra. Double D. They give a nice comfy fit for Pam and Dolly." She cupped her sizable implants and gave them an affectionate squeeze. "I bet they would hold a lot of beer, don't you think?"

"He might not be in a beer mood tonight," Eve heard herself say. "He might not be drinking at all, for that matter."

Yeah, right.

From the stories being printed in the tabloids and broadcast on every major show from CMT's fun *Celebrity Homes* to ESPN's more serious *Live and in Color,* NASCAR's latest and greatest wasn't just racing for the championship. He was drinking and partying his way into the Bad Boys Hall of Fame. Undoubtedly he was drinking tonight, and doing anything and everything else Trina might have in mind.

"He might be the designated driver," Eve added. "Besides, you don't do the jock type, remember? You're all about expensive suits and net worth."

"He's so hot, I'm willing to make an exception for one night and give him a ride home." Trina pulled her shoulders back, pushed out her ample chest, and grinned. "Or just a ride. I think I'll walk over and introduce him to Pam and Dolly." She cast one last glance at Eve. "You'll never hook up sitting in this corner. Men are visual."

"So is my mother, which is why I'm staying right here."

For the next five minutes, Eve watched as Trina made her way through the crowd toward Linc Adams. When her friend reached him and drew his attention away from the reporter, Eve downed the rest of her margarita in one long gulp.

Not that she cared. She was just thirsty.

Linc's gaze swept over Trina and he smiled, and Eve pushed to her feet and headed to the bar. "I'll have another margarita," she told the bartender.

She was *very* thirsty.

She looked back over at Linc while she waited for her drink. The rumors circulating about him *had* to be true. He was a dog, all right. The hound of all hounds. Mr. Tramp himself. Number one on the pound's Most Wanted—

"There you are!" The familiar female voice shattered her thoughts. "I've been looking all over for you."

"On second thought," Eve told the bartender, "forget the margarita and give me a shot of tequila. Straight up." She forced her best smile and turned to greet the woman who'd stepped up behind her. "Hi, Mom."

Chapter 2

Age had done little to soften Jacqueline Farrel. At fifty-six, she looked every bit as imposing as she had when Eve was thirteen. The years had added a little weight to her mother's tall frame and turned her shoulder-length blond bob slightly gray. But she still wore her signature silver-framed glasses that had always been too large for her narrow face, and her dress was its usual beige. Bottom line, she still scared the hell out of Eve. Particularly when she tried to look pleasant. Like now.

"Where have you been?" Jacqueline asked, her expression concerned rather than irritated.

"Right over there." Eve made a sweeping gesture with her arm and tried to quiet the alarm bells suddenly ringing in her head.

"Where *exactly*?" Her mother's gaze scanned the area.

"There." Eve pointed in the opposite direction of her hiding spot, toward her mother's table and the ice sculpture.

"I didn't see you," Jacqueline said. "And your father and I have been at the same table for the past hour."

"Or maybe it was over there." Eve pointed toward the far side of the dance floor. "I'm a little disoriented from all the flashing cameras. I'm practically blind. Hey, maybe that's why you haven't seen me." Well, it sounded good.

Her mother looked as if she wanted to argue, but then shrugged. "I *have* been the victim of far too many pictures." She smiled. "But that's neither here nor there. The important thing is that I've finally found you."

"Your mother is a busy woman. I doubt she'll have the time to torture you more than she already does." Trina's words echoed and hope blossomed in the pit of Eve's stomach, only to burst and deflate when she heard her mother's voice.

"I've been thinking. We really don't spend nearly enough time together, dear."

"Sure we do. I see you every week."

"Only for a fifteen-minute coffee break. That's not nearly enough time to really connect. We need to visit in a more substantial manner. We need lunch."

"Lunch?" Eve swallowed and tried to draw air into her lungs. *Slow, easy. It's just an occasional lunch. No reason to hyperventilate.*

"A weekly lunch."

Okay, now you can hyperventilate.

"A nice, long, leisurely lunch first thing every week in addition to our Friday coffee breaks. We can start tomorrow at that divine new bistro down on the corner of Hollywood Boulevard and Market. It'll be our special mother-daughter place."

First a ritual lunch. Now a ritual place.

"I can't." At her mother's narrowed gaze, Eve rushed on, "I mean, I can't do it *every* week. I'm really busy right now with this new project." *The* project. A career-maker. Or breaker.

She licked her suddenly dry lips and shifted her weight. Yellow tulle moved with her and clung to her clammy legs.

Clammy?

Oh God, she *was* clammy.

Her fingers balled and she became acutely aware of her damp palms. Her pulse raced.

Breathe, she told herself again. But the breathing was getting her nowhere. She needed to think. To say something, *anything,* to send her mother running in the opposite direction.

"Here you go." The bartender's voice drew her around and she downed the tequila shot in one gulp.

"Dear, you really should watch your alcohol intake. Otherwise, your father and I will have to drive you home."

"I'm fine. Really, Mom." Eve turned toward the woman. "That wasn't even a real shot. They water those things down so much that you have to drink a half dozen to get the full effect of one." She moved away from the bar and her mother followed. "Oops, I think I see Skye motioning for me."

Jacqueline turned and glanced toward the head table where Xandra and Beau sat flanked by the other members of their wedding party. Skye sat just to Xandra's left, her attention fixed on the tall, dark, handsome man who sat beside her. Clint lifted a forkful of wedding cake and fed it to his smiling wife.

"It's brainwashing, I tell you." Jacqueline shook her head. "Skye looks like a lapdog."

"A really lucky lapdog." The words were out before Eve could stop them. Despite her upbringing, Eve envied the happiness her sister seemed to have found with her brother-in-law.

Her mother turned an *Et tu, Brute?* gaze on her. "*Clint* is the lucky one. He's managed to undermine your sister's free, independent thinking with a few sexy smiles and charming words. Why, he's probably a card-carrying Himanist." The Himanists were a group of Bubba Beer–drinking men who relished the old days when men were men—clueless and chauvinistic and insensitive—and didn't have to apologize for it. Their ideas were in direct opposition to those of her mother's famed Womanist organization. The Himanists were as much a thorn in Jacqueline's side as Cherry Chandler, the ultra-femme talk show host and best-selling author of the *Sensitive* series. Cherry taught women how they could find the man of their dreams; meanwhile Jacqueline was a firm believer that no such man existed.

"I'm sure Clint's not a Himanist." Eve tugged at the sweetheart neckline of her dress. "And even if he is, he's still good to her. He takes out the trash and rubs Skye's feet."

Jacqueline smoothed the beige satin jacket that matched her floor-length shift. "True, but in turn, she's cooking and cleaning—*for a man*—and she's given up her membership in Womanists, Inc."

"She had to. The bylaws forbid married women to maintain membership."

"That's my point. She's gone completely off the deep end, and now Xandra has followed her." Jacqueline sighed. "But not you. You're still free and independent and sane."

Okay, Eve had been called many things by many

people, but sane wasn't usually one of them. Creative, yes. Inventive, always. Daring, of course. Once she'd stripped down to her underwear and marched down the halls of Georgetown High to protest their new gym uniforms.

"I'm really not sane, Mom. I have weird, distorted, *wild* thoughts."

"I realize you're a little bold, dear, as in the way you dress and behave, but that can be a good thing. You're unique."

"I'm an oddball. A spontaneous, do-any-and-everything nutcase. A total nonconformist."

"You're a little artsy, that's all." Hearing her mother say this with such a calm, patient voice totally undermined the entire concept of being artsy. She was supposed to be the only tornado in an otherwise cloud-free sky. The only Dorito in a bag of plain Baked Lays potato chips.

"But I wear too much makeup rather than glorifying in my natural beauty," Eve blurted out.

"You're simply a victim of the impossible plastic image our male-dominated society has created for women."

"I think Van Halen was and always will be the best rock band in history." A declaration that always received a horrified look, followed by a *Why am I being punished?* headshake.

But Jacqueline only smiled. "While they have been known to objectify women, I must admit they are a talented group of musicians."

Eve's mind raced. "Hooters is my all-time favorite restaurant," she declared.

"I've been thinking of trying the wings there myself."

"My favorite movie is *Grease*."

Jacqueline opened her mouth, only to close it again. Her jaw ticked. *Bingo.*

"Sandy *did* turn herself into a stronger woman," she finally said.

"To please her man," Eve pointed out. Desperation pumped her heart faster and she licked her lips. This was *not* happening. Her mother simply could not be agreeing with her. She never agreed with her. *Ever.*

"Perhaps consciously, but subconsciously I believe Sandy had the true desire to shed society's stereotype and break the rules. I say more power to—"

"There's Skye waving at me again," Eve cut in. "I really have to go." That would be a first. Jacqueline was always the one who walked away from Eve, usually shocked and bewildered and cursing the hospital that undoubtedly had sent her home with the wrong child.

"She's not even looking this way," Jacqueline said as she turned.

"Sure she is. It must be time for the *Modern Bride* layout."

"*Modern* what?"

"*Modern Bride.*" As Eve said the name of Jacqueline's least favorite magazine, the wheels in her brain started to turn and an idea struck. "They're working on their annual Notable Weddings issue," she heard herself say. "It's where they hand out various matrimonial awards for stuff like Best Flowers, Best Dress, Best Cake." Clammy or not, she could still think on her feet. "They're giving the *Get Sexed Up!* Valentine's special the silver-plated Ball and Chainy."

"What in heaven's name is a Ball and Chainy?"

Good question. "It's, um, the, um, matrimonial equivalent of an Oscar." Eve hadn't taken an ad-lib acting elective for nothing. "You're winning the award for Most Innovative Wedding." Horror lit her mother's eyes and Eve smiled. "Congratulations, Mom. You're responsible for taking the whole matrimony thing to an entirely different level."

"Over my dead, decayed body. I'll just have a word with Barbara about this and have those awful people thrown out this very instant." Jacqueline turned and made a beeline for the garden outside, where a group of her producers were gathered in a smoking circle.

Eve drew in a deep breath and tried to calm her pounding heart. She'd done it. She'd successfully diverted her mother.

But it was only temporary. Eve knew once Jacqueline realized that she'd made up the whole Ball and Chainy awards story, the woman would come looking for her again.

Eve's stomach jumped and her hands trembled and she was back to the nervous mess she'd been during the ceremony. Only she wasn't fool enough to think another drink would calm her. Since she didn't normally drink, the few she'd already had were sloshing around in her empty stomach and making her feel slightly sick. If she added another to the mix, she might actually throw up. Or pass out.

Throwing up would send her to the ladies' room, and her mother was sure to look for her there. Passing out would leave her out in the open, unconscious, and in full view of her mother, not to mention her sisters.

Eve didn't need a drink. She needed a taxi.

She glanced toward the wedding party and caught Skye's eye. Her older sister motioned her over. Eve waved and held up her hand as if to say, *In just a minute.*

Okay, so she couldn't *leave* leave. Someone would see her walk out the entrance and they would know she'd bolted from her baby sister's wedding and she would have hell to pay with Skye, not to mention she would surely hurt Xandra's feelings. Normally, her sisters would understand her behavior when it came to their mother. They'd always understood; like when Eve had dyed her hair and worn her first leopard-print miniskirt and taken the most obnoxious football player to the prom. Even if they hadn't agreed with her choices, her sisters had always understood. But they were now living on Planet Marital Bliss and so Eve wasn't placing any bets on getting their sympathy.

Her gaze went to the ladies' room. Maybe there would be a window she could crawl through . . .

The thought faded as a waiter rushed from a nearby swinging door. *A kitchen!* Where there was a kitchen, there had to be a back door for food deliveries. *An exit.* A way out that wouldn't draw the attention of the pack of photographers floating throughout the ballroom, much less any member of her family.

After a quick glance around to make sure no one was watching, she pushed through the door and nearly collided with a waiter carrying a tray of hot meatballs.

"Sorry," she mumbled at the man's back as he hurried past her into the ballroom. "Could you point me toward the nearest *exit?*" she asked aloud, hoping someone would answer.

"Straight ahead to the left." The voice sounded directly in back of her. She whirled as a photographer came up behind her, his assistant in tow. So much for avoiding the press.

But the pair didn't look the least bit interested in her, despite the fact that her telltale yellow dress indicated she was a wedding party somebody. A quick glance at the press pass dangling around the photographer's neck told her why he didn't so much as blink when he walked past her.

Sports Illustrated.

He wanted pictures of Clint and the NASCAR men, not the freaked-out maid of honor. So why was he lurking in the kitchen?

"I've searched from one end of the kitchen to the other. We must have missed him," the man told another photographer who wore a black-and-white-checkered race flag tie, camera in hand.

"Let's check the patio." The *Sports Illustrated* guy nodded and followed Mr. Race Flag Tie. Both men disappeared through the swinging doors, back into the ballroom.

Eve blew out the deep breath she'd been holding and turned to make her way through the massive square-shaped kitchen. Burners and ovens lined the outer perimeter. The inner area was a maze of preparation tables. People clustered here and there, busily arranging everything from trays of speared shrimp to platters of caviar to cold vegetables and various gourmet cheese spreads. She passed the groom's cake, which had been ushered back into the kitchen after the traditional cake-cutting pictures. A woman in a white chef's hat fed slices onto individual crystal cake plates.

The smell of chocolate teased her nostrils as she walked past. Ordinarily, Eve didn't do chocolate. She'd learned a long time ago that it killed her complexion, and so she'd sworn off the stuff in favor of the occasional caf-feine-free alternative like Sugar Babies or candy corn. But after a few drinks, she wasn't thinking clearly and so the chocolate seemed to be calling her name.

She blew out a deep breath, resisted the urge to grab a slice, and headed for the end of the aisle. She needed her apartment and her sweatpants and her thick cotton socks and—

The thought stalled as she walked past a giant freezer and an image beyond the frost-covered square of glass caught her eye.

She stopped and stared through the small window.

Okay, she was either a real lightweight and consider-ably more drunk than she felt, or there was a man sitting in the freezer.

She blinked, but he didn't disappear.

Gripping the handle, she lifted and pulled. The door gasped and creaked open.

Sure enough, a man was sitting on the edge of a giant cardboard box marked *Frozen Crab Cakes*. He held a plate of half-eaten chocolate cake in one hand and a fork in the other. A black tuxedo accented his broad shoulders. His crisp white shirt hugged the strong column of his throat and provided a stark contrast against his deeply tanned skin. Whiskey-blond hair, the top streaked from too much time spent in the sun, brushed his collar and framed his strong face. At the sound of the door opening, he lifted his head.

Familiar blue eyes collided with hers, and his expres-sion went from angry dismay to pure delight in one fast, furious heartbeat. His full lips curved into a grin. A dim-ple cut into his freshly shaven cheek. His gaze sparkled, so bright and vivid and enticing, like the Caribbean on a hot summer day.

Despite the freezing temperature, a wave of heat washed through Eve. Her breath caught and her tummy hollowed out, and for a split second, she felt a dreaded tummy tremor.

But then he opened his mouth, his deep southern drawl sweet and dripping with charm, and the moment faded in a wave of irritation.

"Hey there, sunshine."

Chapter 3

Linc Adams didn't think his day could get much worse.

A friggin' crazy turn of events since things had started out with such promise, it being his first day as the reigning Daytona 500 champion. First thing that morning, he'd seen on CNN that he'd been named the hottest NASCAR prospect for the upcoming season on Bill Biloxi's *Sunday Post-Race Extreme Sports* show. Then he'd opened his e-mail to find he'd been voted NASCAR's hottest hunk and the driver Most Likely to Jump and Dump—a new term for a noncommital man who liked to be with a different woman every night—by the members of Race Girls, Inc., NASCAR's Internet-based legion of female fans.

Yep, he'd started off riding a major high. And why not? His hard work was finally paying off. Not only was he being recognized for his driving ability, but he was making it as plain as a sunshiny Georgia day to the fine, upstanding voters of Adams, Georgia, that he was the black sheep of the rich, powerful Adams clan.

The bad boy who loved being free and single as much as he loved a case of ice-cold Coors Light, a loud party, and a warm, willing, wicked woman.

The rebellious son who would make about as good a mayor as he would the deacon of the Adams First Baptist Church.

But at noon—just before Linc had left for the airport to fly to L.A.—he'd received the phone call from his father informing him that he was ahead in the mayoral race by thirty-three percentage points.

Rather than seeing him as a totally immature, love-'em-and-leave-'em asshole, the voters of Adams were dismissing his reputation with a shrug and a boys-will-be-boys attitude. He was going through a phase. Sowing his wild oats. Having one last *yee-hawww!* before settling down and taking his rightful place as leader of the town, like his father and his grandfather before him, and his great-grandfather before that. He was an Adams, after all. Born to be a politician. There'd been an Adams in office for as long as the town had been in existence. It was the way of things, and it seemed that no amount of bad behavior could convince folks otherwise.

But all Linc wanted was to win a Nextel Cup Championship. Not the fancy clothes or the country-club friends or the political legacy pressed on him since he'd turned four years old and attended his first political fund-raising dinner.

He wanted to live his own dream rather than everyone else's.

He'd entered the sport later than most drivers—after attempting to be the good son by graduating with a law degree and taking over the family practice. It had been a hard battle to prove himself in the six years since. But he'd been hungry enough to push himself up the ranks into the top ten. As of yesterday's season-opening win at Daytona, he was the favored driver to win this year's Cup.

He was this close to achieving his own dream for the first time in his life.

The thought of trading it in to walk into city hall day after day made him sick to his stomach.

Thirty-three points.

How much worse could it get?

It couldn't, or so he'd thought. Until he was caught red-handed in the freezer by Eve Farrel.

She wasn't wearing the short black leather miniskirt or tight T-shirt she'd worn on their disastrous blind date after the Sears Point race in Sonoma, but she still looked every bit as sexy and exotic. She had long, dark hair, a curvaceous body, and a sultry air that reminded him of Angelina Jolie. Dark eye makeup emphasized her vivid green eyes and gave her that intense come-and-do-me look that had dominated his fantasies since he'd first met her. Dark red lipstick plumped her already full lips. Everything about her screamed sex, which suited him to a *T.*

When he had his race face on, that is. But he wasn't gunning for publicity at the moment. He was hiding from it.

Linc pasted on his most charming grin and did his damnedest to hide the cake plate behind his back. The last thing, the very *last* thing he needed was to blow his cover in front of Eve Farrel. It was hard enough play-ing the bad boy in front of the nosy press, but Eve had a gaze that seemed to push aside all the nonsense and cut straight to the chase. A gaze that unnerved the hell out of him.

"Sunshine," he said, unleashing his best southern drawl. "Anyone ever tell you that yellow is definitely your color?"

"My name isn't sunshine and yellow is nobody's color, especially mine."

Linc narrowed his gaze and made a show of studying her. "I don't know. It really makes the rest of you stand out."

"I see you're as obnoxious as ever."

"I meant that as a compliment."

"And I just won Miss Congeniality." Eve shook her head. "You're sitting in the freezer, you know."

"I needed a little fresh air."

"It's not fresh. It's cold."

"I needed a little cold air. It's damned hot out there."

Actually, it was pretty damned hot in here.

The thought struck Eve just as Linc smiled again, and heat fired in her cheeks. Blushing? She was actually *blushing?*

The thought was almost as depressing as the fact that she was now the one and only Great Farrel Hope. She was seriously delusional. Otherwise, why in the world would she be standing in the freezer talking to a man who stirred her anger and made her want to commit a felony?

That, or kiss him.

Hello? You do not want to kiss Linc Adams. Choking him is fine. Kissing is a definite no-no.

"You're eating cake," Eve said as she noticed a brown speck at the corner of his mouth.

Linc held his hands behind his back and tried to look innocent. "You're crazy."

"Yeah, and you're eating cake." She studied him. "You are, aren't you?"

He looked as if he wanted to deny it, but instead he finally shrugged. His right arm came around, revealing the crystal plate and a half-eaten piece of chocolate cake.

"Give it up," she said, trying to stare around him.

When he finally stood, she saw a large glass of what looked like milk sitting on the box. She arched an eyebrow. "A White Russian?"

"You know it."

Something about the way he said the words roused her suspicion. She stepped toward him, grabbed the glass before he could snatch it out of her reach, and lifted it to her lips. "You're drinking *milk*?"

Linc smiled, but it didn't touch his eyes. "Hey, it does a body good."

"Since when have you been interested in doing your body good? You party all night and get totally wasted when you're not on the track."

"Damn straight."

But here he was sitting in the freezer, chasing chocolate cake with a cold glass of milk.

Understanding dawned. "You're hiding," Eve told him. "You're hiding in here so that no one will see you drinking milk and eating chocolate cake."

"I'm not hiding. I'm trying to have a moment of peace and quiet, and you've shot that to hell and back."

"You *are* hiding. Those reporters I saw in the kitchen . . . They were looking for you."

"Did they see you come in here?" Linc set his cake

plate on the box and walked to the small window. He peeked out only to duck back. "Dammit, you're going to lead them right to me."

"No one saw me come in."

He turned and gave Eve a *get real* look. "Sure they didn't." He eyed the layers of tulle. "It's not like you're wearing a bright yellow dress with a skirt big enough to house a family of five or anything like that."

"Has anyone ever told you how charming you are?"

He grinned and the tummy tremor started again. "Actually, everyone."

He was standing so close that Eve could smell the sweet scent of chocolate cake on his breath. "Well"—she swallowed and did her best to look totally unaffected— "they lied."

"Has anyone ever told you how pleasant you are?"

"No. Now what's the big deal with the cake and the milk? I could see if you were eating quiche or foie gras, or something equally unmacho, but it's just cake."

"It's chocolate cake, and it's whole milk. As in whole-*some*." His mouth drew into a thin line and he shook his head, as if he'd already said more than he wanted to.

"And Linc Adams can't be wholesome, is that it? He doesn't drink milk, and he especially doesn't do it with a big slice of cake?"

Linc didn't seem as if he wanted to talk, but then he finally shrugged. "I've got an image to maintain." He walked back over to the box and retrieved his plate.

"So chase the cake with a six-pack."

He looked at her as if she'd grown two heads. "A man can't eat cake with *beer.* Do you know how bad that would taste?"

"I don't do beer. Just tequila." And speaking of tequila . . . In that next instant, a wave of dizziness swept her, and Eve reached a hand out to a nearby wall to steady herself. Not that she was drunk, but she was definitely tipsy. Otherwise, she would have turned and left Linc without so much as a backward glance.

At the moment, however, she couldn't *not* look at him as he forked some cake and took a bite. The speck of fudge frosting still sat at the corner of his mouth as he chewed.

Eve had the sudden urge to cross the few feet between them and taste the sweet crumbs. Her mouth watered, and she tightened her fingers against the fierce hunger.

This is insane, she reminded herself. *As in totally whacked. As in you can't stand this guy, remember?*

True. Unfortunately, her hormones had a very short memory and they couldn't seem to get past the warmth in Linc's smile and the twinkle in his eyes and the fact that she'd been totally celibate for over seven months—since her last date with a semicute cameraman who worked for This Little Piggy, Inc., a video company that catered to feet fetishists. While Eve hadn't been even the tiniest bit turned on by his sterling-silver monogrammed toe ring, she'd fallen for his soft, dark hair and wounded expression. He'd been the classic struggling artist, and his eye for camera angles had truly impressed her.

Unfortunately, the only impressive thing about him had been his talent with a Nikon. He'd turned out to be too selfish in the sack, which meant that it had been seven months since Eve had had sex and over three years since she'd had any really *good* sex. Three *long* years . . . since she'd given up wild and wicked bad boys—the type she always attracted—to focus on her career.

You don't need sex, she had told herself countless times. *You need space and concentration and focus.*

She drew in a deep breath and tried to weather the sudden tilt in the floor. Actually, what she really needed at the moment was a place to sit down.

"You don't look so good."

"I feel good. A little too good, I think."

Linc grinned and patted the seat next to him. "Take a load off."

Eve hesitated.

"I won't bite," he added. "Unless you ask me real nice."

"You're so full of yourself," she muttered as she sank down next to him. "Don't you get tired of being so obnoxious?"

"Don't you get tired of being so unpleasant?"

"I asked you first."

"On occasion, but a man's gotta do what a man's gotta do. Shit," he muttered, shaking his head. "Can you believe I'm up in the polls by thirty-three points?"

"What polls?"

"I'm running for mayor of Adams, Georgia. That's my hometown."

"That's great. Mystifying, but great."

"It's not great. It's a pain in the ass. I don't want to be mayor. I can't be mayor. I barely get a day off now. I can't drive for the championship and be the mayor."

"So why are you running?"

"Because I want my best friend to be mayor. He's running opposite me."

"I'm not getting this."

"You're not supposed to get it." He ran a hand through his hair. "I shouldn't be talking to you about this."

Amen. Eve didn't need to hear his problems when she had so many of her own. At the same time, she heard herself say, "Sometimes it helps to talk things through. Then they don't seem so huge or tragic." So much for staying indifferent.

He seemed to consider her words. "It's like this. I'm running for mayor, but I don't want to be mayor. I want Craig Sanders to be mayor. He's my best friend and the best man for the job, which was why I agreed to enter the race as his opposition. If I didn't, my father would have picked someone else. Hell, he did pick someone, and that someone—with the Adams name and money behind him—would have won. But Craig should win, and so I agreed to run. My dad wouldn't *not* endorse his own son, not when politics are a tradition in our family."

"So you act like a jackass on purpose."

"I don't act like a jackass. I'm just laid back and easygoing and more interested in fun than politics. I'm the worst possible choice for mayor, but damned if anyone sees it. They like me."

"There's no accounting for taste."

"I can't win this damned election."

"So act worse. Be a *monstrous* jackass. Do something scandalous to sully the good Adams name and shock your family."

"And how am I supposed to do that?"

"If I knew, I would try it myself. You've only got a bunch of registered voters on your case. I've got a determined mother." She closed her eyes and tried to ignore the warmth of Linc's body as they sat side by side. "I've got a project to work on. I can't work with my mother on my back, which means I have to figure out a way to get her to leave me alone. And all because my sisters are married."

Eve wasn't sure if it was the drinks or the warmth of Linc's hard body that sparked the next thought. Maybe it was a little of both. Regardless, an idea rooted and Eve found herself smiling.

"I should get married," she told him. "My mother's given up on Skye and Xandra because they did. If I jumped the Womanist ship, too, and married some man she totally disapproved of, then she wouldn't have any reason to hold out hope." Eve's gaze shifted to Linc with his blond good looks and his charming smile and his bad-boy attitude. "I've got an idea that might save us both."

"I do," Eve said a half hour later as she stood in a corner of the Crystal Ballroom and faced Linc.

Xandra and Beau had already left in a flurry of bird-seed to catch a plane to Hawaii for their honeymoon. Skye and Clint had called it a night, as well, and so Eve had lucked out. She wouldn't have to explain anything to her sisters tonight.

Only a handful of reporters remained. They stood on the sidelines, snapping pictures of the spontaneous wedding between the very unlikely pair.

Which was the entire point. It wasn't enough to just get married; Eve needed someone who would truly horrify her mother, and Linc, who oozed testosterone, was just the man for the job.

With Eve's sexy, exotic looks, her scandalous profession, and her notoriety as the daughter of famed sexologist

Jacqueline Farrel, she was just what the conservative voters of Adams didn't need. Which made *her* perfect for the job.

After Eve's proposition and Linc's acceptance, they'd ironed out the details of their "marriage." They were going to help each other over the next nine months until the election in November. Eve's project was due at the beginning of December, so the timing was perfect. Her mother would stay angry and outraged and distant, and Eve would have the focus needed to complete her documentary. Likewise, Linc's family and voters would be equally angered and outraged up until the polls closed. Linc would lose, Eve would turn in her project, then they would make a public announcement of their split. A quickie divorce and it would all be over.

Until then, they would play the newlywed couple, spending part of their time in L.A. and part in Georgia. Eve would also put in a few appearances along the NASCAR trail to keep the press buzzing.

First things first, however. They'd had to make their union official. They'd left the freezer and gone in search of the judge who'd married the other couples. Eager for more publicity and the five hundred dollars Linc had pressed into his hand for his trouble, he'd readily agreed to perform the impromptu ceremony.

While there was no actual marriage license, Eve and Linc could apply for it after the fact and still have a legal marriage as long as they both agreed, and the judge consented to sign. Which he did.

And so the deed was done.

"I now pronounce you husband and wife," the judge declared. "You may now kiss the bride."

The minute the words were out, panic rushed through Eve, along with a flutter of anticipation. While she'd thought most of the details through, she hadn't counted on the kiss.

Eve closed her eyes as Linc's lips touched hers. *A peck.* That's what she told herself. *He'll give you a peck and then it will be over and . . .*

Her lips softened under the pressure of his mouth. His tongue swept her bottom lip and slipped past to deepen the connection. He pulled her closer, his hands at the base of her spine, burning through the thin material of her dress and stirring her deprived hormones.

The chemistry between them was instant and explosive and she couldn't help herself. She kissed him back, her tongue tangling with his. She slid her hands up his chest, her palms flat against the stiff material of his jacket until she reached the solid warmth of his neck. Her fingers curled around, holding him close.

The floor fell away as she leaned into him. His warmth overwhelmed her. His scent filled her nostrils and made her heart pound and—

"Eve Elizabeth Ruella Farrel!" Her mother's voice shattered the passionate haze surrounding Eve, and her eyes popped open. She whirled to see Jacqueline walking toward them, her expression outraged. Her father, Donovan, followed, surprise gleaming in his eyes. Her grandmother wore a startled look as she hurried to keep up with Jacqueline and Donovan.

"You didn't . . . ," Jacqueline sputtered. "You couldn't . . ."

Before Eve could respond, Linc stepped around her.

He caught her mother in a gigantic bear hug. "Mom!" he declared, planting a huge kiss on her lips.

And then he did the one thing that would cinch Eve's freedom and secure his place on Jacqueline's list of the most rotten chauvinists on earth. He pulled out a Sharpie from his pocket and attempted to give Jacqueline the signature Linc Adams autograph—smack-dab on her ample cleavage.

Chapter 4

Eve didn't want to kiss Linc Adams again.

Not yet, that is.

Not until they'd reached the safety of her apartment. At the very least, the elevator that led to her apartment. The key was privacy. No taxi driver stealing glances at them through the rearview mirror. No photographers tailing them.

They left the Beverly Hills Hotel fifteen minutes after the autographing incident. Her mother had been so shocked that she'd rushed off to the ladies' room, her face red with outrage. Thankfully. For a few seconds there, Eve had actually expected the woman to cry. And while Eve lived to shock the woman, making her mad and making her cry were two very different things. But Jacqueline had reacted in the usual fashion, which meant things just might go as planned.

Before leaving, Eve had pulled her father aside and explained that she and Linc had this cosmic connection and so she'd tied the knot to explore it further. Donovan Martin had been doubtful, but not at all surprised. He'd stopped being surprised by Eve when she was eleven years old and she'd sung Tammy Wynette's "Stand by Your Man" in an impromptu performance during Jacqueline's first *Good Morning America* interview.

In front of the hotel, Eve climbed into the backseat of a waiting cab. She gave the driver instructions to her apartment and leaned back against the vinyl seat. Taking a deep breath, she focused all of her attention on trying to ignore the man who followed her inside.

Her husband.

The thought rooted in her mind as he settled next to her. Not that theirs was a typical marriage, but it *was* their wedding night.

And she was feeling uncommonly good, thanks to that shot of tequila and the fact that she'd managed to reclaim her Rebellious Daughter title.

And Linc's lips were so close and he smelled so good—like rich, chocolaty groom's cake and ripe strawberries—and it had been a long time since she'd had a really great kiss.

Twenty minutes, to be exact, since they'd said "I do."

"I think we're off to a good start," Linc said as the cab pulled away from the curb. He half turned. A grin tilted the corner of his mouth as he pinned her with a gaze.

Eve's heart stalled and she couldn't help herself.

She leaned forward and touched her lips to his. It was nothing short of explosive. The chemistry ignited and mushroomed, and what started as a subtle press of mouths soon morphed into a deep, urgent, delicious probing of tongues that seemed to go on forever.

No, no, *no,* a voice whispered. This was too fast, too soon. At the same time, she'd wanted to kiss him like this since she'd seen him at the Sonoma race the night of their first date. Caution melted away in the face of so much heat as arousal washed through Eve from her head to the tips of her bright red toenails. The pulsing awareness started in her scalp and spread through her body, pausing at every major erogenous zone. Her nipples tightened and hardened. Pressure hummed between her legs. Her thighs quivered. Her heart pounded as loud and as fast as the drummer for Limp Bizkit, and her blood rushed at an alarming rate.

Linc's hand found its way under her skirt and swept a burning path up the inside of her thigh. His finger traced the lace edge of her panties before dipping underneath. His finger ran back and forth, his calloused skin arousing Eve's sensitized flesh. Back and forth. Up and . . . ahhh.

He pushed into her and she gasped. She wiggled, pivoting her hips, desperate to feel him deeper and harder and . . . There. Just like that. And that. And *that* . . .

His lips left her mouth to blaze a trail down her throat to her pulse beat. He rasped the tip of his tongue against her skin and worked his finger inside her body. A moan vibrated from her throat. Linc caught the sound with his mouth and devoured her in another luscious kiss.

Suddenly, the cab swerved and the cabdriver's muttered curse penetrated the haze of desire that enveloped them. Not that the cabdriver could actually see anything. With the massive yellow dress, the specifics of what Linc was doing to her were hidden from prying eyes. But it was still obvious that he was doing *something,* and that she was enjoying it and—

The thought scattered as a flash lit up the dark interior of the cab. Awareness skittered over Eve and she pulled away long enough to take a deep gulp of air. Another flash went off from outside, to her left. She jerked her head around to see a photographer hanging out the window of a car keeping time next to them. He flashed another picture and black dots danced in front of Eve's eyes.

"I don't think—," she started.

"Don't think," Linc murmured before kissing her again.

The small bit of consciousness she'd regained quickly drowned in a rush of desire. He was simply too close and too warm and too intoxicating and she was too turned on.

Eve relished his deep, thrusting touch for a few more delicious moments before he pulled out of her completely. The tips of his fingers skimmed her swollen flesh as he caught her thigh. She trembled as he urged her leg up and over his lap until she straddled him. They faced one another, her dress bunched around her waist.

Linc's gaze drilled into hers, his eyes dilated with hunger and a deep appreciation. Warmth bubbled inside her, a feeling that might have spooked her if she hadn't been so hot and bothered in the first place.

Eve didn't do bubbling warmth. Or soft fuzzies. Or any of those girly feelings that tended to undermine even the most strong, confident woman when it came to men. She didn't let herself get involved in the emotional aspect of sex because that would only make it harder to walk away the next day. And she always walked away. While she'd had a few relationships that lasted more than one night, the connection had always been the sex.

But at the moment, Eve was too needy to worry over the way her heart skipped a beat and her hands trembled at the look on Linc's face. As if he *liked* her. He felt too good and she wanted to feel more.

As if he read her mind, his strong hands cupped her bottom and he worked her against the rock-hard bulge pressing tight against his tuxedo trousers. The friction was incredible and stirring. Her head fell back and her eyes closed as pleasure ripped through her.

She shimmied her hips and spread her legs even wider, settling more fully on top of him. He let loose a low growl and leaned forward, his hot mouth going to the plump cleavage pushing against the low neckline of her dress. His tongue traced the edge of the material before he reached his hand up to grasp the edge of the neckline. He was just about to pull it down and free her aching breast when an all-important fact registered.

Eve wasn't clutching at his shoulders to keep from swaying to the side anymore. They were sitting stock-still, the cab engine idling, the driver waiting.

"We're here," she breathed.

Linc's hands stilled as his gaze met hers. They stared at each other for a long moment, their breaths coming in quick, frantic gulps.

"We're here," he echoed. He sounded disappointed.

Until reality seemed to hit, and then it was as if someone lit a fire under them. She scrambled from his lap and pushed open the door to step out onto the curb while he paid the cabdriver. The photographers had pulled up to the curb on the opposite side of the street and had already climbed out to follow. Eve picked up her pace, but not to outrun the paparazzi. She needed to get into the elevator and into her apartment and back into Linc's arms.

Linc followed and soon they'd retreated into the safety of her apartment building. The elevator wasn't working, unfortunately, and so they took the stairs up to the fifth floor as if the devil himself were chasing them.

Eve fumbled with her key for a few moments before Linc stepped up behind her and wrapped his arms around her waist. His long, lean fingers closed over hers, and he steadied her long enough to slide the key into the lock. Metal clicked and hinges creaked and then they were inside. The door slammed behind them and before she could draw a breath, he whirled her around and pulled her into his arms.

He kissed her, his tongue delving deep as he pulled her close. Her thighs quivered and her bosom heaved and she came dangerously close to fainting from the desire swamping her. But this was too good to miss, and she wasn't about to forfeit what was surely to be a really incredible orgasm.

She reached for the waistband of his pants as he reached behind for the hooks on her dress. They both worked at the clothes until all the pieces had been pulled away. The yellow nightmare landed in a heap somewhere across the room. The matching hoop slip ricocheted against the far wall and nearly smacked Eve upside the head. But Linc took the brunt against one solid shoulder and it hit the floor like a hula hoop. Eve's corsetlike bra put up a fight, but Linc eventually emerged the victor. The edges sagged and groaned with relief as he tossed it near her massive DVD collection in the far corner. She wasn't sure what happened to her stockings or shoes. She could only hope they developed a life of their own and dead-man-walked their way to the trash compactor in the kitchen.

Likewise, Linc's clothes followed hers. His jacket hit the floor along with his belt and trousers. Buttons popped, and she shoved the shirt down his arms and sent the white material flying in the opposite direction. She paused only to discover whether he was a boxer, brief, or au naturel man—crisp white BVDs, just for the record—before shoving the elastic waistband down and freeing a massive erection.

She wanted to look. But even more she wanted to feel, and so she threw herself against him. Her body went flush against his as bare skin met bare skin. His lips found hers again for a long endless moment before he pulled away to fish a condom from his pocket and slide it on his throbbing length. He kissed her as he swept her into his arms and started for the bedroom.

They ended up in the kitchen, and while she had nothing against a little tabletop action, her small glass-topped breakfast table could barely accomodate her laptop, a pot of coffee, and her supersized mug. She tore her mouth from his long enough to murmur, "The hallway. Third door to the left," before plunging back into the kiss.

There was just something about the way his mouth ate at her lips and his tongue tangled with hers, stroking this way and that, up and down, deeper and stronger, that took her breath away. She'd never met a man who kissed with such passion and intensity. As if he liked it. As if he liked *her.*

The last thought rooted in her mind as he tumbled her back onto her king-sized bed. Her dog, Killer, who'd been curled up on her pillow, jumped to the floor with a loud, surprised yelp. She then let loose a grumpy growl—usually elicited by dry dog food and the *Live with Regis and Kelly* show—before scurrying off toward the walk-in closet that housed her doggy pillow.

Linc's body covered Eve's and she spread her legs, ready for the wondrous Big O that would undoubtedly follow such heated, frantic foreplay. She wrapped her legs around him as he readied himself and plunged fast and deep inside her.

She expected it to be good. Fantastic, even, with a man like Linc.

A wild man.

Eve tried to force aside the last thought. So what if he was the exact type she'd sworn off? They were stuck in a relationship together, however temporary, and so they might as well make the most of it.

Enjoy yourself, a voice whispered. Unfortunately, her conscience said something completely different.

"Are you going to move or just lay there?" His deep voice slid into her ears and shattered her thoughts.

"I'm moving." She frowned up at him and shifted her pelvis for emphasis. "You're just moving too much."

"Too much?" He plunged into her and stilled. "That's the craziest thing I've ever heard." He stared down at her, a disbelieving look in his gaze. The same look he'd given her when she'd tossed the breadstick at him during their first date. A look NASCAR's hottest commodity undoubtedly reserved for any female stupid enough to resist his southern charm.

She stiffened. "Too much as in quick on the draw."

His brows furrowed together. "Who are you calling quick on the draw?"

"You're the only one cocked and ready, so that would be you."

"You might not be cocked, sunshine, but I'd say you're pretty ready, yourself." He moved to prove his point, and her body welcomed him deeper. He grinned the infuriating grin that never failed to make her heart beat faster and her bloodlust rise to dangerous levels. "Just relax and enjoy."

She tried. She met him thrust for thrust until sweat beaded on his forehead and her breaths came faster and shorter and she moved closer toward a climax. Just . . . a . . . few . . . more . . . and . . .

"Ahhh." His groan filled her ears and she knew he was close. Determined not to miss out, she shimmied and swayed and rode him for the next few seconds, waiting for the light to splinter her vision. She closed her eyes, anticipating a wave of sensation.

Or at least a ripple.

Nothing. Her eyes popped open and she saw Linc looming over her, his neck muscles taut, his gaze deep and hungry and expectant. He was waiting for her.

The realization sent a burst of warmth through her, followed by a rush of panic because she wasn't even close to the edge.

Before she could stop herself, she closed her eyes, opened her mouth, and let loose a deep moan that quickly morphed into screaming encouragement. Linc pounded into her a few more times and her voice, louder with each thrust, echoed off the walls surrounding them.

"Yes! Yes! Yesssssssssssss!"

Linc collapsed on top of her for several long moments, his heart hammering against hers while Eve did her best to breathe beneath the full press of his weight.

Finally, he rolled onto his back next to her and Eve managed to breathe again. Unfortunately, the supply of oxygen helped calm her frantic thoughts, and all too soon reality hit her.

Ugh. Not only had she violated her No More Meaningless Sex rule, but she'd had *bad* meaningless sex.

A half hour later, Eve listened to the steady sound of Linc's breathing and inched her way to the edge of the bed. Her feet touched the rug a breathless moment later. The old T-shirt she'd slept in the previous night sat in a heap in a nearby corner and she snatched it up. She slid the soft cotton over her naked body. It didn't quite cover her bottom, but she didn't care. It was dark and she was desperate. Snatching up the cordless phone that sat on her dresser, she tiptoed to the window, eased the glass up, and crawled out onto the fire escape for some privacy.

While her apartment wasn't small, it certainly wasn't large, and she was terribly afraid her voice would carry. Not to mention, if Killer heard her up and around, the dog was sure to abandon the closet and come after her. And bark. Eve didn't want to wake Linc, because then she would have to face him and she couldn't do that right now. She couldn't even face herself.

Forget the whole meaningless sex thing. It was even worse. She, Eve Farrel, an expert when it came to sex, had *faked* an orgasm.

The darkness outside her apartment swallowed her up. There were no buildings directly behind hers. Just a great view of the Hollywood Hills and a spray of twinkling lights, for which she paid through the nose despite the small size of her place.

Her hands trembled around the cordless phone as anxiety rushed through her. Of all the terrible things she'd done in her lifetime, this had to be the worst. A total violation of her sense of self, not to mention a grave injustice to her partner.

Even if he didn't know it.

She turned and peered back through the window. Her gaze shot to the bed where he lay sprawled on his back, the sheet pulled over his lap. He had his arms folded under the pillow, cradling his head. His biceps bulged, his chest rising and falling to a steady rhythm. Carefully, Eve slid the window closed and moved away to sit Indian-style on the metal scaffolding.

"I think I just made a huge mistake," Eve blurted out when Skye's groggy voice sounded on the other end.

"Eve?"

"*The* worst mistake of my life."

"You're damned straight you did. You married a stranger, for heaven's sake!"

"That's not the— Wait a second, how do you know?"

"I'm on the other line with Mom. She's really freaked. Hold on." The line clicked. In a few seconds, she clicked back. "I told her it was an emergency for Clint. You've done some crazy things, but this takes the cake. How could you—"

"Would you just listen?" Eve cut in. "I'm having a major crisis here. I can't believe it. I faked it."

"You faked what?"

"What do you think?"

"Oh, honey, I'm so sorry." Skye's tone quickly changed as she realized the severity of Eve's problem. "Was he really that bad?"

"No and yes." Eve pulled her knees to her chest and tugged the T-shirt down around her folded legs.

"I'm not following you."

"He wasn't bad leading up to the sex, but once we started, it was totally downhill." Eve felt an inkling of guilt as she said the words. Then again, this was a major crisis. The lowest point of her life. If a girl couldn't turn to her own flesh and blood in a time of need, who could she turn to? That's what sisters were for. Besides, Skye was her most loyal ally. The only person other than Xandra that Eve could trust to keep such personal information in the strictest confidence.

"Clint," came Skye's muffled voice. "Wake up, honey. She did it. She didn't just marry him. She *slept* with him."

Okay, so the whole marriage thing had obviously loosened Skye's lips.

"You're not going to tell anyone else, are you?" Eve asked after listening to more of Skye's whispering.

"Who? Me? Of course not." A few moments of silence ticked by, and Skye's conscience obviously got the best of her. "Just Clint, but the buck stops there. I swear."

"He's Linc's boss."

"So?"

"So nobody wants their boss to know what a dud they are in the sack. Not to mention, you absolutely cannot tell him that I faked it."

"I won't tell him you faked it."

"Skye."

"Sorry. Listen, Clint doesn't care if you faked it. Everybody fakes it at one time or another." More whispering and Skye's muffled voice carried over the line. "Everybody except me, honey. Believe me, I couldn't fake it if I tried. Now"—her voice grew loud and distinct again as she turned her attention back to Eve—"I know you're feeling down right now, but that's no cause to panic or do anything stupid."

"I've never faked it."

"This is not a big deal."

"I suck."

"You do not suck."

"I'm a liar."

"You're sensitive."

"You're not making me feel better."

"Obviously, Linc just wasn't all that skilled, otherwise, you never would have faked it."

"You think?"

"Heck, yes. My little sister doesn't fake orgasms unless she has a really good reason. Now, let's go through the events leading up to the bad part."

"Okay." Eve blinked back a swell of tears. *Tears?* She didn't cry, especially over a sexual encounter. Then again, she was doing a lot of things she didn't normally do in the short amount of time she'd been married to Linc Adams. She sniffled. "The kissing was good, but once the clothes came off . . ." Her mind flashed back to the stripping they'd done in her living room and her glimpse of him in nothing but his BVDs. "Okay, so there were a few hot moments while we were naked, too, but once we hit the sheets, that's when everything went to hell."

"*To hell,* as in he lost his erection?"

"No."

"Premature ejaculation?"

"No."

"Eve, honey, I can't say that I see the problem."

"He just got tense and then he didn't move right." Eve stared at the twinkling lights that dotted the Hollywood Hills. "It wasn't deep enough or fast enough. Then again, it could have been too fast and too deep. I don't know. It just wasn't right."

"You two weren't in sync. That happens sometimes."

"I know that, but it's never been cause for me to fake it in the past." A cool February breeze found its way under Eve's T-shirt and she pulled at the hem. The metal of the fire escape felt cold against her bare bottom, yet it wasn't enough to cool her flushed skin. She was still hot. Still needy.

"Don't beat yourself up," Skye told her. "It happened, and there's nothing you can do about it now. Maybe Linc has a mattress phobia that interfered with his concentration. You know, concentration is key for a lot of guys. You guys should just do it someplace else. . . . What am I saying?" she blurted out after a few seconds. "You shouldn't do it anyplace else. You shouldn't do it at all. You don't know him and he doesn't know you, and I can't believe you actually *married* him."

"Just until November." Eve tugged at the neckline of her T-shirt and spent the next several minutes giving Skye the lowdown on their arrangement.

"I knew it," Skye finally said. "You don't love him."

"Who said anything about love?"

"You've been living too close to Mom for too long. Love is everything."

"Maybe in a real marriage, but this is just for show. I don't need love right now."

"Everybody needs love."

"You've definitely watched *Casablanca* one too many times." Eve leaned back against the brick of the building and stretched her legs out, her feet dangling over the ledge.

"I don't watch movies. I read. Since the doctor found out about the twins, he instructed me to take it easy, which translates into staying off my feet. So I've been reading a lot lately."

"*101 Nights of Great Sex*?"

"*A Knight in Shining Armor* by Jude Devereaux. Clint's grandma Willemina gave me an old box of romance novels. Her keepers. I'm right in the middle of *Heaven, Texas* by Susan Elizabeth Phillips. It's so wonderful. He's this football player and she's this plain Jane and—"

"I'm going to ignore all of this because I know you're pregnant and not thinking clearly." Eve blew out a deep breath. The sound faded into the surrounding city noise so typical of an L.A. night—the roar of cars on a nearby expressway, the occasional barking dog, the late night news drifting from a neighbor's apartment. *Typical,* all right. At the same time, it all seemed different. *She* was different. "Can we get back to the subject?" she asked Skye.

"About how you tainted one of the most sacred forms of commitment between a man and a woman?"

"Mom decided we should spend more time together." Eve swallowed past the sudden lump in her throat. "Lunch. Every week."

"Okay, so marrying Linc might not be that bad an idea," Skye agreed. "But sleeping with him is positively the worst, and not because he's a dud. That's bad enough. You still don't know him, and while I have nothing against a one-night stand, you two aren't strangers passing in the night. Two lost souls who've lost their way and found each other. A pair of hungry bodies desperate for companionship, however brief."

"You've really been reading too many romance novels." Eve flexed her feet and marveled at the way her toes still tingled. The same way they'd tingled when Linc had been inside her. She shook her head. Tingling toes, but no orgasm. Go figure.

"What's happening to me?" Eve blurted out. "If I don't orgasm, I don't orgasm. I'm open and honest and I *never* put on a show just to make some man feel better about his performance."

"This isn't just a man. It's your husband."

"A stranger," Eve reminded her. "You said so yourself."

"True, but you guys *did* tie the knot, and you are going to spend some time together. It's not like you can kick him out and try again with someone else. So maybe it's a good thing that you faked it. You wouldn't want to hurt his feelings when you have to see him again."

"That's true. I wouldn't want to scar him for life, which would surely happen because he obviously thinks it was really incredible."

"How do you know?"

"Because he's sleeping. And snoring. And probably dreaming about all the ways he wants to do me." She stiffened and gathered her control. "I'm an idiot."

"You're not an idiot. But I do think you've bitten off more than you can chew with this marriage business. I hope you know what you're doing."

But Eve had all her bases covered. She knew exactly what she was doing—preserving her sanity and finishing a winning documentary—and what she wasn't doing— having sex with Linc Adams again.

One fake orgasm was plenty. She was cutting her losses and keeping things strictly platonic from here on out.

At least, that's what she intended to do just as soon as she climbed back inside.

Eve said good-bye, punched the OFF button, and hauled herself to her feet. She tucked the phone under her arm, turned toward the window, and pushed at the pane. It didn't so much as budge, and a wave of dread rolled over her.

Not because she was locked out; she'd been locked out before. The glass was forever slipping when she climbed out on the fire escape to enjoy the sunset, which was why she kept a key hidden under a planter just to the left of the front door to her building.

Click. Click. Click.

The noise drew Eve's gaze, and she glanced down to see a photographer hanging over the edge of the fence that surrounded the back of the building.

Dread rolled through her, followed by a flutter of panic.

Being locked out was no big deal for Eve Farrel. But being photographed minus her undies . . . Now that was a different story altogether.

Chapter 5

Linc barely made it back to the bed before he heard Eve's fingertips on the window. He hit the sheets and went totally still, feigning sleep. He listened as she pushed at the glass, but she didn't knock. Obviously, she didn't realize he was wide awake. Or that he'd been the one to lock her out in the first place.

He waited for her to knock. That was the whole point, after all. He didn't want her to get away with sneaking out on him. Better that she should have to face him and explain why she'd felt the need to slip out of bed. Instead, he heard the groan of metal as she started descending the fire escape steps.

He climbed out of bed and walked to the window in time to see the top of her head as she descended to the third floor. The metal kept groaning as she went lower. He turned to pull on his black tuxedo trousers. He had half a mind to go out front and help her with the reporters camped out on the front steps. Then again, his appearance would only compound the problem and, with the mood he was in, he was sure to say something he would regret.

Besides, she had no business being outside in the first place.

Did she go out to call a girlfriend? To brag?

He wanted to think so, but something didn't sit right in his gut. She'd been too stiff afterward. Too uptight.

She was nervous, his ego whispered. *She'd just had sex with a famous NASCAR driver.*

It made sense. He'd met women before who went all googly-eyed and freaky when they got close to him. One minute, they were panting to get into his pants and the next, starstruck.

The thing is, Eve wasn't the groupie type. Sure, he'd thought so when he'd first met her. With her hot body and skimpy clothes and do anything attitude, she'd seemed like another one of those trophy girls who followed him around from track to track. And so he'd been his typical bad-boy self. She'd been totally turned off, however, enough to walk out on him, and he'd realized then that she wasn't like the other women in his life.

There was an air of self-confidence about her that had nothing to do with sex appeal and everything to do with self-respect.

Linc walked into the living room and retrieved his pants. A wall-to-wall entertainment center that included a projection screen TV and DVD player filled the opposite side of the small room. A red velvet sofa and matching chair took up the rest of the space. Pillows in various animal prints covered the plush furniture and gave the room an exotic feel. The entire space screamed hot and wild and primitive.

Exactly what he would have expected.

At the same time, he couldn't help but wonder about the white wicker basket that sat in the far corner looking extremely out of place. A pale blue quilt patterned with sailboats peeked over the edge.

Sweet.

As soon as the thought struck, he pushed it back out. There was nothing sweet about Eve Farrel. She was as hot as spice.

He walked over to the glass entertainment center and the shelves that held her DVD collection. The top shelf held music CDs, everything from vintage Mötley Crüe and Guns N' Roses, to Creed and Nickelback. The bottom held her movie collection. Or so he thought.

After scanning the various titles—from *Fantastic Foreplay* to *Bedtime and Bondage*—he quickly realized that the DVDs were part of the How-to series, produced and directed by Sugar & Spice Sinema.

He slid the *Panting, Screaming, and After-Sex Dreaming* DVD free from its case and read the content description: "Surefire signs to recognize a thoroughly satisfied lover."

Linc inserted the DVD into the player and punched the ON button. The screen filled, and he spent the next few minutes watching a man and a woman called Jack and Candace have incredible sex. But it wasn't the sex that made Linc's heart pound faster. It was Candace's reaction to the sex, before, during, and after.

". . . A lover on the cusp of climax will have dilatated pupils, a telltale flush to the face, trembling lips—particularly during penetration—and frantic fingers."

Mentally, Linc rushed back through the encounter with Eve. While she'd had flushed cheeks, all right, and grasping fingers—at least during the undressing phase—she hadn't been the least bit frantic when he'd been inside her. No nails digging into his shoulders or his back. And she certainly hadn't had dilated pupils. If anything, her eyes had been wider, which could only mean . . .

Nah.

". . . orgasmic scream will be different for every female, but a common trait is the uncontrollable nature of it. It comes and goes with each thrust, the pitch often escalating. It can differ in range, as well, from a throaty moan to a high-pitched shriek . . ."

He frowned as he remembered Eve's loud chant of *"Yes!"*

". . . After sex, the muscles are spent and so the body lapses into a state of blissful lethargy . . ."

Translation: no jumping up to dash out the window and talk on the phone.

"Son of a bitch," he growled.

She'd *faked* it.

Possibly.

Probably.

Linc was about to hit PLAY again to go over the specifics—just to be sure—when he heard a knock on the front door. He quickly pushed the EJECT button on the DVD player, retrieved the disk, and replaced it on the shelf before heading to the door.

He opened the door to find Eve, a blanket wrapped around her waist. Two police officers flanked her.

"Holy cannoli," one of the officers blurted out. "It *is* him. You're Linc Adams." The man grabbed Linc's hand and pumped for all he was worth. "He's the NASCAR driver who just won the Daytona 500 yesterday," he told the other officer.

"Like I don't know that," Officer Number Two said. "Damn fine job you did. Damn fine."

"I thought you were a Mark Martin fan?" the first officer asked the second.

"Ain't no better driver out there than Shooter Adams. Blows all them barely legal rookies clean out of the water. This man's got maturity to go with his talent."

"Thanks, fellas."

The man continued to pump Linc's hand a few more seconds before realizing what he was doing. "Sorry there, Shooter."

"So what can I do for you guys?" Linc asked.

"Someone in the neighborhood called complaining about the reporters camped out in front of the building. We came to check things out and found your new missus here smack-dab in the middle of a bunch of photographers."

"I was trying to get my spare key," Eve said. "I locked myself out."

"My new missus?" Linc didn't mean to play dumb, but the notion that she'd faked it kept niggling inside him, distracting him.

"You two are married," Officer Number One declared, his gaze going from Linc to Eve and back again. "You *are* married, aren't you?" Before Linc could reply, the officer shook his head. "Dammit to hell. I knew it had to be a rumor. We heard it on this late-night talk show we always listen to. The host is usually on the money with his news, but I knew this was too far out to be true. No way would Linc Adams saddle himself to one woman. She's one of them groupies," he said to his partner. "Crazy women are always trying to get close to Linc. Why, I saw this gal parachute into Victory Lane last year after the Bud Shootout. She was wearing an itty-bitty bikini, and she was all over Linc here before security could pull her off."

"That was you?" The second officer looked awestruck.

Linc shrugged. "It's a tough job, but somebody's got to do it."

The men laughed and Eve stiffened. "Look, I'd love to stand here and keep listening to *Life and Times of the Conceited and Famous,* but I'm a little cold and almost naked."

Linc's gaze shifted to her. Her eye makeup was smudged, her dark hair tousled, and her lips still swollen from his kisses. She looked as if she'd just rolled out of bed after a really good orgasm.

Yeah, right.

Linc forced a smile. "You know, I think I do recognize her." He peered closer, and he had the feeling she was this close to slapping his face. "Why, it *is* her. She's the new little woman, all right. Sorry, sunshine." He winked at Eve and she scowled. "I didn't recognize you with the police-issue blanket and all. She's usually wearing a lot less," he told the officers. "You know how it is with newlyweds."

"Sure thing, Mr. Adams."

"Thanks for finding her before she wandered off somewhere." Linc lowered his voice. "It's all that medication."

"Medication?"

"For the sex addiction," he whispered. "It calms her down long enough for me to get some sleep, but it makes her sort of"—he let loose a low whistle—"*crazy.*"

"Oh, well, yeah, I think I've heard about that," Officer Number One said.

"Me, too," the second man added. "We'll clear out the press camped in front, but I'm sure they'll be back. You folks have a nice night, and be sure to call us if there are any disturbances."

"Sure thing." Linc smiled, pulled Eve inside, and shut the door.

She turned on him. "A *sex* addiction?"

"Would you rather I told them you were schizophrenic or delusional, or some other story to account for the fact that you were dangling naked from the fire escape?"

"I'm not naked. I'm *almost* naked, and I didn't need you to tell them anything except that I'm your wife. I already had a convincing story for the fire escape."

"That's good, because I'd love to hear it. First off, why didn't you just knock on the window?"

"Because I didn't want to wake you . . ." Her words faded as her gaze drilled into his. Realization brightened her gaze. "You were awake, weren't you? You locked me out on purpose."

He had half a mind to deny it, but when she looked at him it was as if she could see right through him. He shrugged. "You shouldn't have been outside in the first place."

"I needed some fresh air, that's all."

"And here I thought you were trying to gossip on the phone so I couldn't hear you."

"Well, that, too, but—" The words stalled as her gaze collided with his. Guilt filled her expression before it faded into a passive look and she shrugged. "I don't gossip. I was simply relaying the facts to my sister."

"Gossip."

"It wasn't gossip. I needed to explain things to Skye. I wanted her to know what was going on."

"So you had to call her five minutes after we finished having sex?"

"It wasn't five minutes. It was twenty-eight minutes, and I didn't think you would mind because you were asleep. I, on the other hand, couldn't sleep, so I thought I would just give my sister a call."

"To talk about me."

"I don't kiss and tell," Eve told him, and she meant it. She never found anything gossip-worthy about mere kisses.

"Some people like to brag," Linc continued. "Especially when it's really incredible. You were pretty worked up and pretty loud."

"I was?" The memory of the fake orgasm rushed at her full-force and she blurted out, "Yes, um, I guess I was."

"So you liked it?"

There was something oddly desperate about the question, and instead of coming clean and telling him the truth—that, yes, she'd *liked* it, but she hadn't loved it, not enough to actually reach la-la land—she heard herself say, "What's not to like?"

He eyed her for a full moment, and she had the strange feeling that he knew.

He couldn't know. She was the sexpert here. Not to mention, she was a woman. She knew how to fake an orgasm as well as she knew how to tie her own shoes. Not that she did it very often. Or ever. If she came, she came. If not, she simply finished herself off after the man went his way and she went hers. This time, however, she was stuck with Linc.

Temporarily, of course. But stuck nonetheless.

Silence stretched between them for a few frantic heartbeats. She gripped the blanket tighter around her. "Look, about the sex. While it *was* good"—*the foreplay, that is*—"and we've obviously got really good chemistry"—*go figure*—"it was still just sex. It didn't mean anything." *Especially not an orgasm.*

"It meant you wanted me and I wanted you." Linc walked around the living room and eyed the contents, from the leopard-print velvet table lamp to the penis-shaped nutcracker hand-carved out of tiki wood that sat on her coffee table.

"That's right. *Wanted* being the key word. As in past tense. The last thing I have time for in my life is an ongoing relationship. Not that I have anything against relationships," Eve rushed on, eager to set the record straight so that he knew up front she wasn't an antimarriage activist like her mother. "I fully intend to have one someday when Mr. Kaboom comes along."

"Mr. Who?"

"My soul mate. He'll be tall, dark and handsome—sort of a cross between Johnny Depp and Benicio Del Toro with a smidgeon of Vin Diesel thrown in to give him that dangerous edge. But he won't be all brawn and no brains. Nor will he be an egotistical cretin. He'll be an intellectual who's not only thoughtful and smart, but artistic as well. He'll also be very sensitive to me and my needs. We'll have instant chemistry to go with the meeting of minds and *kaboom,* it'll be fireworks. In the meantime, I need to focus on my work."

"I know the feeling." Linc fingered the black velvet painting of Van Halen—pre–Sammy Hagar—that hung on her wall. "This was my favorite band back in high school."

"You and every other guy I've ever known. Look, the point I'm trying to make is since you have to focus and I have to focus, we shouldn't be wasting time focusing on each other."

"What you're saying is no more sex." He continued to eyeball the velvet painting.

Eve frowned. Linc didn't have to look so unaffected by the bomb she'd just dropped.

Not that she wanted him to be affected, mind you. It was the principle of the thing. She'd pulled out all the stops to give him a stellar performance. The least he could do was look a little disappointed.

"They just weren't the same after David Lee Roth left," he finally said.

"He *was* the driving force." Eve inhaled deeply and tried to ignore the faint scent of warm male that teased her nostrils. "You can sleep in the guest bedroom"—she pointed toward the doorway that led to the short hall and the two bedrooms—"when you're here. I'm sure you have a spare room at your place. That, or I can just sleep on the couch. That way we'll avoid temptation."

"Actually, I thought Eddie Van Halen was the driving force. His guitar riffs were incredible."

"Right." She drew another deep breath. Her breasts pressed against the soft cotton of her T-shirt, and she became instantly aware that she was standing there without any underwear on. Sure, she had the blanket wrapped around her waist, but suddenly it didn't seem like nearly enough. Not with Linc so close, filling up her small living room. "Can we get back to the matter at hand, please?"

He spared her a look and arched an eyebrow. "Your screaming orgasm?"

She frowned. "That and the fact that I don't think I should have another, not with you, that is."

"Not with anyone while we're married." He pinned her with a stare. "I don't need the sympathy vote because my wife is out cheating on me."

"I won't have time to cheat. I have a project to finish." She watched him resume his study of her living room. He bypassed the painting and stopped near the white wicker basket she'd left out last week. He fingered the baby blanket that sat inside.

"Is this part of your documentary?"

"It's a baby quilt. I'm making it for Skye's twins. Actually, I'm going to make two. The first one's almost finished."

"You did this?" He held up the hand-sewn quilt and surprise flickered in his gaze.

"I want to give her something special. Besides, the quilting helps me de-stress after a long day."

"It's . . . nice." Linc stared at the quilt as if he couldn't quite believe his eyes before the expression disappeared. "I never would have figured you for the quilting type."

"Yeah? Well, I never would have figured you for the milk type, either. So we're even."

Eve watched as he placed the blanket back into her basket before turning toward her stereo system. Muscles rippled in his arms and chest as he pressed the ON button and Avril Lavigne's "Happy Ending" blared from the speakers.

"You can't cheat, either," she said after he'd turned the volume down. "My mother has to think we have the perfect marriage. If there's trouble in paradise, she'll get her hopes up, and that will mean she'll pay me more attention because she thinks there's a chance to save me."

"No cheating," he agreed, killing the music and walking over to her. He stopped just a few inches from her, and she had the crazy thought that he meant to kiss her.

Even worse, she *wanted* him to kiss her.

She tightened her grip on the blanket around her waist. "Just be your obnoxious self like you did tonight. It's bad enough that I enslaved myself, but doing it with someone like you makes it that much worse."

He grinned. "No problem, sunshine."

"And one other thing. Since we're sort of playing on the same team, you can stop trying to irritate me. No more *sunshine,* except in front of my mother. She'll hate it."

"No sex. No pet names." Linc stared at her lips as if debating over the kiss. "I can see this is going to be a long nine months," he finally said before turning toward the guest bedroom.

And how, Eve thought as she watched him walk down the hall, her gaze on the sway of his tush beneath his fitted pants. Bad sex aside, he *was* attractive. And exciting.

And totally *not* her type, she reminded herself. Which meant he was completely off-limits from here on out.

Had she really *faked* it?

The question echoed in Linc's head as he stretched out on the bed in Eve's guest room and stared at the ceiling. Sure, it hadn't been the best race of his life—she'd tensed up toward the end and it had thrown off his stroke—but he sure as hell hadn't had to fake it. He'd simply floored the gas, moved a little faster, and sailed right over the finish line.

He knew women were different and that sometimes it took more than just picking up the pace to make things happen. More kissing and touching and rubbing. He would have been more than happy to try all three to help her get off, but then she'd opened her mouth and started with the whole *yes* thing.

A put-on?

Eve didn't seem like the type. She was too out there and in your face and too damned knowledgeable on the subject.

Then again, maybe that was the reason itself. Her very nature stirred expectations that she might have felt hard-pressed to live up to. She looked wild and wicked, and so she'd done her best to be wild and wicked.

Maybe.

And maybe it had been so good that she feared doing it again because she didn't want to let herself fall for a man like Linc. He didn't look a thing like Johnny Depp or Benicio Del Toro or Vin Diesel, even though he did appreciate the man's taste in sunglasses. To fall for Linc would make her a hypocrite, and so she'd come up with the whole No Sex rule to keep from having another orgasm with a man so totally unlike her ideal.

He weighed the two options and would have been inclined to lean toward the latter—he was a man, after all, and his pride was at stake.

But he couldn't forget the DVD about the surefire signs of a well-satisfied partner. Eve had had none of them except for the panting and the scream. Two out of five didn't make for a convincing argument.

Who the hell cares? This isn't about sex. It's about keeping your freedom, buddy. And your focus. You can't win a championship if you're attending city council meetings and dedicating new libraries.

Damn straight.

And so it was a fine idea that they weren't going to do it again. The last thing Linc needed was another distraction. He couldn't afford to think about the way her bottom lip trembled beneath his when he kissed her, or the way her fingers clenched when he licked her pulse beat, or the way she'd looked so soft and vulnerable wrapped in that police blanket.

He wasn't as young as the other new drivers out there, and so he felt he had more to prove and less time to do it. He'd entered the sport with an impressive showing—he'd won a whopping ten out of the thirty-six races his first year, and at least that many in the four years since—but he'd never won the Daytona 500.

Until yesterday. He'd set a precedent for himself. This was his year.

He knew it.

He felt it.

He *needed* it.

To erase the regret that still ate at him for not pursuing his dream sooner, and to reassure himself that giving up the solid foundation of a law practice to pursue a crazy, out-of-this-world dream hadn't been a mistake.

Right now he needed to think about this Sunday at the Rock—the drivers' term for North Carolina Speedway in Rockingham   and the second season race, which would be even more of a challenge than the first. The drivers who'd had a poor showing at Daytona would be out to prove something. The ones who'd raced well would be out to maintain their standing. The competition would be fierce.

Linc was up to the challenge. He was hungry and focused, and he wasn't the least bit worried about Eve Farrel and her orgasm. Real or not.

At least that's what he told himself.

Chapter 6

It had to be a dream.

That was Eve's first thought when she opened her eyes the next morning and the sex episode with Linc rushed through her head.

She'd had a little too much to drink and way too much of her mother, and so she'd come home and had a really awful nightmare.

But as she climbed out of bed and stumbled over Killer, who lay amid a pile of clothes—a man's tuxedo jacket and shirt—she knew beyond a doubt that last night had been all too real.

Everything, that is, except for her orgasm.

Guilt churned inside her and she did her best to tamp it back down. She pulled on a pair of black leggings and an oversized black T-shirt imprinted with the title of her last video. Then she headed to the kitchen.

Fifteen minutes later, after two cups of strong black coffee, she called Trina.

"Why didn't you tell me you and Linc Adams had a thing?" Trina demanded.

"We don't have a thing." Eve stood at her kitchen counter and poured herself another cup of java.

"You married him."

"Okay, so we have a thing. But it's just a little thing. Listen, I need you to handle the office for the next few days."

"You're not changing the subject. You *married* Linc Adams and totally ruined him as fantasy material for me."

"What are you talking about?"

"I won't be able to picture Linc without picturing you, and while I've swung both ways on occasion, we're talking *you*. While you *are* pretty hot in a Guns N' Roses video sort of way, you're like my sister."

"Since when do you fantasize about NASCAR drivers? You don't do anyone who doesn't live in a three-piece suit and have a seven-figure bank account." Eve sipped her coffee. The hot black liquid sent a rush of warmth through her body and a *wake-up* jolt to her brain.

"A seven-figure bank account supersedes the three-piece suit. You wouldn't believe how much some of those guys make. And women—NASCAR finally has a female driver. She aced the Bud Shootout last year and walked away with a pretty nice paycheck. Which brings me back to the money. The weekly purse for each race is incredible. On top of that, you've got bonus money from various race sponsors and—"

"Hold on a second." Eve took another sip. "Since when do you know anything about NASCAR?"

"Since I read the sports section of the *L.A. Times* this morning. I know that Linc won ten races last year, and made an amazing finish overall. I know that he's the favorite to win the Nextel Cup this year, thanks to a win this past weekend at the Daytona 500, which, I might add, is the first race of the NASCAR season and has one of the biggest paychecks. I also know that Linc closes his eyes when he kisses and that you don't photograph well in yellow."

Eve set her cup on the ceramic countertop and leaned against the edge. "You know that last part from reading the sports section?"

"Actually, I know that by watching late-night E! How they got pictures of you and Linc locked at the lips so fast is totally beyond me. I guess that's why I'm in marketing and not production. Did you know that he's been linked romantically to three different actresses? He's also been with a Victoria's Secret model and two girls from *Hooters Magazine.* Not at the same time, of course, and the affairs were all very brief. But that still doesn't erase the fact that he's strictly a flavor-of-the-week kind of guy. He doesn't do relationships, and he sure as hell doesn't do marriage. Which makes me, and the host of late-night E!, think there's something funny about this marriage."

Eve picked up her cup and downed the rest of the strong liquid. "Maybe it was love at first sight," she finally managed.

"And maybe I'll just forgo my next collagen injection in the name of natural beauty." Trina sighed. "*Not.* So give with the details."

"You have to swear you won't tell anyone." She set the cup back on the counter and mindlessly traced the rim as the memory of the past night rushed at her.

"I swear on my uncle Duke's collector's edition Ferrari."

"We're not really married," Eve blurted out. "I mean, we are. But we aren't." She spent the next several minutes filling Trina in on the details of the pretend marriage. "So you can't tell anyone," she finished, "otherwise, my mother will know it's a lie and she'll go back to thinking I'm the good daughter."

"My lips are sealed."

"Good." Eve shifted the subject back to the reason for her phone call. "Now—I've left a stack of catalog samples sitting on my desk."

"Hold on. You can't just drop a bomb like this and then start talking work. You know I can't work without my coffee."

"So get your butt to the kitchen."

"All right, all right. I'm here," Trina told her after a lot of grumbling.

Eve went over the work details that needed immediate attention. The rest she would handle herself via e-mail. "I'll be back on Monday. I'm meeting the in-laws today, then I'm going to put in an appearance at the racetrack in North Carolina. Rockingham or something like that. I should have the basic documentary layout done by the time I get back so that we can start expanding on each of the segments."

"You really expect to work with Linc Adams within arm's reach?"

"The man's a barbarian, and I don't do barbarian anymore. I'm not even attracted to him."

That's what Eve wanted to think, but when Linc walked into the kitchen a few minutes after she hung up the phone her interest sparked again.

He wore only the black tuxedo slacks from the night before. His bare feet were long and tanned against Eve's white marble tile. At well over six feet tall, he dominated her small kitchen. The enticing aroma of fresh soap and raw male filled her nostrils.

She steeled herself and tried to focus on all the reasons why she shouldn't be attracted to him.

He was a total cretin. An old-fashioned, chauvinistic caveman who changed women as often as he changed his socks. Ordinarily, he dressed like a beach bum. He also grinned way too much. As for the winking . . . Well, that irritated her as much as the word *sunshine.*

She watched as he opened three cabinets before finding a glass and turning toward the fridge. He poured some milk and started to lift the glass to his lips when she stopped him.

"You don't have to mind your manners on my account." *Please don't mind them,* she pleaded silently. *I need all the ammunition I can get.*

"I don't drink out of the carton." Linc gave her a knowing look. "But if you want to lend me your bra . . ."

"I wouldn't lend you my bra if you were the last man on the planet and needed a drinking vessel in order to avoid severe dehydration."

His lips curved up at the corners and her heart stalled. "Your can't lend me your bra because you're not wearing one." His gaze dropped to the telltale twin points outlined by the thin material of Eve's black T-shirt.

"I was speaking figuratively." Okay, so she sounded like a snotty bitch. But better to sound snotty than interested. "You do know what *figuratively* means, don't you? Never mind, I forgot that you graduated from the University of T & A."

"If I didn't know better, I'd say you were calling me a chauvinist."

"If the Bubba Beer ball cap fits . . ." She was referring to the latest picture of Linc to circulate in the tabloids. Him wearing a Bubba Beer ball cap, an inebriated grin, and a Hooters girl on each arm. He'd attended an all-you-can-eat wing fest down in Houston, and had been the deciding judge at a bikini contest.

"That was a publicity stunt."

"No one can pretend to be that obnoxious."

He frowned. "I don't drink Bubba Beer, and I don't drive for them. Jason Dancer's their golden boy with his number ninety-seven Ford. Someone just stuck that cap on my head when I wasn't paying attention."

"Sure, and I'm the spokesperson for prim, proper virgins everywhere."

"Keep that to yourself. We're trying to shock my parents, not make them fall in love with you. And speaking of my parents, we're due at the airport in an— What the hell is *that*?"

Linc stared past her at the kitchen doorway.

She followed Linc's stare and smiled as Killer walked into the room. "It's my labradoodle."

"Your what?"

"You know, part Lab, part poodle."

"You mean a mutt."

"Killer is not a mutt." Eve leaned down and the dog walked right into her arms. The animal was medium-sized, with wavy gold hair and long, fluffy poodle ears. "Don't listen to him, girl. You're not a mutt. She's very sensitive and her feelings get hurt really easy," she told Linc as she stroked her pet.

"She's a dog."

Eve nuzzled Killer and eyed Linc. "Don't listen to him,

girl. He's one of *those*." When Linc cocked an eyebrow at her, Eve added in a whisper, "A dog hater."

"I don't hate dogs. I just don't put them on the same level as people. They're animals."

"Then you two ought to get along really well." Eve meant it as a joke. She didn't expect Killer to walk right over to Linc and start licking his toes as if she'd been doing so every day of her life. Eve shook her head and eyed the suddenly affectionate dog. "Killer?"

"What's wrong?" Linc asked as he knelt to pet the animal.

"She's not supposed to like you. I mean, she usually doesn't like strangers."

"Maybe she's sick?"

"She doesn't look sick."

"Maybe she's pregnant."

"It would be miracle puppies because the only other dog she has any contact with is Mr. Wilkie's blue heeler, Lady and the Tramp, who happens to be a female."

"Maybe she doesn't see me as a stranger. You and I *are* married. Maybe Killer senses the new connection." Linc pushed to his feet. "We've got a plane to catch in less than two hours." He grinned. "It's showtime."

She'd had a dream. A really *bad* dream.

Jacqueline Farrel held tight to the thought as she climbed out of bed early Tuesday morning. A soft snore floated through the dim bedroom. She glanced at her significant other, who lay sprawled across the king-sized bed.

No wonder she'd had a bad dream. With Donovan tossing and turning and invading her side of the bed, it was impossible to get a decent night's rest. Certainly he was warm, and she did enjoy cuddling up against him when they first climbed beneath the covers, but those joys didn't last long. Once Donovan fell asleep, it was every man for himself.

Of course, the bad dream could have been due to the fact that she was off her schedule and out of her comfort zone. Ordinarily, she would have been halfway to the studio by now. Because of the previous night's festivities, however, the show's executives had given everyone the morning off. Thankfully. Jacqueline had a million things to do before she was expected at the studio later that afternoon. At the top of her list was putting her mother on a plane bound for Texas.

Jacqueline drew in a deep breath and walked toward the bathroom. Some coffee should dispel the exhaustion clouding her senses and the uneasiness in the pit of her stomach.

Imagine Eve getting *married*, of all things. And to a virtual stranger. Even worse, to a stranger who was a womanizing, hell-raising, lewd, crude, out-of-control male chauvinist like—

Her thoughts screeched to a halt as she caught sight of the newspaper that was crumpled on the kitchen table next to her mother's #1 GRANDMA mug. The front page of the sports section peeked around the edge of the food and entertainment section. Air stalled in her lungs and her heart threw up a picket sign and went on strike. Her trembling hands reached for the newspaper. She tugged it free to see the full color photograph of Eve and Linc Adams in a passionate kiss. The caption beneath read: NASCAR'S WILD MAN PULLS YET ANOTHER STUNT AND TIES THE

KNOT IN AN IMPROMPTU WEDDING TO L.A.'S OWN HOW-
TO SEX DIVA.

Jacqueline entertained a few seconds of denial before her mind rushed back to the previous night. To Linc Adams and her precious Eve. To Linc Adams and her precious Eve kissing. To Linc Adams and her precious Eve saying "I do."

"I think I'm going to be sick." Jacqueline turned and made a beeline for the bathroom. She'd just shut the door when she heard Donovan's voice on the other side.

"Jacqueline?"

"I'm okay," she called out as she tried to catch her breath. She was not going to be sick. What's more, she was not going to have a nervous breakdown.

The doorknob clicked and Donovan ducked his head inside. Though in his fifties, he was every bit as handsome as the day they'd met. His dark hair was now sprinkled with gray, but still thick and soft. He had the same intense brown eyes that had first turned her knees to Jell-O, even though crow's-feet now fanned from the corners. Morning stubble covered his strong jaw.

Concern drew his brows together. "Honey? Is anything wrong?"

She wanted to say no. She wanted to *feel* no. But the only thing she felt was a churning stomach and a strange sense of doom.

"It's not that bad." His deep voice drew her gaze back to the mirror and his reflection just over her shoulder. "Maybe Eve loves him. Maybe he loves her."

"They hardly know each other. Not to mention that love has nothing to do with any of this. They're *married,* Donovan. It's not like they've moved in together and decided to share a cable bill." At his raised eyebrows, she added, "While a shared cable bill is extremely serious, it's not an out-and-out travesty." What was she saying? She didn't even share a cable bill, or any other utility account, with Donovan, who was as close to perfection as a man could get.

Or rather, he used to be her ideal male. Before he'd shown up on her doorstep in L.A. a few months back and decided to press her for a more serious commitment. Why, they already shared three daughters and a house in Georgetown, Texas—at least for half the year. The other six months she spent in her own apartment in L.A., where she taped her hit talk show, *Get Sexed Up!*—the very same apartment Donovan had recently invaded.

"Marriage isn't so bad. Skye's happy. And Xandra looked positively radiant yesterday."

"They're both still riding the lust high, not to mention Skye's hormones are raging thanks to the pregnancy. Neither one of them is thinking clearly. But Eve . . . She knows better than to give up everything for some man."

"Not if he's *the man.*"

"What are you trying to say?"

"That I've been thinking about this, and I think that when someone finds the right person there's nothing wrong with declaring it to the world. I've been thinking, in fact, that you and I should try it ourselves."

Jacqueline's churning stomach did a complete flip and she swallowed. He couldn't be . . . He wouldn't dream of actually suggesting . . .

"We've been together for a long time," he went on. "I think it's high time we—"

"Do you always have to leave the lid up?" she cut in,

effectively killing his next words. She slammed the toilet seat down and pushed past him before he could say another word. "What kind of effort does it take to simply pop it back down when you're finished? Sheesh, you would think I was asking for a miracle." She headed for the kitchen again. When she got there, she scooped the newspaper into a pile and shoved it into the trash before moving on to her next order of business.

She needed caffeine. Lots of caffeine. Enough to kick-start her brain from its present funk and get it moving as fast as her heart and the adrenaline that pumped through her body. She needed to think. To digest.

"You're changing the subject," Donovan said, following her.

"I'm not changing anything. I was in the bathroom," Jacqueline said as she hauled open a cabinet and rummaged inside. "There was the toilet seat in its usual upright position, gawking at me like always. *That* was the subject."

"I'm talking about marriage. About you and me—"

"Where the hell are the coffee filters?"

"In the cabinet over the sink next to the Coffee-mate. Now about you and I—"

"I keep the coffee filters right here, not over the sink. I keep them right next to the extra napkins and the Ziploc baggies and the Bounty."

"I moved them. I think we should get—"

"You moved my coffee filters?" She whirled on him. "How could you do such a thing?"

"You're blowing this way out of proportion. I just thought it made more sense to keep them next to the coffee."

"*You* thought it made more sense. This is my apartment, yet I don't have any say-so in anything anymore. You leave the toilet seat up and your socks in a pile and you hog the entire bed. You've taken over the answering machine and now the kitchen. The next thing you know, I'll be chained in the laundry room, living on bread and water and—"

"Hold on a second. I think you should just take a deep breath and—"

"It's not about what you think," she screeched. "Doesn't anybody care about what *I* think? I'm on the edge, Donovan." She yanked the coffee filters from the cabinet and switched her attention to the coffee. Her hands shook as she started to spoon in the dark grounds. One. Two. Three.

"You're just scared," his deep voice sounded behind her. He came up, his chest against her back. He smelled so good that she actually closed her eyes for a brief moment and simply drank in the rich aroma of coffee and warm male.

"It's understandable, given your deep-seated fear of commitment," he went on. Her eyes snapped open to find that she'd spooned the grounds onto the countertop.

"Would you just give me some space," Jacqueline muttered, scooting to the side, away from his scent and warmth. "We're not joined at the hip."

"We should be. We should be joined in holy—"

"Coffee?" she cut in. "Speak now or forever hold your peace." Cripes, why had she said that? "This is your last chance. I'll add some for you, or you can just watch me drink it."

"I'll watch. Look, I think we should just do it."

"Fine with me, but don't go begging for a sip when you see me enjoying myself."

"Would you forget the coffee? I'm talking about us. Let's just go to a justice of the peace and get it over with as quickly and as painlessly as possible, and you'll see that being married— Ouch!" He rubbed his shoulder where the coffee scoop hit him. "What did you do that for?"

"You talk too much, Donovan."

"You're trying to avoid the subject, but I'm not going to let you. Not this time. This is it." He dropped to his knees, and panic bolted through her. "Jacqueline Dawnette Farrel, will you—"

"Mom!" Jacqueline called out as she whirled and started down the hallway. "Are you up yet? Your plane leaves at noon. We need to get a move on!"

"Heavens to Betsy, what is all this racket?" Ruella Farrel pulled open the bedroom door. She was wearing a white cover-everything-up cotton nightgown, her silvery white hair wrapped up in pink sponge rollers.

Jacqueline came to a halt. Surprise mixed with the panic already winding her insides tight. "Mom, why aren't you up? I put an alarm clock on your night table last night."

"I know. The blasted thing nearly gave me a heart attack this morning."

"So you heard it?"

"Of course I heard it. I may be old, but I'm not deaf."

"So why aren't you dressed?"

"I am dressed."

"For bed."

"That's because I'm *in* bed."

"But we leave for the airport soon."

"I'm not going home."

"Of course you're going home."

"I've cashed in my ticket and decided to stay awhile. Los Angeles really is a lovely city. So many people." Ruella smiled. "I think a lengthy visit is in order."

Surprise turned into full-blown dread. "Lengthy? How lengthy?"

"A week at least."

"A week?"

"Maybe two. Or even three. Why, I just might pack up and move in for good. It's so much more exciting here than back home. Now keep it down. I was up reading late last night, and I need my beauty sleep." The slam of the door punctuated her sentence, and Jacqueline found herself staring at a closed door.

"Jacqueline?" Donovan's voice sounded from the opposite end of the hallway. A very short, narrow hallway that had always been just the right size for one person. Large even. But now it seemed crowded, as if the walls were closing in. "We're not finished talking."

Forget closing in. The walls of Jacqueline Farrel's carefully constructed world were now falling down on top of her.

Chapter 7

Ruella Bethany Farrel needed to find a grade-A, 100 percent, snow-on-the-rooftop-but-fire-still-blazing-in-the-cookstove man. And quick.

She would even settle for one of those Viagra-stoked fires, just so long as there were enough sparks to keep the old equipment functioning nice and proper.

At seventy-one (and counting), Ruella wasn't sure exactly how much time she had left. Her three older sisters had all been diagnosed with diabetes by the age of seventy-two. Likewise, all three had passed away due to diabetes-related causes by the age of seventy-four. Ruella had thought that maybe, for the first time in her life, she might get lucky. After all, she'd made it to seventy-one with a clean bill of health. The occasional stomach upset, but nothing to get her britches in a twist about.

Two weeks ago, however, she'd received the bad news, and she didn't need a crystal ball to predict what was likely to happen next. Sure, she would feel fine for a while. She would take the appropriate medications, follow a very restricted diet, and do everything the doctor told her, but it wouldn't make any difference. Sometime within the next two and a half years, she was going to kick the bucket just like her sisters. End of story.

Ruella had never been a lucky woman. She'd married the first man she'd ever kissed. She'd gotten knocked up the first time she'd ever had sex. She'd been duped by a coldhearted, callous man who'd disguised himself as Prince Charming. She'd gone on to endure years of emotional and physical abuse from that same man. And just when she'd gotten used to both—a small price to pay for a roof over her head and clothes on her back—the Lord had struck down her rat bastard of a husband, and she'd found herself left with a mountain of debt and a child to raise on her own. Luck? Bah, humbug.

Ruella was an expert when it came to the worst case, and so she saw no need to try to be optimistic now. Her clock was ticking and the good Lord was *this close* to calling her home. She had to do something. *Now.*

She glanced at the newspaper she'd picked up yesterday on her way home from Xandra's wedding. The classifieds section sat on her nightstand, the paper folded open to the personals. She'd circled several ads the night before and was trying to compose one of her own.

Single white widow seeks mature, experienced, attractive, single male for fantastic sex.

She eyed the words thoughtfully before scribbling an extra sentence. "Lots of fantastic sex." Okay, so it wasn't as poetic as she might have liked, but she was a woman whose days were numbered. She didn't have time to sugarcoat things. She needed as many replies as possible in the shortest amount of time, which was why she'd called an 800 number late last night and left a prerecorded message for other sexy singles. She didn't want to waste even a moment while waiting for her ad to run. Likewise, she didn't have time for a long courtship with any of her respondents. Courtships were for falling in like and finding common interests and sharing lifelong goals and forging long-term commitments. Ruella wasn't interested in long term. She wanted right now. She wanted excitement. She wanted to go to her grave having felt her heart pound and her stomach flutter and her knees tremble and her palms sweat for a reason other than a thyroid condition, a stroke, or underactive sweat glands. She wanted to feel alive, truly *alive,* for once in her life.

Because Ruella had never had a climax while having sex. During her marriage, she'd always been focused on pleasing the rat bastard, fearful of disappointing him and suffering the consequences, and so her own pleasure had never come into the equation. After his death, she'd been so busy making ends meet and putting Jacqueline through school, and then looking after her granddaughters, that she'd never had time for a date, much less sex.

Until now.

Now it was all she could think about. Could it really be as pleasurable as it was described in all of those romance novels? Her gut said no, but there were too many people out there doing it for it to be all that bad. And so she intended to find out firsthand.

Since her hometown of Georgetown, Texas, wasn't exactly overflowing with possibilities, she'd decided to stay in Los Angeles. It was one of the biggest cities in the United States, a veritable smorgasbord of gentlemen.

With her mind made up, she hummed that old George Michael song that had been all the rage when her grand-daughters had been young. "I Want Your Sex."

She went about pulling on a pair of cream-colored support hose. Next she struggled into a beige girdle and a heavy-duty underwire bra. She pulled on one of her new pantsuits, then a strand of pearls and matching earrings. Later, she surveyed herself in the mirror. She wasn't even close to winning Miss Ripe and Ready at Georgetown's yearly watermelon fest, as her late husband had always been quick to point out. She never had been. But she'd certainly seen worse.

She leaned closer to the mirror, and her gaze lit on the tiny, threadlike scar that ran from her temple and bisected one silver eyebrow. She had a dozen others here and there. Battle scars from her marriage. They'd faded over time, so now it was hard to tell them from the wrinkles on her face.

Ruella forced aside the negative thought. So she was old? And a little worn? Nobody was perfect unless they had at least a half million dollars invested in cosmetic surgery—an option she'd actually considered at one point to erase all signs of her bad marriage. But the bottom line was, Ruella hadn't wanted to erase the scars or forget her past for fear that she would find herself making the same mistake again, and so she'd kept them as a reminder. Looking back, she supposed she should have followed through with the surgery for Jacqueline's sake. Perhaps that would have softened her daughter's view of love and marriage and commitment.

Then again, maybe not. While Ruella could have erased the scars on her face, she couldn't erase the scars on her daughter's childhood. The nights when Jacqueline had lain awake and listened to her father yelling. The times she'd hidden beneath the stairs and watched him work out his aggression with his fists. The times she'd cried because she'd wanted Ruella to take her far, far away. But Ruella had been stuck. She'd had no money and a family that had frowned on divorce. And so she'd stayed and endured, and at the same time, she'd fed her young daughter's mistrust.

Regret welled inside and tears blurred her eyes. She blinked frantically until her reflection came back into focus. There was no sense dwelling on the past. She couldn't change things, but she could change the future.

She blinked again and eyed the old woman who stared back at her. Wrinkles and scars aside, she had good skin. No age spots or spider veins. And she had nice eyes. No cataracts to cloud things over. Her eyes were still as blue as Sinatra's were, as sexy even.

She held fast to the notion, slicked on some pale lipstick to match her suit, and gathered up her handbag. She was going to the post office first thing to mail her ad and the money for its placement, and then she was heading to the nearest coffee shop. There she would have a nice, steaming cup, her usual black with no cream, and make herself very open and visible to the male population that strolled by.

She might even have a piece of apple pie, provided they served the kind made with a sugar substitute. Men liked apple pie, and so she was sure to snag the attention of at least one observant, hungry male. Meanwhile she would brainstorm a list of possible places to meet men. She definitely needed a list of local bingo parlors. She might even visit a sporting goods store on her way home. Most of the men her age were too frail to cast a fishing rod or too weak to paddle a kayak or too blind to see down the scope of a rifle, but she was open to the possibility of cradle-robbing and finding herself someone in his sixties. Maybe even his fifties.

The notion sent a burst of adrenaline through her and she smiled. She might be on her way to kicking the bucket, but she wasn't a goner yet.

"You've got a lot of explaining to do," Clint said the moment Linc answered his cell phone on Tuesday morning.

"Are you speaking as my boss or as my brother-in-law?" Linc asked as he slid into his first-class seat on the flight to Atlanta. Eve was busy settling in next to him.

"Both," Clint told him. "Would you mind telling me what the hell you were thinking last night?" Without waiting for a reply, Clint rushed on, "You've pulled a lot of stunts before, but this takes the cake. I thought you liked being single. I thought you thrived on it."

"Maybe I'm tired of it. Maybe I'm trying to clean up my image."

Eve gave him a *yeah, right* look before leaning over to rummage through her purse.

"By marrying *Eve Farrel*?" Clint's voice came over the line.

"Okay, so maybe I'm trying to do damage to my image."

Clint let loose an exasperated breath. "That much I understand. What about your popularity with NASCAR fans? Going from playboy bachelor to devoted husband is

bound to kill enthusiasm. Danielle's called fourteen times in the past hour. She's this close to having a heart attack."
Danielle Savoy was the racing team's publicist and the woman responsible for Linc's bad-boy bachelor image.

"After winning the Daytona 500, the only thing that's going to kill enthusiasm is losing the next race. Everybody loves a winner, boss. Single or otherwise."

"I hope so. Speaking of which, I'll see you at the Rock first thing tomorrow morning. We've got some PR stuff to do with some of the local radio stations and then a meeting with Big Tex." Big Tex was the main MacAllister Magic racing team sponsor.

"I'll be there."

"Are you staying in L.A. the rest of today?"

"We're flying to Adams to spend the night, then we'll head for the track at daybreak."

"We? You and Eve?"

"We *are* married."

"I hope you know what you're doing with all of this."

"So do I." Linc hung up the phone and watched Eve pop three pieces of gum into her mouth before leaning over to stuff the rest of the package back into her purse. His gaze fixed on her mouth as she chewed. She had a really great mouth.

"Why are you staring at me?" she asked after several seconds ticked by.

"I'm not staring at you."

"You're definitely staring at me."

"You look nervous," Linc told her. "You're not afraid to fly, are you?"

"I'm not afraid to fly." *If only,* Eve thought. But she had much bigger problems at the moment.

She was stressed from having to pack in less than fifteen minutes. And tired from having to tote Killer down to Mr. Wilkie's apartment for an impromptu sleepover with Lady and the Tramp—her neighbor had agreed to dog-sit while she was away. Eve was also nearly blind, thanks to the three photographers still camped out on the front steps of her apartment building. The trio had followed Eve and Linc all the way to the airport and snapped picture after picture while they'd headed for the gate. She was also eager to pull out her laptop and get to work. And thirsty since she hadn't had a sip of anything since they'd left the house. And hungry for a major sugar fix since she'd missed her midmorning package of Sugar Babies.

"It's okay," Linc went on. "My brake man, Jim, can bench-press four hundred pounds, but he's terrified of heights. Just the thought makes him break out in a sweat."

"I am *not* afraid to fly."

"Then what are you afraid of?"

"I'm afraid of Teletubbies, conservative Republicans, and men who name their penises. That's about it." Eve tried to sound nonchalant as she forced her knuckles to loosen their death grip on the armrests of her seat.

The last thing, the very last thing Eve needed was for him to realize that she was, indeed, nervous. But not about flying. About him. He was too close and he smelled too good.

"Why are you afraid of Teletubbies?" Linc asked as he rested his elbows on the armrests of his seat. His arm brushed hers and she did her best not to jump.

"One of my cameramen belongs to this group that thinks all the babbling they do is some secret code used by aliens to communicate with fellow aliens stationed on earth. They've even got members dedicated to deciphering the code, which they report in a monthly e-mail newsletter to all members." She busied herself fastening her seat belt.

"And you believe that?"

"No, but the fact that over two hundred and fifty supposedly rational adults buy into such a thing makes me terribly afraid of the state of our society."

"What about conservative Republicans?" Eve gave him a *get real* look and he shrugged. "Okay, that's a given. What about men who name their penises?"

"It's a sign of insecurity."

"How do you figure?"

"Men develop pet names for their members because they're too embarrassed to use the correct term. It smacks of immaturity, which indicates that society will never fully evolve into a peaceful, rational world where all are created equal."

"You get all that just from a guy referring to his Baby Huey?"

"Baby Huey?"

"Or Captain America. Or Grave Digger. Or even the Titanic." His gaze hooked with hers. "Has it ever occurred to you that maybe the nickname isn't a sign of immaturity, but practicality?"

"Meaning?"

"Maybe men just like using a term that's more individual and appropriate. *Penis* is such a generic word for something that comes in all shapes and sizes. Besides, it's a damned sight special to most men, so it deserves a name all its own."

"So what do you call yours?" The words were out before Eve could stop them.

He grinned. "I've already told you."

"Baby Huey?"

He gave her a *you know better* look.

"I might understand Grave Digger, but Titanic is a bit ambitious, don't you think?"

Linc frowned and it was Eve's turn to smile. His thigh bumped hers as he stretched his legs. His forearm, all hard muscle dusted with golden hair, grazed her bare skin again and she sucked in her breath.

Breath-sucking because of a gold-dusted, muscular arm? Cripes, she hated everything gold, and she'd overcome her weakness for muscles. Now it was all about mind over matter when it came to men. Intelligence over physique. Men who pondered the state of the world rather than the state of their abs. Men who didn't have long legs and muscular thighs and a tiny scar that bisected the back of their right index finger.

Eve tore her gaze away from the strong, large hand resting atop Linc's upper thigh and distracted herself by pulling every magazine from the seat pocket in front of her. She flipped through several pages and tried to forget about Linc, who sat next to her and stared out the window. Heat rolled off his body and teased her closer. The delicious scent of him—an intoxicating mix of raw sensuality and wildness—stole her breath away.

She squirmed and searched for a more comfortable position. One would think that first class would be a bit easier on the bottom.

"You really do look nervous."

"I am *not* nervous."

He surveyed her for a few moments before the flight attendant serving the first-class passengers stopped near their seats and drew his attention. The woman carried a bottle of Dom Pérignon, a lacey white bow tied around the neck.

"On behalf of the crew and everyone at the airline, we would like to extend our deepest congratulations!" The attendant presented them with the bubbly. "We're so thrilled to have you and the new Mrs. Adams flying with us today!"

"It's not *missus*," Eve cut in. "It's Eve. Eve Farrel. *Mizzz* Eve Farrel."

"But you're married."

"I'm also a strong, independent, fully competent woman who happens to like her name. I've had it a lot longer than I've had him."

"But that's all going to change," Linc said, sliding his arm around Eve's shoulders and pulling her against him for a tight squeeze. "We're joined at the hip now, ain't that right, lamb chop? Two peas in the same pod. Two bottles of Coors Light sharing the same six-pack." Another squeeze. "Till death do us part."

"That could be a lot sooner than you think," Eve muttered for his ears only.

Linc wasn't intimidated. He squeezed her once more for good measure before sliding his arm free. "Tell everyone I'm mighty obliged," he told the flight attendant. He winked and the woman blushed. "Me and the missus, here, appreciate everybody's support."

The flight attendant's curious stare slipped over Eve, appraising the woman who'd managed to snag NASCAR's hottest bachelor.

Surprise registered in the woman's gaze, and Eve gave herself a mental high five. She'd purposely gone out of her way to tramp it up before leaving her apartment, and she'd obviously succeeded. While she still wore short skirts and clingy tops—old habits died hard—she now dressed with designer clothes and great accessories. Today, however, she'd traded her Gucci and Prada for a black spandex miniskirt, a Madonna bustier, fishnet stockings, and thigh-high black boots. She looked more like a biker chick than a Victoria's Secret model, or any of the other blond, blue-eyed babes Linc had been seen with.

Today she'd left her jet-black hair long and straight. A dozen bangle bracelets dangled from one wrist. The only other jewelry Eve wore was a honker of a wedding ring. They'd made the purchase on the way to the airport after stopping off at Linc's hotel so that he could change and pick up his luggage. The ring was platinum gold with a huge marquise diamond. Very traditional, which made it stand out even more since Eve herself was very nontraditional.

She smiled, her bloodred lips parting as she took the bottle of champagne from the curious flight attendant. "Thank you so much. But where's his?"

"Excuse me?"

"This is barely enough to get me through takeoff, and I hate drinking alone. That's one common interest we both share, isn't it, love monkey?" The flight attendant arched an eyebrow at the nickname Eve gave Linc. "Trust me, you don't want to know," Eve told the woman as she patted Linc's thigh and then wished she hadn't. It was too hard. And too hot. And too close. "We love to get sloshed."

"I'll, um, see if I can dig up another bottle before we take off." She glanced at her watch. "We've still got a good twenty minutes before the rest of the passengers finish boarding and we get into the air."

"No need," Linc quickly told the shocked flight attendant after shooting Eve a *behave yourself will ya?* look. "We can share the bottle."

"The *entire* bottle," Eve called out as the attractive woman turned to walk back up the aisle to retrieve glasses and a corkscrew. Forget walked: She sashayed, swaying this way and that, obviously determined to give Linc the Love Monkey a nice parting view.

Eve frowned and barely ignored the urge to chuck the champagne bottle at the woman. Not that she was jealous, mind you. It was the principle of the thing. Eve felt outrage on behalf of all married women everywhere. The flight attendant had a heck of a lot of nerve flaunting herself in front of a committed man.

At least that's what Eve told herself as she fought back her feelings, unfolded her lap tray, and tried to mentally prepare herself for the flight ahead.

Chapter 8

Y ou're not really going to drink that entire bottle, are you?" Linc asked a few minutes later.

"I might, if there was an extra-large athletic cup handy. But since there isn't, I'll content myself with a teeny, tiny glass." Eve meant to wipe the smile off his face, but the expression only widened.

"You're good, but you can save the really outrageous comments for my parents."

"I didn't say that for shock value. I'm dead serious." At Linc's skeptical look, she added, "What? Women can't be just as obnoxious as men?"

"Drinking beer out of a bra isn't obnoxious. It was supposed to be, but the only thing it did was garner more attention. It seems ninety-nine percent of the female population think it's a turn-on. I've got women mailing me their bras."

"There's no accounting for taste these days."

He grinned and winked at her. "That's a fact I'm banking on, sunshine."

"So give me some background on your parents,"

Eve said after a heart-pounding moment. Better to talk and keep her mind busy than sit silently by and lust after him. "If I'm going to pull this off, I need to be prepared."

"My dad's a career politician. He started small as a city councilman and worked his way up. He served several terms as the mayor and now he's a state senator, second term. He's handpicked each of the last three mayors of our town, and was about to endorse the fourth when I stepped up to the plate and agreed to run."

"To help your friend win."

Linc nodded. "It's time we had someone to shake things up and start looking after the little people. Craig knows what it's like to work his ass off to make ends meet, and he's got some pretty good plans."

"I get the feeling that's not the only reason you're endorsing him," Eve told him.

Linc grinned and shrugged. "I grew up going to polo matches and golf tournaments at the Adams Country Club. I never even knew NASCAR existed until I saw a race over at Craig's. My parents weren't very happy about me hanging out with Craig because he didn't have money. But he was the coolest boy in the eighth grade. He came to school in old faded jeans and T-shirts and played ball at recess, while I was stuck in Dockers and polo shirts, my lunchtime spent studying for the academic decathlon team. He was everything I'd always wanted to be. He was a kid, just being a kid."

"You were a kid, too."

"Not in my family. I was an extension of Jackson Adams, and I was expected to act appropriately."

"I know that feeling."

Linc eyed her. "I can't imagine you ever doing an appropriate thing in your life."

"I realized early on that the only way to escape the expectation was to be a huge disappointment. So here I am."

"A disappointment?" He arched an eyebrow at her. "I'd say you've got it going on."

"Very funny."

He grinned before his expression went serious. "You own a highly successful production company, and you're on the verge of breaking into the big time. That's far from disappointing."

"Professionally. I'm talking personally. I don't dress the way my mother thinks I should, I don't look the way she wants me to, and I certainly don't act it."

"I don't, either. Not anymore. But I did. I dressed the part, and I even earned a law degree from Yale."

"You're a *lawyer*? From *Yale*?" *Don't panic,* she told herself. *Just because he didn't get a degree in partying from some mail-order college, doesn't mean he's an actual thinker. He's probably an ambulance chaser who specializes in sucking money out of insurance companies for fake injuries.*

"I *was* a lawyer—a public defender. Now I'm NASCAR's latest and greatest."

Uh-oh.

"When I was fifteen, Craig's dad let us take turns driving his old souped-up Ford Impala in the field back behind the shop." Linc grinned. "There was just such a feeling of freedom when I climbed into the driver's seat and felt that wheel in my hands . . ." He shook his head. "I know it sounds crazy."

Unfortunately, it didn't sound crazy at all. Or insensitive. Or chauvinistic.

"I felt the same way the first time I dyed my hair black," Eve heard herself say before she could think better of it. "Up until then, I'd been a miniature version of my mother. But then I dumped on the dye and suddenly, I was different. Me." *Free.*

Linc shifted and turned in his seat. His gaze burned into her, his eyes bright and assessing. She moved away from him and folded her hands in her lap at the intense speculation. "What?"

"I'm trying to picture you with blond hair."

"Trust me. It's not a pretty sight."

"I don't know about that."

The compliment slid into her ears and Eve felt a rush of heat. A crazy reaction because that's what men like Linc Adams did. They smiled and charmed and complimented their way into a woman's heart, only to turn right around and eat hot wings with a voluptuous Hooters girl.

It didn't mean anything.

"So you owe your whole NASCAR career to Craig," she went on, eager to ignore the strange warmth creeping through her.

"I wouldn't be here today if it weren't for him."

"What about your mother? What does she do?"

"She's the wife of a career politician. She goes to all the obligatory fund-raising lunches and heads the local women voters league and does anything and everything to ensure that my father stays in power and that his image remains untarnished. That's what my grandmother did for my grandfather. What my great-grandmother did for my great-grandfather. What every Adams woman has done for every Adams man since the town's founding in the early eighteen hundreds."

"Sounds like a true calling."

"It's a lot harder than it sounds. You know the saying 'Behind every good man is a good woman'? Well, it's true. My father wouldn't be where he is without my mother, and he knows it."

"I bet your parents were thrilled when you agreed to run."

"They were happy, but not surprised. They don't take my racing seriously. They figured I would outgrow it sooner or later the way my dad did his fishing—he won several amateur bass competitions back in his day—and settle down into career politics."

"But you just won the *Daytona 500*. How can they expect you to just walk away?"

"They're politicians, not NASCAR fans."

She wanted to point out the fact that they were his parents, too, but she kept her mouth shut. Judging by the stern set to his jaw, she had no doubt that Linc had already thought the same thing himself, and he wasn't all that pleased about it.

"My mother was thrilled when I started Sugar & Spice Sinema," Eve said instead. "But that's about the only thing I've ever done that she didn't totally hate. She's a sex guru, after all."

"Have you always wanted to make sex education films?"

Yes. It was there on the tip of her tongue, but instead she heard herself say, "Actually, I've always wanted to make movies. Not the sex-ed kind, but the big-screen, 20th Century Fox, box-office-hit kind."

"So what are you doing filming a documentary?"

"It's for a major cable network. Hopefully, it will get my production company some much-needed exposure and our big break."

"It doesn't work that way."

"What do you mean?"

"It's not about getting a break. It's about cracking that mother yourself. Luck doesn't just happen. It's made. You decide what you want and you go after it."

There was a truth to his words that made her chest tighten. She forced the feeling aside. "Any brothers and sisters?" she asked.

"One sister. She still lives with my folks, along with my grandmother. My grandfather died five years ago."

"I'm sorry."

"Thanks. It was unexpected—a car accident—which made it that much harder on everyone. Especially my dad. What about you? Grandparents still living?"

"Just my mother's mother. My gram is seventy-one going on twenty-three."

"She's fun?"

"She's fun and sweet and wonderful. She practically raised me and my sisters when we were growing up. Our mother was always off on some book tour, and my dad had various conservationist projects that he worked on when he wasn't teaching a seminar on the mating habits of the Guatemalan pin monkey at the university of some-thing or other. Gram was our only touchstone. She was always there."

"My parents were always home, but they weren't, if you know what I mean."

She knew all too well what he was saying, and it

bothered her. Because bad boy Linc Adams wasn't supposed to talk about things she could actually relate to, any more than he was supposed to be a public defender who went to Yale. His conversations should involve sports, how much Bubba Beer he could drink in a single sitting, and whether or not Jessica Simpson was actually wearing underwear in her latest video. They weren't supposed to have anything in common.

But they did.

Before she could dwell on the notion, a middle-aged man leaned over her and handed Linc a cocktail napkin and a pen.

"Um, excuse me, Linc, but I was wondering if you would autograph this for my boy."

"Sure thing."

Just as the man moved to the side with an excited "Thanks!" another appeared. And then another. They were all in a hurry to get Linc's signature before the plane took off and they would be forced into their seats.

Thankfully.

But while she felt grateful that her conversation with Linc had ended, it was a double-edged sword because she was left with nothing to do but remember the feel of his mouth on hers and the way he'd nibbled her bottom lip and the way he'd sucked on it just enough to make her nerves tingle.

To make matters worse, he kept smiling at his fans. Even worse, he was actually *nice* to them. No temperamental star syndrome. He made small talk and he made everyone feel comfortable, which made Eve that much more uncomfortable. How was she supposed to focus on his negatives when he kept wiping them clean off her mental slate?

The question echoed in her head and before she knew what had happened, she'd popped open the bottle of champagne with the corkscrew the flight attendant handed her, and poured herself a glass.

She was busy sipping her way to a calmer state when a voice over the speaker finally ordered everyone to their seats. The bottle of bubbly was promptly plucked from her hands, along with the glass, and she was left without any distraction.

"You're sure you're not afraid to fly?" Linc asked again as she clutched her hands in her lap and barely resisted the urge to chew at her fingernails.

"Of course not."

"Just breathe and relax."

"I'm breathing just fine and I'm relaxed, too . . ." The sentence trailed off as his strong fingers closed around her neck and started to knead.

"You're definitely uptight."

Amen.

"And tense."

And this close to exploding.

"I'm really fine with flying." She stiffened and his hand fell away. "Actually, I'm looking forward to it. I'm going to use the time to get started on my project."

"I think I'll try to get some shut-eye. We've got a lot to do in a short amount of time. I figure you'll make a really bad first impression, which should be all over town by the time we fly out tomorrow morning for Rockingham."

"Good news travels fast in a small town."

"And bad news travels even faster." He leaned back and closed his eyes.

Once they were safely in the air, Eve retrieved her laptop

and tried to ignore the sudden urge to crawl into Linc's lap and kiss him. She hit the POWER button and watched the screen fire to life. She already had the initial pitch she'd used to sell the documentary, which meant she simply had to turn each key point into a sixty-minute episode.

Key point: Sex isn't what it used to be.

She typed a few ideas of how to portray the notion of sex twenty years ago. The taboos. The gender bias. The—

Whew, it really is hot in here.

She readjusted the air nozzle and tried to steady her pounding heart. Linc was snoring softly next to her, the sound sliding into her ears and skimming her nerve endings. She'd always hated men who snored, but his was so soft and steady that it didn't make her want to poke him. Rather, she wanted to lean even closer and feel the soft rush of his breath against her ear. And then her mouth. And then—

Clackkk! She snapped the laptop closed, but he didn't so much as flinch. He just kept snoring softly and soundly. His handsome face so passive and peaceful. His chest, so solid and muscular beneath the soft cotton T-shirt, rose and fell in a steady rhythm. With each intake of oxygen, his muscles flexed and his shoulders expanded. His pulse beat methodically at the base of his muscular neck.

She licked her lips. She wanted to taste the saltiness of his skin. And feel the raspy stubble against her mouth. And—

Ugh. This was going to be the longest plane ride of her entire life.

Eve wasn't surprised to see the press waiting for them when they arrived at Atlanta International Airport. She slid her hand into Linc's—they were newlyweds, after all—as they headed for another gate, where a charter plane waited to fly them the eighty-five miles to Adams. Linc paused twice to scribble his name—once when a young kid asked for his John Hancock on a ball cap, and the other when a gushing twenty-something shoved her chest into his face, along with a felt-tip pen, obviously eager for Linc's legendary cleavage autograph.

Eve frowned. "If you weren't so accommodating, you might lose a little more popularity," she told him once the fan had rushed off.

"I'm not going to totally kill my career with NASCAR for the sake of losing a small-town election. I plan to be driving long after Craig has taken office. Besides, I don't have to worry anymore about tarnishing my image with the good voters of Adams. You'll do that for me."

"Great. You get to play the guy sowing his wild oats and I get to be Medusa." Eve already knew this, but somehow saying it now left a funny taste in her mouth. "I love Medusa," she murmured to herself while Linc stopped yet again to sign someone else's cleavage. And a few shoulders. And the naked patch of skin beneath some woman's pierced belly button.

"I *am* Medusa," Eve muttered as a strange clawing started in her gut.

Meanwhile Linc was a total chauvinistic jackass.

Not.

The truth followed her to the charter gate and onto the small plane. They climbed into the small cabin and settled into two chairs that took up the same amount of space as her one roomy seat had in the first-class section of the previous plane. Her thigh settled firmly against his. Her arm rested along the length of his. Heat skimmed along her nerve endings.

She'd been dead wrong before. *This* was going to be the longest plane ride of her life.

Eve practically raced to the gate when they landed at a small airstrip just outside Adams, Georgia. She needed distance and perspective and something to remind her that Linc was still the lowest form of life.

Her reminder arrived in the form of a young groupie who threw herself into Linc's arms the minute he reached the gate.

"Hey, hot stuff," he told the girl as he lifted her in a massive hug that made Eve stiffen.

Enthusiastically hugging a woman young enough to be his daughter.

Definitely a negative.

And calling her hot stuff.

Ditto.

"You looked so radical on CNN yesterday morning. Janie Blueberry's oldest sister said you're the hottest driver on the circuit," the young girl told him as he set her on her feet.

"And what did you say?"

"That you are *so* not all that. Ryan Newman is where it's at. Young and—"

He caught her in a headlock and stifled the rest of her words. "You're a pain, you know that?"

"And you're a butthead," she managed when he finally released her. She frowned. "A big one. An *old* one. The daddy of all buttheads. The *granddaddy* of them."

Linc looked up at a now-puzzled Eve. "This is my kid sister, Betsy Mae."

"I'm not a kid," Betsy said. "I'm seventeen, and if you don't stop bossing me you'll be walking home." She dangled a set of car keys.

"Sixteen and two months," Linc said, grabbing the car keys before she could pull her hand away.

"That's practically seventeen, and give those back. It's my car."

"It's nearly a year away, and it's not your car. It's my car. You're just looking after it while I'm gone."

"Butthead."

"Short stuff."

"Boogerhead."

"Piglet."

"Pleased to meet you, Betsy Mae," Eve said, effectively killing their verbal sparring, which reminded her too much of her own relationships with Skye and Xandra.

"Call me Jake," the girl said.

"Your name's not Jake. It's Betsy Mae. It's a family name," he told Eve. "My grandmother's on my dad's side."

"One I fully intend to change," Jake informed Eve, "along with my hair color and these horrible clothes." She motioned to the pink button-down polo shirt, khaki shorts, and loafers that she wore. "Just as soon as I reach legal age, make my first million, and leave this lame town behind." At Eve's questioning look, she added, "I'm going to be a rap artist." A dimple cut into the side of Betsy's cheek and her eyes crinkled just like her older brother's when she smiled.

"She's going to be a lawyer," Linc said, and Betsy's expression turned to a frown.

"I think I'd prefer rap artist to lawyer, myself." Linc

gave Eve a look that said *You're not helping matters.* "It sounds more exciting."

"Exactly," Betsy declared. "I know I don't exactly look like the rap type, but that's my folks' fault. I've got some good jams. My real name is Betsy 'cause my folks are really lame, but that's all irrelevant when it comes to money and fame." Her smile faded into a frown. "I'm still working on that one."

Eve wanted to tell her that no amount of work would save that particular rhyme, but Betsy looked so hopeful that she heard herself say, "Sounds like you're on the right track."

"Thanks."

"This is Eve," Linc told Betsy. "My wife."

Betsy's eyes widened and her cheeks turned an even darker shade of red underneath the three inches or so of makeup she had caked on. "Then it *is* true." Surprise turned to guarded skepticism as she turned on Eve. "I saw it on the news this morning, but I didn't believe it. You're not at all my brother's type. You're nothing like the women my brother used to date."

"That's the point," Linc told her.

Betsy glanced at her brother before turning back to Eve. A knowing look dawned in her eyes. "Mom and Dad are *so* going to freak. They heard about it, too, but they're convinced it's a rumor."

"Did they see any pictures?"

Betsy shook her head. "I don't think so. But even if they did, they wouldn't believe them. I didn't believe them." She shook her head. "You're *really* not my brother's type."

Actually she was exactly his type now, and she was fast discovering that Linc just might be her type, after all.

Before Eve could dwell on the thought, Betsy's voice drew her attention. "So you live in L.A.?" the girl asked as they started toward the parking lot.

"For the past eight years."

"L.A. is the heart of the hip-hop scene. I'm going to live in L.A. someday."

The girl looked so determined that Eve couldn't help but smile. Particularly because she'd said and thought the same thing herself all those years ago.

"Keep telling yourself that and you will."

"You think so?"

"I know so. It's all about focus."

Hello? Can we practice what we preach?

She was trying, but Linc wasn't making it very easy. When they reached the parking lot several yards away and stopped in front of a black Lincoln Navigator, she turned on him. "You're killing me, you know that?"

Linc shrugged. "What? You don't like my SUV?"

"Yes, I like it. It's tasteful without being pretentious. That's the point."

He gave her a knowing grin. "I've got a yellow Hummer with naked lady mud flaps and a rebel flag painted on the back bumper if that helps."

"It would if you were telling the truth. You're not, are you?"

"I do have a Hummer, but it's white. No mud flaps or rebel flag."

"It figures."

Chapter 9

Eve quickly discovered the cure for a bad case of lust—an obnoxious grandmother.

One minute Eve was fantasizing about getting down and dirty with Linc. The next, she was sitting on the veranda of a monstrous antebellum home, sipping a mint julep with Lucille Abigail Schmidt-Adams, and praying for a Valium.

". . . Your mother voted to do away with the entire program," Lucille Abigail Schmidt-Adams said, her rose-colored lips pursed in a frown, "which left me no choice but to stand up for what's right."

"Meaning you tactfully pointed out all of the reasons the Cinnamon Bake-Off should be preserved?" Linc asked as he took a long gulp of his drink and grinned at the old woman sitting in the white wicker rocker opposite him.

"Of course." Grandma Lucy was a small but regal woman, her snow-white hair piled on top of her head in an old-fashioned updo. She wore a rose-colored pantsuit and smelled of Chanel No. 5. An expensive-looking strand of pearls hung around her thin neck. Small, gold-rimmed glasses, anchored by a gold chain, sat low on her nose. She flicked open the fan that sat in her lap and waved it at her face. A small white dog fidgeted on her lap.

"You called her a lunatic and a communist," Betsy added as she retrieved a petit four from a silver serving tray and settled on a matching wicker love seat, her legs folded up under her. Large flowerpots overflowing with leafy green ferns and lush flowers sat here and there. The scent of jasmine filled the air.

"I had to stand up for myself," Grandma Lucy went on. "Susanna is out to get me. She always has been." Grandma Lucy pointed her fan at Linc. "Why, she told your father that I need to be in the old geezers' home. Can you imagine that? *Me?* In a nursing home?"

"It's too scary for words."

"Exactly. I would be petrified in a place like that."

"I was thinking about the other residents." Linc grinned and Betsy giggled and Grandma Lucy simply shook her head, as if to say *What am I going to do with you?* before turning to Eve.

"Thankfully, my son had the courage to stand up for me," Grandma Lucy went on. "He told Susanna—Lord love him—that he would put me in no such place, because I'm of sounder mind than her mother's aunt Tallulah, who's older than Jesus. That put a wasp up her wazoo, let me tell you. Now she's even more hell-bent on doing away with the whole event, and for no other reason than the fact that my recipe's been walking away with the gold ribbon going on thirty years now. Everybody knows Susanna's against the Bake-Off because she hates me."

"Mom doesn't hate you," Betsy said. "She just thinks

the Bake-Off money could be better spent. We need more day-care facilities."

"More? Why, this town can't fill up the one day care that it has."

"That's because Janice Phelps is an elitist snob who charges way too much for graham crackers and grape drink," Linc said. "She's too expensive for the average day care and too expensive for the average workingman. That's why one of the first things Craig plans to do is to propose two brand-new facilities and allocate several thousand dollars of his own money to help fund them."

"Craig?" Grandma Lucy looked puzzled. "Craig who?"

"The man running for mayor."

"You're running for mayor, dear."

"The man running against me. The man who's likely to win."

"Nonsense. You're going to win. It's a consensus among my bridge club, and we've accurately predicted the winner since 1932."

"That's because you always predict an Adams and it's always been an Adams, or a candidate handpicked by the Adamses."

"A grand tradition that you're going to continue, dear. Your first act as mayor could be to make Janice lower her rates. Then there would be no need to do away with the Bake-Off."

"It doesn't work that way, Grandmother."

"Of course it does. We're Adamses. We can make it work that way. Why, your mother could put the pressure on Janice herself—they belong to the same garden club— but she won't, because she's trying to ruin my life and take my livelihood from me. Meanwhile, I've done nothing from the get-go but welcome her with open arms into this family."

"You spilled cranberry juice on her wedding dress right before the ceremony."

"I wasn't anywhere near her dress." At Linc's knowing look, she added, "And even if I was—which I most definitely *was not*—you would think she would have let it go by now."

"And you left her name off the Christmas cards last year. And the year before that. And the year before that."

"I'm an old woman. I can't be expected to remember everything. So tell me, Eve"—she peered at Eve through her thick bifocals as if she still couldn't quite see—"what is it that you do for a living?"

"I make sex videos."

"*Six* videos?" She hugged the white ball of fluff sitting on her lap. He licked at her cheek and wagged his tail. "What's a six video?"

"*Sex* videos," Eve said again. "As in *s-e-x*." The smile faded from Lucille's face. Where Eve's appearance hadn't been enough to really shock the old woman since she could hardly see, despite her glasses, Eve's comment did the trick.

"Well, I never heard of such a—"

"So where did you say Mom and Dad are today?" Linc cut in, as if he'd decided to change the subject.

"Your mother had a Daughters of the Confederacy luncheon, and your father is dealing with several constituents before the Senate session next week."

Linc grinned and got to his feet. "I think Eve and I will just take a little ride over and surprise Mom." He grabbed Eve's hand and twined his fingers with hers. "News this good shouldn't have to wait. Besides, we're pressed for time. Our plane leaves first thing in the morning. What do you say, sunshine?"

Eve nodded enthusiastically, but not because she was anxious to spread word of their marriage. She wanted off the veranda and into the safe confines of the car where she could retreat to the opposite side of the seat, far, far away from Linc and his long, strong fingers and the warmth of his palm flat against hers. His pulse beat ticked against the inside of her wrist and her heart kicked up a notch.

"A plane?" Grandma Lucy arched an eyebrow and stared in the vicinity of Linc's shoulder. "Where are you rushing off to now, dear?"

"Rockingham, North Carolina."

"Whatever for?"

"The second NASCAR race of the season."

"Are you still fiddling with that stuff?"

Linc stiffened, but Eve didn't miss the flash of disappointment in his gaze. She had the insane urge to squeeze his hand.

Instead, she shoved her hand toward Lucille. "Nice to meet you, Grandma."

"Um, yes." Grandma barely touched Eve's hand, as if she were afraid she might catch something. "Likewise."

"Later, Grandma," Linc said as he tugged Eve toward the walkway.

"Wait for me," Betsy blurted out as she jumped to her feet. "I am *so* not going to miss this."

". . . wraps up the presentation for the new Roosevelt Adams Kiddie Playcare Facility, just one of the many improvement projects slated for development once the mayoral election is over," said the petite blond woman who stood behind the lectern situated at the head of the large banquet room.

At fifty-six, Susanna Adams was trim and well-groomed, her shoulder-length hair worn in a bob that framed her round face and softened the wrinkles fanning from the corners of her eyes. She looked every bit the politician's wife in a blue skirt and jacket, a white blouse, and a red scarf draped around her neck. Several campaign buttons flashed from her lapel.

"Remember, a vote for Adams is a vote for Adams." A round of applause erupted and she smiled, her red lips parting to reveal a row of gleaming white teeth. She turned to retrieve her notes and her gaze snagged on Linc, who stood just inside the doorway off to the side of the room.

Her smile went from polite and practiced to sincere as she turned back to the microphone. "And speaking of the man of the hour, here he is: your next mayor!"

Linc frowned as dozens of gazes turned toward him and another round of applause erupted. Where was Eve when he really needed her?

His gaze swiveled to the lobby and the ladies' room where she'd made a pit stop with Betsy as soon as they'd arrived.

His mother motioned him up to the lectern, but he waved her off. She frowned for a split second before years of practice kicked in and her polished smile bloomed once again. "We'll get a few words from Linc once dessert arrives," she told the audience. "Everyone, please enjoy your lunch." She switched off the microphone and offered a word here and a pat on the shoulder there to the women seated at the head banquet table as she scooted her way down the row. She made a beeline for Linc just as a handful of waiters burst through the kitchen doors on the opposite side of the room, their trays laden with glazed chicken salads.

"Thank heavens you're here," his mother told him as she rushed up. "Do you know how hard it is to sell an absentee candidate?"

"You don't have to sell me, Mom. I can get my own campaign manager."

"Nonsense. I'm the most qualified, and your father is willing to share me for the good of the town. Besides, he's in session right now and it's not an election year for him. And that's not the point, you not being here half the time is." She gave an exasperated shake of her head before flipping open her portfolio and skimming a page of notes. "I've just introduced the list of new projects for your platform and gone over each of them. Having you say a few words will cement them in everyone's mind. I've also got good news about the Founder's Day Celebration." She beamed at him. "They've picked you as the Most Prominent Citizen."

Linc smiled. If he didn't, his folks might suspect that he didn't want the title and, ultimately, the office of mayor. Then they would surely pick and endorse another candidate, and Craig would lose the election. "I've got some good news of my own," he told his mother.

"It's such perfect timing, since Founder's Day will be the weekend before the election," she rushed on as if Linc hadn't said a word. "You'll be the guest of honor Saturday and Sunday, and I've actually booked Margo Sinatra for the Saturday night gala."

"Margo Sinatra?"

"She's Frank's cousin three times removed, with just as intoxicating a voice. Why, your grandmother has every record she's ever released, which means I won't have to listen to her complain all evening."

"Mom, they don't make records anymore."

"That's beside the point. She's a star, at least according to the over-sixty set, which accounts for thirty-three and a half percent of the voting population of this town. Which reminds me, we need to come up with something effective for the under-twenty-five set. Maybe you could use your NASCAR connections while you've still got them to get some free race tickets to donate to the Baptist Community Church Youth Group. Which brings me to my next bit of news: Reverend Mitchell wasn't very happy about that whole beer thing you did on the television last week. While I know you're not declaring any specific religious affiliation so as not to alienate the other church groups in town, we have to do something very special to prove to him that you're every bit as competent as your father."

"Mom," Linc said, trying to draw her attention.

"Maybe you could donate a portion of your racing proceeds to the new gymnasium," she went on. "That way you'll be making something positive out of all that negative notoriety. That would give a nice spin to this whole NASCAR episode."

"Mother."

"And you'll definitely have to send Reverend Mitchell a letter of apology."

"*Susanna.*"

"Yes, dear?" She glanced up before directing her attention back to the notes.

"I'm married."

"No you're not, dear. That's just a rumor I heard on the radio this morning. Now, the letter should say I'm sorry in a nice, sincere way without saying we're just trying to save—"

"I'm really married." He held up his hand and waved the simple gold band he'd purchased along with Eve's ring. "Chained for life. Out of the running as Adams's Most Eligible Bachelor."

The surprised look on Susanna's face slowly morphed into one of pure delight. "That's wonderful, dear!" She hugged him. "Settling down shows you're committed and that you support basic family values. Why, it's just the ticket to winning this— Who's that?" She pulled back and stared past him at Eve, who was pushing and pulling against a burly security guard who held her firmly by the arm. Betsy stood just to the side, a smile on her face.

"This is discrimination," Eve's raised voice carried the distance to them. "And it's against the law. You can't boot me out of here just because I don't look like a Stepford wife. I know my rights. If you want to pick on someone, you should go after that lady over there with the yellow daisy hat and the white patent-leather pumps. Talk about a crime . . ."

"Who *is* that?" Susanna's mouth drew into a thin line and her eyes narrowed.

Linc smiled and slid his arm around his mother's shoulders for an affectionate squeeze. "That's my wife."

"I've never seen Mom throw up in public before," Betsy said later that afternoon as she sat on Linc's bed. They were at the large home Linc owned, several miles outside Adams. The girl eyed Eve. "That was *so* priceless."

"It was definitely interesting." Eve pulled a black T-shirt and a neon-blue leather miniskirt from her hanging bag. She draped the outfit on Linc's bed and rummaged in her suitcase for a pair of black stockings and three-inch stiletto heels. With Betsy in tow, Linc had had no choice but to place Eve's luggage in his room rather than the nearby guest bedroom. For now. After they took Betsy home and had dinner with Linc's folks, they would come back to Linc's place and Eve and her things would move to the next room for the night.

"Mom's always so together," Betsy went on. "Why, I swear she looked on the verge of tears."

She had, which had sparked Eve's guilt. Crazy. It was Linc's mother, so it should be his guilt. She had her own mother to deal with.

She retrieved her cell phone and checked her caller ID. Four phone calls from her mother, several from Xandra—who'd probably heard about the marriage by now—and one from Skye. Eve made a mental note to call her sisters as soon as possible—she wasn't ready to hear her mother rail about her marriage just yet—and stuffed her cell phone back into her purse. Then she busied herself getting ready for today's grand finale—dinner—where she would not only see Linc's mother again, but meet his father for the first time.

After the throwing-up incident, they'd left Susanna Adams to deal with the wave of newly stirred-up gossip at the luncheon and headed over to city hall to see his father. But Senator Adams had already left for a private afternoon golf meeting with the city comptroller, and so they'd spent the next few hours making themselves very visible around the small town.

They'd stopped at the local diner and the dry cleaners and the mechanic shop owned by Linc's friend Craig. Craig had been out meeting with his own supporters, and so Eve hadn't been able to meet her new husband's long-time friend. But she'd seen him in the dozens of pictures lining the walls of his office.

Craig and Linc in the sixth grade. Craig and Linc winning a medal for first place in freshman shop class. Craig and Linc leaning under the hood of a rusted-out Ford Mustang. Craig and Linc on Victory Lane following Linc's first NASCAR win.

Craig was not just a buddy, but Linc's only supporter, it seemed, when it came to the NASCAR racing. Eve could easily understand why Linc would go to such an extreme to help the man win the mayoral election, and so she'd stepped up her efforts to play the imperfect wife. She'd handed out brochures promoting her newest video to everyone they'd met, and had even offered Reverend Mitchell's wife a guest appearance in her *Generation seX* documentary. And she'd posed for picture after picture for the handful of photographers that had tailed them throughout the afternoon.

Obviously, she'd shaken things up as Linc had hoped. The phone had been ringing nonstop with calls from outraged citizens since they'd stopped off at Linc's to change for dinner.

Eve had expected a massive, sprawling playboy-type mansion in keeping with Linc's bad-boy image. Something complete with a hot tub in the living room, posters of naked girls covering the walls, pizza boxes piled high in the kitchen, and beer cans stacked to the ceiling.

What she'd found was a single-story, ranch-style house

with a wraparound porch. The large den hosted a beige leather sofa and two matching chairs. There wasn't a poster in sight, or anything else to detract from the architectural beauty of the stained cedar walls and massive rock fireplace. The kitchen was state-of-the-art with gleaming stainless-steel appliances and a marble-topped island. Two guest bedrooms had been decorated in various shades of beige and hunter green. Linc's bedroom had been done in navy-and-green plaid, from the down comforter that topped the king-sized bed to the woven rugs covering the hardwood floor.

There was nothing loud or obnoxious about the place, with the exception of a large, state-of-the-art sound system and a plasma movie screen in the den. Overall, the house looked more like a feature in *Southern Living,* rather than the home of NASCAR's baddest bad boy.

Eve glanced at her reflection in the mirror before adding an extra layer of black around her eyes. She topped off the sex kitten look with a layer of Vivid Valentine lipstick to accent the fullness of her lips.

"Cool necklace," Betsy said as she watched Eve pull a chain of safety pins from her overnight bag. "L.A. must be the most bitchin' place to live."

"It's okay as long as you stay off the freeway during rush hour. And this isn't really a necklace. I just fasten them together so they don't scatter in the bottom of my . . ." Her words faded as an idea struck. "You know, this does sort of go with my outfit."

"Totally. Check this out," Betsy said as Eve fastened the chain around her neck. "Safety pins are the new thing in town, 'cause Eve's in the house and she's ready to party down."

"I like it."

"So do I." Linc's voice sounded in the doorway and Eve's heart kick-started. She turned to find him looking at her—or through her, it seemed. Appreciation glimmered in his gaze.

"The safety pins are a nice touch," he said, eyeing her necklace. "If something rips, we're all set."

"Or we could just use them for the good of all womankind and fasten your lips together."

Betsy giggled and Linc smiled.

"Careful there, sunshine," he whispered for Eve's ears only when she walked past him to leave the room. "I'm liable to think you're actually starting to like me."

"When the devil gets his first brain freeze."

Linc pulled Eve to a halt just shy of the doorway to his parents' dining room. The minute they'd arrived at the monstrous colonial where Linc had grown up, Betsy had rushed up to her bedroom to get in a few phone calls before dinner. Thankfully, Linc needed a few quiet moments to psych himself up. While he'd tried to mentally prepare himself for the coming dinner during the fifteen-minute drive over, he hadn't been able to focus. Not with Betsy chattering away in the backseat, rapping about everything from Celia Martin's new John Deere tractor to the latest boy in her biology class. And not with Eve smiling damn near the whole way.

He hadn't expected his stomach to hollow out at the sight of her smile, but it had. It wasn't as if he was a damned stranger when it came to good-looking, sexy women. He'd had more than his share, particularly over the past few years since he'd started beefing up his NASCAR notoriety. He didn't go all hard at the sight of a pair of long legs, or a nice ass, or even a substantial pair of breasts. And he sure as hell didn't get all hot and bothered over a woman's smile.

But Eve's lips were just so full and lush, her teeth straight and white. And she had this dimple that cut into her upper cheek and softened her entire expression. He hadn't noticed it before because he'd been too busy focusing on the overall package. But it was there, even more pronounced when she actually laughed out loud.

Which made matters worse, because the soft, melodic sound bothered him almost as much as her smile did.

Almost as much as the fact that he'd lied to his mother earlier that day and was about to perpetuate the same lie to his father.

Despite his reason for the deception, the whole thing didn't sit well with him. He didn't like deceiving people, especially the people he loved. And now that very love was at stake.

"I hope you're happy now, because I'm not. I never will be, thanks to you." Jackson Adams had spoken those bitter words not five years ago to his own father.

Linc didn't want to end up saying the same thing to Jackson. Worse, he didn't want to *feel* the same bitterness long after it was too late to make things right.

He drew in a deep breath and tried to ignore the scent of warm vanilla sugar that filled his nostrils.

Concentrate on your points, man, a voice whispered. *It's all about hitting those points.*

In racing, and in life.

When he wanted to successfully navigate a track, he mentally mapped the quickest and most efficient way to get through a lap. If he hit just the right points lap after lap, he could keep his pace and win the race.

Now was no different.

It was all about losing votes from now until November and winning his first Nextel Cup. That meant—point A— keeping up appearances with Eve, while—point B— keeping his mind on the next race. And the next. And that meant no thinking about her or the chemistry that sizzled between them.

Or the sex that had fizzled.

He shook away the sudden notion and tried to concentrate on the voices that carried from inside the dining room.

"Why, she's totally unacceptable. What with all that makeup and those clothes. You saw her picture in the newspaper."

"You can't believe the press. You know that. They're always out to smear candidates."

"In this case, they have some really great ammunition. She makes *sex tapes* for a living. It's people like her who are killing family values and sending this country straight to hell in a handbasket. I can't imagine what Lincoln was thinking marrying someone like her."

"Maybe he loves her."

"And maybe he's smelled too much exhaust."

"She really makes sex tapes for a living?"

"Explicit how-to videos. *Very* explicit. And she doesn't just make them. She talks about them. She calls herself a sexpert."

"Well, that explains it then. The boy's thinking with his Willy Wonka."

"I might agree with you, but she's just as frightening as

she is sexy. I've never seen so much black eyeliner in my life. Why, she could be one of those devil worshipers, for all we know."

Before Susanna Adams could say anything else, Linc steered Eve forward and they entered the dining room.

"We're here," he announced as he guided Eve toward a chair. "Mom, you and Eve have already met."

"Why, yes. Lovely to, um, see you again, dear."

"Dad," Linc went on, "meet Eve. Eve, meet my dad, Senator Jackson Roosevelt Adams."

Jackson Adams looked every bit his sixty-two years and then some. It wasn't so much his appearance; while he did have snow-white hair, it was cut in a stylish fashion and slicked back. He wore a nicely cut dark gray suit, his tie a mix of red and navy pinstripes. If anything, he was an attractive man who'd aged well. It was his eyes that betrayed his years. They were dark and knowing. As if he'd seen too much and worried over even more.

Judging by the sudden narrowing of his gaze as he stared at Eve, Linc had just added a heap of worry to the mix.

"Nice to, um, meet you, young lady."

"The pleasure's all mine, sir. I've always wanted to marry into politics."

Jackson's expression went from worried to pleasantly surprised. "Is that so?"

"It's always been my absolute fantasy to fall head over heels for a handsome Democrat. In fact, I'm going to use the idea for my very next video. *Sexual Positions for the Adventurous Democrat.*"

Linc tried to hide his smile while his father nearly choked on a mouthful of iced tea.

"We're not Democrats, young lady," the conservative Adams told his new daughter-in-law when he finally found his voice.

"You're not?" Eve looked hopeful. "Independent Party?"

"No, ma'am."

"Liberal something or other?"

"Not in this lifetime or any other. Son"—he turned to Linc—"you mean to tell me you married a Demo—"

"Let's not talk politics," Susanna cut in. "Or work," she said, nailing Eve with a gaze that said *Please, no more talk about s-e-x.* "Let's just have a nice dinner." She patted her husband's arm. "I told you so," she murmured under her breath.

"My, but that's an interesting necklace," his mother said once the salad had been passed around.

"Oh, my necklace." Eve fingered the silver safety pins. "It's very sentimental."

"Sentimental safety pins?" Susanna frowned. "I don't know that I've ever heard of such a thing."

"I have a total of twenty-two piercings, each of which I did myself with these babies. This is sort of a keepsake to mark each occasion."

"*Twenty-two?*" Jackson Adams took another sip of iced tea and eyed her. "Why, I only see two holes—one in each ear."

"The other twenty are in various *other* places."

"Other places?" Jackson cast a puzzled look at his wife, who shook her head as if to say *Drop it.* "How many other places can you put an earring, for Jesus' sake?"

Eve winked at Linc and smiled. "Well, sir, since you asked . . ."

Chapter 10

Eve was not going to think about Linc. Or the way he looked. Or the way he smelled. Or the fact that he was sleeping in the room right next to hers.

That's what she told herself as she lay in the comfortable king-sized bed in Linc's guest bedroom and stared at the ceiling.

Comfortable, as in she should be sleeping right now. It was midnight and she was exhausted. Dinner had been a huge success—Linc's parents were sufficiently horrified by their new daughter-in-law and her never-ending sex advice—and so she felt extremely satisfied. Comfortable plus exhausted plus satisfied usually equaled sleep.

Not this time. Not with Linc's image firmly entrenched in her brain. She could still see him staring back at her across the dinner table, a smile on his handsome face, his eyes glittering with humor and admiration and lust.

Despite their agreement, he still wanted her.

Despite the bad sex, she still wanted him.

Her eyes snapped open and she stared at the ceiling again. She rolled onto her right side and punched the pillow a few times before snuggling down. There. She was going to close her eyes, and she wasn't going to remember the heat in his fingertips when he'd brushed against her while opening the car door. She'd been surprised by the gesture and startled by the contact and amazed at her fierce response . . .

Her skin prickled and her eyes popped open. She rolled onto her left side, scrunched the pillow under her head and snuggled down. There. *Now* she was going to close her eyes, and she wasn't going to remember the way he'd smelled when he'd come up behind her at his front door. An intoxicating mixture of cologne and fresh soap . . .

Her nostrils flared and her eyes popped open again and she rolled onto her back.

A sharp ache echoed between her legs and her heart raced and her tummy trembled and . . . Geez, who was she trying to kid?

She sat up and climbed out of the bed. A few steps and she found herself in the hallway. The hardwood floor was cool beneath her bare feet, but it did nothing to ease the fire burning inside her as she poised outside his door.

Now what?

She was going to knock, that's what. And then she was going to go inside. And then she was going to tell him that she couldn't stop thinking about him or how much she wanted a real orgasm and could he please, please, *please* give her one.

You do not need a man to give you anything. Own your orgasm, a voice whispered.

Her mother's voice.

She reached for the doorknob.

"Can't sleep?" The deep, husky timbre stirred the hair

on the back of her neck and stalled her hand on the cold brass.

She whirled to find Linc standing in the doorway that led to the kitchen. The sight of him wearing nothing but a pair of snug, faded jeans stalled her heart for a long moment. Soft denim molded to his lean hips and strong thighs, and cupped his crotch. A frayed rip in the denim on his left thigh gave her a glimpse of silky blond hair and tanned skin and . . . *Yum.*

She'd seen him without a shirt before, but she hadn't really *seen* him. She'd been too hot and bothered the night before, too eager for the next moment to take a good, long look, and too determined the morning after to ignore him.

He had an athlete's body, his shoulders broad, his arms muscular. Gold hair sprinkled his chest from nipple to nipple before narrowing into a thin line that bisected his six-pack abs and disappeared into the waistband of his jeans. Her gaze riveted on the hard bulge beneath his zipper for several fast, furious heartbeats before shifting north.

"Hungry?" he asked.

"In the worst way."

"Me, too." He held up a sandwich. The aroma of peanut butter and grape jelly slid into her nostrils. Her stomach grumbled and he grinned. "I've got plenty if you want some." She didn't miss the heat that simmered in the bright blue depths of his eyes. As if the offer had nothing to do with food and everything to do with him.

But then his gaze darkened and he stiffened, as if he'd just remembered some all-important fact.

Duh. You two have an agreement. No more sex.

Yeah, right.

He was a Yale-educated public defender who drove a modest but tasteful Navigator, treated his fans with dignity and respect, doted on his little sister, went above and beyond the call of duty for his best friend, ate peanut butter and jelly sandwiches, *and* kept his word.

Eve was definitely in trouble.

Linc had never been a big believer in luck. Good fortune came through hard work and talent, and when things went wrong, there was usually a damned good reason behind it. Lack of motivation. Fear. Laziness.

But as he watched Eve walk past him into the kitchen, he couldn't help but reevaluate his position.

He blinked and stared at the woman standing near the kitchen island. He'd expected her to be wearing a slinky leopard-print bra and panty set, or a see-through black teddy, or something equally exotic and racy when climbing beneath the covers. The last thing he'd anticipated was a pair of pink boxer shorts with yellow smiley faces and a matching tank top.

Not that he liked pink boxer shorts. Not at this point in his life. He liked his women hot and spicy and temporary. Eve looked just the opposite with her hair pulled up in a ponytail and her face free of makeup. Forget spicy. She looked as sweet as sugar, and damned if he didn't want a taste anyway.

Of all the rotten luck.

"Help yourself," he told her, motioning to the peanut butter and jelly that sat on the countertop. "I'm afraid it's all I've got. I don't get home too often and so I don't keep the refrigerator stocked."

"This is fine. I was too busy trying to keep from laughing

to really eat tonight," she told him as she untwisted the bread tie and pulled two slices from the loaf.

"You kept a straight face the entire time."

"I knew those acting classes would pay off someday." She set her bread on the counter and reached for a knife.

"You took acting classes?"

"Every film student takes acting classes. I took a few more than the norm, however." She dipped the knife into the peanut butter and spread a layer onto one slice of bread. "Acting is my second love." She smiled as if she had a secret. "At one point in college, I actually considered giving it a shot. I met this producer while I was waitressing at this restaurant down on Hollywood Boulevard. He offered me a small part in a movie he was casting. He said he liked my look and my attitude, and he could make me a star if I would just say yes." She set the knife on the counter and topped the peanut butter layer with her second slice of bread.

He took a bite of his own sandwich and chewed before asking, "What did you do?"

She shrugged. "What could I do? I was two months shy of finishing film school, and I couldn't spare the time without jeopardizing my degree."

"That was smart." He took another bite and watched as she cut her sandwich into two halves.

Regret gleamed in her eyes. "Actually, it was the dumbest thing I ever did. I spent the next two years scraping by, barely making enough to pay my rent while I apprenticed for Justin Coleman, an executive producer for FOX. The acting gig paid ten times more than the apprenticeship."

"What movie was it for?" He arched an eyebrow. "One

of those kick-ass flicks like *Amazon Biker Babes* or *Buffy the Vampire Slayer*?"

She frowned and retrieved a nearby napkin. "It doesn't matter. It was a paying job."

"Paying or not, it was a gamble. The odds of making it to the top as an actress are slim."

"True, but the odds of making it as a producer are practically nonexistent. There are hundreds of working actresses, but only a handful of working female producers."

"I never really thought about that."

"I think about it every day." She placed one half of the sandwich on her napkin and took a bite of the other.

He eyed her. "But you do it anyway, despite the odds."

She swallowed her mouthful. "What can I say? I'm a sucker for punishment. You have another one of those?" She eyed his bottle of Sweet Leaf Tea sitting on the counter next to him.

He nodded. "Man cannot live by bread and Bubba Beer alone." He watched her retrieve a bottle of tea from the refrigerator. "So the masochist in you keeps you in the production biz?"

"That, and I've always dreamed about sitting in a movie theater and seeing my name roll across the credits at the beginning of the movie." Her full lips hinted at a grin. "I know it sounds egotistical." She set her sandwich down and twisted the cap off the tea bottle.

"There's nothing egotistical about having goals. Everybody needs something to push them out of bed in the morning." He watched her sip the tea before he took another bite of his own sandwich. He marveled at the sudden feeling of companionable silence that engulfed them for the next few moments.

Now *that* was crazy. Linc Adams didn't get comfortable with a woman. For him, it was always about getting hot and bothered.

Then again, this wasn't just any woman. This was his wife.

For now.

"What pushes you?" she finally asked him after eating several bites of her sandwich and washing them down with a long sip of tea. "The thought of winning the Nextel Cup?"

He nodded. "And not turning into my father."

"I wouldn't worry about that. You couldn't be farther from the schmoozing politician."

"Not now, but I was close." He took a bite of his sandwich and swallowed. "I'm still close."

"Your mother and father might overlook your wild ways in the name of youth and immaturity, but I make sex videos for a living. Trust me, you can kiss the mayor's race good-bye."

"I'm not talking about politics." The words were out before he could think better of them.

"Then what are you talking about?"

Nothing. That's what he meant to say. But with Eve looking so soft and vulnerable, and staring back at him as if she really cared about what he had to say, as if she understood, he couldn't help himself. "Up until five years ago, I was following in my dad's footsteps. My law career was taking off. I was networking with the right people and running in the right social circles and I'd just entered the race for city council."

"And then your grandfather died and everything changed."

"My grandfather died and *I* changed."

"Death has that effect on people."

"It wasn't his death that woke me up. It was my father's reaction to his death." At her questioning gaze, he added, "I never even considered that my dad might be unhappy. He'd lived and breathed politics for as long as I could remember. I'd always thought it was because he wanted to. Not because he had to."

"What do you mean?"

"The funeral home had just closed after the evening viewing hours. I had stayed behind and was sitting in the back of the room when my father came in. He didn't know I was there. He'd kept his distance most of the evening, doing the typical meet-and-greet thing near the front door. But with the place empty, I guess he felt free to say his last good-bye." Linc shook his head, remembering the dimly lit room and the smell of white roses. "At least that's what I thought he was going to say." His gaze met hers. "He told him that he hated him. He hated him because he'd raised him to carry on the family tradition of law and politics and responsibility. He hated him because he'd never given him a choice otherwise." Linc shook his head, hearing the words as clearly as he'd heard them that night.

"I hope you're happy now, because I'm not."

"He'd given up his love of bass fishing because his father had pressed him to, not because he'd wanted to, and he regretted it."

"That must have been terrible for you."

"What was worse than hearing him say it, was knowing how he felt." His gaze met hers again. "Because I felt the same way." Silence settled for several long moments before he finally added, "That's when I realized that I was turning into my father, just like he'd turned into his father."

"But not anymore."

"I promised myself then and there that I wouldn't be the same bitter, resentful man twenty years from now. I love my dad. I don't want to end up hating him and feeling guilty for it."

She grinned. "He might end up hating you if he has to sit through another dinner with me."

He smiled, but then the expression faded. "I really don't like lying to him, but it's for his own good. One day he'll realize that he tried to do the same thing to me that his father did to him, and he'll be glad that I kept it from happening."

"You mean *if* he realizes it." She eyed him. "Maybe he won't ever recognize his ways and regret them."

Linc had thought the same thing himself more times than he cared to admit, but like always, he pushed the possibility aside. "He will, and then he'll understand my choices."

"I should be so lucky. My mother thinks she's right and she'll always think that, which is why I keep my distance and my sanity, and do my own thing."

"Or what you think will piss her off the most."

"What's that supposed to mean?"

"That you're not half as wild and bold as you pretend to be."

"I am so."

"Yeah?" He gave her a knowing look. "Nice boxer shorts."

She glanced down as if realizing what she was wearing

for the first time. She looked so distraught that he had the sudden urge to step forward and pull her into his arms.

Her expression quickly faded into a frown. "My leather teddy was dirty tonight."

"That's too bad. But if it's any consolation, you look even better in the boxers."

He didn't mean to step toward her. He was supposed to walk the other way and put as much distance as possible between them. He knew that, but he couldn't seem to help himself.

He stopped just shy of touching her. Her heat curled toward him, begging him closer. He pressed a kiss to her forehead before turning toward the door. It was that or kiss her smack-dab on her full lips, which he was dangerously close to doing.

"*Steel Magnolias*," she blurted out as he reached the doorway.

He glanced over his shoulder.

"The movie that bigwig producer wanted to cast me in. It was *Steel Magnolias*. He said I had a sweet and sentimental nature wrapped up in a package of strength that would have made me perfect for Julia Roberts's part. Crazy, huh?"

"Certifiable." That's what Linc said, but he couldn't help thinking what a genius that producer had been.

Of all the *really* rotten luck.

Chapter 11

Are you okay?" Linc asked the next morning as he followed Eve onto a monstrous RV-like black and silver bus, that had his name and sponsor blazing in full color on the side. The bus, like dozens of others dedicated to various NASCAR drivers, was parked in the motor home lot for drivers and owners near the Rockingham racetrack.

"I'm fine." Eve stalled on the top step and stared at the interior. "Don't I look fine?"

"No, you look nervous." He came up directly behind her, dwarfing her with his large frame.

She should be used to his nearness by now, especially after their early morning plane ride, where she'd all but sat on his lap while he did an in-flight interview with a traveling journalist. They'd held hands and stared meaningfully into each other's eyes.

But that was an act, she told herself. A charade for the press.

This . . . Her gaze shifted in time to see him close the door behind them. This was just the two of them. Alone. Together.

She dropped her bag to the side and stepped forward to survey the interior and put some distance between them. She bypassed a small eating area that consisted of a boothlike table on one side and a refrigerator, stove, and sink on the other. Next came a small living area with two plush leather recliners on one side and a large TV on the other. A few more steps and she reached a sleeping space with a full-sized bed on one side and a large closet on the other. Two more steps and the aisle dead-ended into a second bed.

"You're definitely nervous." Linc's voice sounded directly behind her and she stiffened.

"Well, I'm not, and if you start with the whole *Are you afraid to ride on a bus?* thing, I'm going to find the nearest firearm and start shooting." She turned and ducked under his arm to put a few blessed footsteps between them again.

"I didn't think you were afraid of riding on a bus. We're not going to ride in it. We're going to sleep in it."

"Well, I'm not afraid of that, either." *Liar.*

It was one thing to have a nice solid wall between them and a small portion of hallway and, God bless 'em, an actual door, and quite another to be less than a few feet away, and in full view.

She opened the one doorway that set between the beds and eyed the small shower, which was just tall enough to accommodate Linc and flanked by a small toilet.

"It's kind of small in here."

"It's about the same size as Clint's."

Eve's mind rushed back to the moment she'd caught sight of her brother-in-law's red, white, and blue RV on the outskirts of the racetrack. It *had* looked large at first glance, but if it was the same size as this, she couldn't possibly imagine how Skye ever fit into the interior with him.

Then again, Skye and Clint had the whole real marriage thing going on, and so close confines were no problem.

"My crew chief usually bunks out in here, too, but since we're newlyweds, he didn't want to impose, so we'll have the bus all to ourselves."

"Lucky us." She closed the bathroom door and checked out the small television and stereo built into the wall at the foot of the first bed. She punched a few buttons on the remote and the stereo lit up. A rock song burst from the speakers.

"Cal likes Nickelback." Linc came up and pressed a button. The stereo fell silent.

"At least he has good taste in music." She inched to the side, away from him.

"I'll pass on the compliment." He headed up the aisle toward the refrigerator. "Can I get you something to drink?"

"I've had all the Sweet Leaf Tea I can handle right now, thanks."

He grinned and retrieved a bottle. Twisting off the cap, he took a long drink and Eve tried to ignore the picture he made standing there, head thrown back, guzzling the icy liquid.

Are you deaf? a voice whispered. *I said "Ignore." That means no noticing the way his throat muscles work, or the way that single drop of tea glides down his tanned skin, or the way his muscles flex as he tightens his hand around the bottle.*

She tore her gaze away and folded down the covers on her bed before she had to face the next challenge—retrieving her overnight bag from near the front doorway. The walkway accommodated one person, no problem. But two? Maybe. If she plastered herself against the far side and eased past just so, she might avoid any actual contact.

Yeah, right.

He stepped to the side, but there simply wasn't enough room. One hard, sinewy shoulder brushed hers and his muscled bicep touched the side of her breast. Her breath caught and her heart revved.

Strong fingers closed around her upper arm and he stared down at her.

Okay, so accidental touching was bad enough, but the fingers on her arm were there on purpose. Strong. Sure. Comforting.

The air stalled in her lungs.

"Hey, are you really okay?"

"Fine," she blurted out, expelling the breath. The floor seemed to tilt and it got really hot, really fast.

Just breathe. In and out. In and out.

His gaze narrowed as he studied her. "You're hyperventilating."

"I am not." Was she? Oh, cripes, she *was.*

She tried to slow her sudden breathing. Impossible considering the fact that he was still touching her arm. His fingers burned into her flesh, sending a rush of heat to every major erogenous zone.

"Yes, you are. You're hyperventilating."

"I am *not*"—*breathe in, breathe out*—"even close to"—*breathe in, breathe out*—"hyperventilating"—*breathe in, breathe out*—"I'm just breathing"—*breathe in, breathe out*—"a little heavily, that's all." She gulped for air after the last rush of words.

His gaze narrowed. "You're not claustrophobic, are you?"

"No. Yes. I mean, I never thought so, but maybe I am." Okay, why was she lying?

For the same reason she'd faked it. She was a sexpert. A calm, cool, controlled professional. Sex. The idea of sex. The eagerness for it shouldn't freak her out like it did everyone else, let alone intimidate her. And it sure as hell shouldn't make her hyperventilate.

"We could go to a hotel," he told her. "It's not really convenient because I need to be on site for practice tomorrow, then Saturday's the qualifier and Sunday's the race, and there's always a bunch of stuff in between the actual driving, which makes it pretty hard to stay out of the mix. But if it's really freaking you out—"

"No. No hotel." That would mean getting one room, because no way could they register for separate rooms. The press, who'd been a constant presence in one form or another for the past few days, would have a field day, and all the headway they'd made convincing everyone they were blissfully married would be for naught.

She forced a slow, deep breath and clung to the one and only bright side of sleeping on the team bus—at least they had separate beds.

Separate, she told herself for the rest of the night. And she might have believed it if it didn't feel as if they were practically in the same room. Above the hum of the air conditioner, she could actually hear his soft snores. The brush of skin against cotton as he rolled one way and then the other.

She did some rolling of her own, tossing this way and that, counting everything from the various sexual positions to the dreaded sheep in an effort to hypnotize herself to sleep. Fat chance. Her body stayed in a constant state of awareness and by the time the sun topped the horizon early the next morning, Eve was so exhausted she could barely walk, much less scowl. Throughout the morning she hid behind a pair of sunglasses and wore an *I'm a cold bitch and I can't be bothered to acknowledge you* persona as she got her first up close and personal look at NASCAR's hottest new driver in action.

Watching Linc do the first few practice laps was extremely exciting.

Watching him do one hundred, however, was downright boring.

Eve's stomach grumbled for the countless time and she turned to the young woman in a T-shirt and jeans who was standing near a portable fuel pump. The only woman, in fact, she'd seen at the track other than a few wives and significant others.

"Is there a snack bar or something around here?"

"There are some vending machines near the mechanics' lounge." The young woman pointed toward a large silver garage in the not-too-far distance. "Just go inside and take a left. You can't miss it."

"Thanks."

Fifteen minutes later, Eve had scarfed down a full bag of Doritos, a pack of Twinkies, and was busy reevaluating her chocolate ban—a Snickers bar would really hit the spot—when a young woman wearing jeans, a racing jacket, and biker boots pushed through the doorway. She had a dollar in her hand, tears in her eyes, and a frown on her face as she headed for the candy machine.

She blinked several times as she fed the dollar unsuccessfully into the machine. She shoved the dollar between her teeth, hauled off her gloves, and tossed them to the floor before giving the dollar another try. Her hands trembled and the paper kept rolling back out at her.

"Here. Let me." Eve took the dollar and fed it into the machine. The cash registered and the young woman stabbed a button.

"Thanks," she growled as she tore open a Reese's Peanut Butter Cup. She blinked frantically, as if determined not to shed any one of the tears swimming in her eyes. "The low-down, dirty motherfucker," she muttered. "He's an *asshole,* that's what he is." She took a bite and paused for a few chews. "A rat bastard." She popped the other half into her mouth and shook her head. "A *snake,*" she said around the peanut butter cup.

Obviously, the chocolate was having its soothing effect, because the cursing was steadily dropping from DEFCON 1 to temporary alert.

The young woman wadded the wrappers and tossed them in the nearest trash can before turning to Eve.

"Thanks."

"Glad to help. You okay?"

The question seemed to snap the woman to attention. She pulled her shoulders back, pushed her chest out, and nodded. "Yeah, I'm fine. He thinks he's psyching me out, but he's just pissing me off."

"And he would be?"

"Bobby Milton."

"Your husband?"

"Not in this lifetime. He drives for the same team I do."

"*You're* the driver," Eve said. "The woman driver my friend mentioned."

"I'm a driver. A good one, too. Damned good enough to know how many laps I can make before I need replacement tires. I know the limit. I don't need his damned advice on tires, or how to come into a turn or which goddamned way to hold my friggin' steering wheel. I'm the driver of *my* car, even if all these dumb-ass, dick-for-brains, I-have-a-cock-therefore-I-rule-the-world, male-chauvinistic *Bubbas* don't want to admit it. The fact that I happen to be a woman is beside the point. I can drive as well as any of those jocks. Just as fast, as controlled. I don't fucking need them telling me how to do it." Silence settled as she drew several deep breaths.

Eve gave the woman a knowing look. "Feel better?"

The woman blew out an exasperated breath. "I'm getting there."

"Here." Eve fed money into the machine, punched the button, and handed the woman another Reese's. "Eat this and call me in the morning and remember, we're already the superior sex, so we have nothing to prove. They, on the other hand, need constant reinforcement that their shit doesn't stink."

The woman smiled. "I'm Jaycee Anderson."

"Eve Farrel."

"Nice to meet you, Eve Farrel . . ." Her expression faded into disbelief. "Not *Farrel* as in *Jacqueline* Farrel?"

"She's my mother."

"No way. She is so awesome. You wouldn't catch her taking crap from these guys. She doesn't doubt herself. She thinks she's just as good."

"That's my mom." Eve smiled, picked up the woman's

gloves, and handed them to her. "And she doesn't doubt herself because she *knows* she's just as good."

High on a sugar rush, Eve shed the indifferent bitchy persona and put on her sexiest, most confident smile. She headed back to Pit Road. But when she arrived, she found something much more threatening to her charade than a pack of nosy reporters.

Skye Farrel-MacAllister looked very out of place as she stood among the uniformed crew that rushed around Clint's legendary red, white, and blue Chevy. She wore trendy hip-hugger jeans that hit just below her protruding belly and a flowing white peasant blouse that would have made the average pregnant woman look like a blimp. On Skye's petite frame, she looked like she should be walking the runway for the latest in maternity fashion. Her long blond hair was pulled back into a ponytail. Her green eyes sparkled and her cheeks seemed pinker as she touched a protective hand to her belly.

Eve felt a momentary pang of envy that faded into a rush of fear when Skye's gaze found her.

"Hey, Skye," Eve said as she walked up to her sister.

"Hey, yourself." Skye frowned. "You look like hell. Marriage must not be treating you well." Before Eve could say anything, she rushed on, "And why would it? You're making a mockery of a sacred institution."

"If that were my only problem."

"You didn't . . ." Skye studied her before declaring, "You slept with him again."

"I did not"—Eve shrugged, her bravado fading beneath her sister's knowing gaze—"but I want to. What's wrong with me?"

"He's handsome, successful, and charming."

"I know. That's why something has to be wrong with me. I don't lust after men like him. And I don't lust after men who can't even help with a decent orgasm."

"Maybe you should have given him a clue instead of jumping off the deep end and faking it in the heat of the moment. Geez"—Skye touched her face—"is it just me, or is it hot in here?"

"It's hot."

"Thank God. I was afraid the hormone thing was raging again. I'm in month five. I should be even for the next few months. At least I hope so for Clint's sake. Do you know I actually yelled at him for breathing? I mean, he was doing it sort of loudly when I was trying to read the ending of Sandra Brown's *Slow Heat in Heaven*, but that's beside the point. The poor thing. He's been walking on egg shells ever . . . Oh, no." Skye's gaze filled with panic. "I just rambled. Rambling is a sure sign of raging hormones."

"You didn't ramble. You just got off the subject a little, but it's okay." She touched Skye's hand. "Really, sis. It's all right. Breathe."

"I'm breathing." She puffed once, twice, for emphasis. "Okay, I'm okay. Are you sure I wasn't rambling?"

"Rambling is insignificant nonsense. That all had meaning." *Sort of.*

"I'm totally in objection to this whole marriage business," Skye went on, "but I am glad you're here. We don't get to spend nearly the time together that we should." Before Eve could respond, Skye gave her a huge hug.

Okay, one minute she was Captain Ass Kicker and the next she was ready to sing "Kumbayah." Definitely hormonal.

"I love you," Skye murmured and hugged harder, and for whatever reason, it felt good. "I talked to Mom," she said when she finally pulled away.

Eve raised an eyebrow. "You?"

"It's the whole pregnancy thing. Before, all I could think of was avoiding her in the interest of self-preservation. Now I just keep thinking how I'll feel if little Clint and little Cowboy avoid my phone calls, and so I can't help but pick up the phone. That's why I came to the track with Clint despite a ton of work. It's the only way to honestly avoid the phone."

"You have a cell phone."

"Of course, but I accidentally left it at home."

"Accidentally, huh?"

"Actually, I told Clint to hide it so that I couldn't find it. He's good, too. I looked everywhere. So I'm guilt-free right now. Sort of."

"You're naming one of the boys Cowboy?"

"It's just for right now. We can't decide on a second name. We could use Dad's, which is my vote, but that will make Clint's dad jealous." She motioned to her husband, who stood several feet away talking to Cal, the crew chief responsible for Linc's car. "If we use his father's name, it'll make Dad feel ousted. If we do both, then we face a similar situation. Donovan Frank. Frank Donovan. So we've just agreed to disagree for right now. In the meantime, he's Baby Cowboy. Whew." She blew out a breath and touched a hand to her back. "I think I need to sit down." She motioned to a few chairs off to the side, away from the hustle and bustle and noise of the pit area.

After they had settled down into the chairs, Skye turned to Eve. "Mom's really freaked out."

Eve smiled. "Mission accomplished."

"I mean she's more freaked out than usual when it comes to you. She's *mega*-freaked. I'm kind of worried. She sounded stressed when I talked to her. She never sounds stressed."

"She's got Dad underfoot."

"And Grandma," Skye added.

"What?"

"She said Grandma is on some dating quest to find Mr. Right."

"No wonder she sounded stressed."

"I can't help but feel a little sorry for her." Skye slid her feet free of the two-inch sandals she wore and wiggled her toes. "Her whole belief system is on shaky ground."

"Don't you think you're being overly dramatic?"

"Am I?" Worry lit Skye's eyes as she slid her feet back into her shoes. "Drama is a definite sign of out-of-control hormones."

"A shaky belief system sums it up to a *T*," Eve said, trying to steer Skye away from the hormone issue. "I'll call her."

"You will? Because I told her you love her and aren't trying to purposely ruin her life."

"I'm trying to keep her from ruining mine. I just need her to give me some space, and this was the only way to accomplish that. I've got a lot riding on this, Skye. This is my chance to kick my company up to the next level. I can't blow it, and you know what Mom does to me."

"I know . . . I mean, I'm sure she doesn't mean to."

"Little Clint and little Cowboy again?"

Skye nodded and rested a hand on her belly. "Just call her to touch base. You can even act blissfully married, but not too blissful. I don't want her to have a heart attack or anything. Just say hi, tell her you love her despite your life choices, and hang up."

"Like that will reassure her."

"Maybe not, but at least you tried, and she can stop saying you totally hate her."

Eve sat up straighter in her seat. "She said I hated her?"

"No, but she's thinking it. I know because that's what I would think if little Clint or little Cowboy went and married some totally horrible girl that I didn't approve of."

"They won't do that because you won't be so close-minded." Eve eased back against the chair and tucked her long hair behind one ear.

"I tell myself that, but what if I am?" Skye asked. "What if I'm like Mom?"

"Don't even think it," she told her older sister, just the way she'd been telling herself the same thing ever since her sixth-grade gym teacher, Maybeth Sparks, who'd also gone to grade school with Jacqueline Farrel, had told Eve she was the spitting image of her mother.

"Why, it's like being in the sixth grade all over again. You could be her twin, Lord help you. Probably stir things up just the way she did, too, but I'll have none of that in my class. No sirree. The boys have their side of the gym and we have ours. They get the football equipment and we do badminton. End of story."

Eve had hated badminton, but she'd actually gone to the state championships two years in a row because her mother had detested the sport, and so she'd given it her all.

"You're right." Skye's voice drew Eve back to the present. "There's no way I'm going to try to shape and mold my boys to be what I want them to be just because I think they ought to be that way. And no way am I going to get mad just because they're too busy with their lives to talk to me when I call. And I won't be hurt, either. That's just life. And— Geez, I'm really hot. And hungry." A startled expression gripped Skye's face. "Oh, God, I'm doing it again, aren't I?"

"You are not hormonal. You're just hungry. Come with Auntie Eve. I know this perfect little vending machine just around the corner."

A few candy bars later, Skye was laughing and talking and Eve was starting to think being stuck at the racetrack every few weeks, smack-dab in the middle of the whole macho, chest-beating NASCAR thing, might not be so bad if it meant seeing her sister more often. Hormones and all.

Chapter 12

That feels *soooo* good."

Ruella Farrel stared down at her hands, which were clasped in her lap, before shifting her attention to the man who sat on the sofa next to her. "But I'm not even touching you."

"I know. I'm just practicing." Morty Haskins was a seventy-nine-year-old widower who'd only recently gotten back into the dating pool. He'd seen Ruella's ad in a sexy singles section of the paper and responded with a profile of himself. He had four children, nine grandchildren, and three great-grandchildren. He also had a nice apartment in a small suburb on the outskirts of Los Angeles. He'd been the packaging department manager for a cereal company for forty years before retiring. He'd lost his wife seven years ago to a heart attack. He liked *Wheel of Fortune, Reader's Digest,* and crossword puzzles. He enjoyed cooking, bunko, and his favorite color was yellow.

Ruella adjusted her lemon-colored blazer and barely resisted the urge to laugh at the man sitting beside her.

Laughing should be the last thing on her mind while having dinner with her number one orgasm prospect. Why, he'd made a roast, for heaven's sake, complete with little new potatoes and strained spinach. To round off the meal, he'd made individual tapioca puddings sweetened with sugar substitute—bless him. No man had ever done anything for her before, much less taken on the monumental task of making dinner. She should be mesmerized right now. Entranced. *Turned on,* as her sexologist daughter would say.

"Practice makes perfect." He pulled out a small cheat sheet from his pocket and held it up. "See, my memory ain't what it used to be, and to compensate for my short-comings, I just write things down. Since I also ain't too good at verbalizing my feelings, either, I write 'em down."

She set her tapioca aside, took the list, and read the second entry. "Great, baby, I like it just like that." She wasn't sure whether to smile or run as fast as her orthopedic shoes and slightly arthritic knees would permit.

"I was never verbally inclined. So I've been taking some classes here lately down at the seniors' center. This one in particular, Over the Hill and Behind the Times, is all about getting back into the whole courting scene. They tell you how to be successful—give you tips on what to wear, how to act, what to say."

"They told you to wear that rather, um, interesting tie?" She eyed the bright green tie covered with orange shamrocks and again tried to hide her smile.

This is not funny. This is a romantic situation. A simmering pot of seductive stew that should soon be hot and ready.

"Actually, my grandson told me to wear this. He gave it to me for St. Paddy's Day last year and it's his favorite."

Morty wasn't very smooth, but he was a sweet gentleman. "It's nice." Ruella pulled up her sleeve and revealed a handmade bead bracelet with a tiny silver leopard clasp. "This is from my granddaughter Eve. So tell me more about this class of yours, Morty." She was determined to give the situation a good effort. "It sounds really fascinating."

"Well, the main point of it is that you have to change your preconceived notions about the opposite sex and what they want from a relationship. It's different than it was years ago. Before, you could bring a woman a bag of penny candy and a bouquet of handpicked daisies or something, and she was a happy camper. Not anymore. First off, you can't get anything for a penny, and if you try to pick flowers anywhere in L.A., you'll wind up in the pokey. Second of all, women aren't half as interested in a man's taste in candy as they are in his communication skills. Women want you to actually talk to them."

"I can see how that might be helpful if you want to have a relationship with someone."

"You ain't just whistling 'Dixie.' Women want a man who puts himself out there and says what he wants. A man who doesn't assume she knows the meaning behind a full bag of licorice bites. There ain't no such thing as subtlety anymore." He took a bite of his tapioca before wiping his mouth with his napkin. "Women want you to just blurt out everything. They want to crawl inside your head. Speaking of inside, when are we going to do the deed?"

"I . . . You really *want* to do, um, the deed?" About the only thing Ruella wanted was a glass of warm milk, a box of Milk Duds, and her comfy pajamas.

"You bet." He eyed her before adjusting his shamrock necktie. "I mean, I guess I do. I would really like to give it a shot again. Not that I haven't had relations recently, or anything like that. But it's been a while since I've had them with a real woman."

Ruella wasn't going to inquire.

"So I might be a little out of practice," Morty went on, "but I've also been taking this other class, which teaches you all about the female body parts. There's a helluva lot more parts down there than I ever figured, and it's all got its own name. There's the vulva and the . . ." Morty went on for the next ten minutes about a woman's nether regions and Ruella prayed that the racy subject matter would stimulate some sort of reaction. After all, she hadn't put on her new lemon yellow lounging suit, matching sandals, *and* knee-high panty hose for nothing.

Other than learning a few new facts about her own treasure chest, she wasn't any more excited than she'd been when he'd pulled open the door and she'd first glimpsed his necktie.

The most thrilling part of the past two hours had been when she'd accidentally sat down on his grandson's Bouncing Tigger. Other than a quick tingle thanks to Tigger's loud "Woohoo!", she'd felt nothing even close to excitement all night. In fact, she was this close to borrowing Morty's blood pressure cuff—which he kept on the end table next to his bifocals and a bottle of Dr. Scholl's foot powder—just to make sure she hadn't given up the ghost already.

Otherwise, she should feel *something,* shouldn't she? Morty was perfect on paper. And he wasn't half bad in person. He had an average face, thinning gray hair, and watery blue eyes, but she'd seen worse. And he was nice. Maybe a little desperate, but she couldn't blame him for that. At least he was trying.

It wasn't his fault that she kept noticing the age spots just below the long strands of white hair he'd combed over the balding patch on his head. And it certainly wasn't his fault that his dentures clacked every now and then when he laughed. She'd had the same problem herself until she'd switched to a different adhesive cream. And it surely wasn't his fault that he was out of practice when it came to seduction. The man had been married to one woman for fifty years. Why, if it had been fifty years since Ruella, say, had made biscuits, she doubted she could whip up even a halfway decent batch.

Bottom line, he *was* trying.

Which meant that it wasn't his fault the evening wasn't a romantic success. It was hers, because she simply wasn't the type of woman to ever feel such things with a man. She wasn't a woman, period.

"You're damned lucky to have me, Ruella. 'Cause ain't no man would ever have you. You're too plain, too fat, and too dumb, to be good for anything 'cept mopping up after someone. There's no fire in you, gal. No fire a'tall."

Maybe not. But maybe there was and Morty just didn't have a big enough spark to start things flaming.

She clung to the last thought, pushed her doubts and her dead husband's voice aside, and focused on finishing her tapioca. And then she shook Morty's hand, bid him good night, and headed home to go through the dozens of ad responses she'd received that morning.

If at first you don't succeed . . .

* * *

She was not going to panic.

Jacqueline Farrel told herself that as she paced the Berber rug in the front hallway of her apartment and waited for her mother to return.

Her apartment?

The question echoed in her head as she glanced toward the living room and glimpsed Donovan sprawled on her lovely Victorian sofa. White brocade patterned with pale pink tea roses. His sock-clad feet were planted firmly atop one of her favorite books, *The Divine Female,* which sat on her cherrywood coffee table right next to a hand-sculpted female vagina done by one of her favorite New Reality artists.

Conservationist magazines cluttered the rest of the tabletop, along with the leather billfold she'd purchased for Donovan last Christmas, his discarded T-shirt from the previous night, a plate with a half-eaten slice of pizza, and the real bee in her bonnet: an empty Bubba Beer can.

Why, she could barely pass the beverage in the grocery aisle without feeling sick to her stomach, and now he'd brought the stuff into her apartment—yes, *her* apartment because she'd yet to add his name to the lease—and he'd had the gall to actually drink it right in front of her . . .

Her thoughts ground to a halt as the doorknob turned and the door opened. Ruella Farrel walked in, a sheepish look on her face.

"Do you know what time it is?" Without waiting for a reply, Jacqueline blurted out, "It's practically midnight."

"It's ten fifteen," her mother pointed out as she closed the door and set her purse near the coatrack.

"That's practically midnight. I was worried sick, Mother. You can't traipse around Los Angeles at all hours of the night. It isn't safe."

"I'm a grown woman, dear. I'm not defenseless. I have mace. Besides, I wasn't traipsing. I was having dinner."

"With a man you hardly know." Jacqueline waved the note her mother had left, which read simply "Having dinner with my new male friend. Don't wait up." "What if he had turned out to be some serial killer? Which is a very likely possibility, given that ninety-nine point nine percent of all serial killers are male."

"He wasn't a serial killer."

"Obviously, otherwise you would be in pieces in his refrigerator right now instead of here with me."

"He made me dinner. A very delicious dinner. He could really cook."

"That's nice, but—"

"Yes, it *is* nice," Ruella cut in. Her face drew into a frown. "That's the problem. I don't want nice. I mean, I do. But I want nice *and* exciting, and Morty was only one out of two. Of course, if he bought a new tie and changed his denture cream, maybe that would help. What do you think?"

"I think I don't want to think about new ties or denture cream or an exciting man named Morty."

"He wasn't exciting at all. That's the problem."

"No, the problem is that you're running around a strange city looking for men. You're a grandmother, for heaven's sake."

"So?"

"So you're a mother, too. *My* mother." Oh God, had she just said something that close-minded? She had. Even worse, she'd meant it.

Jacqueline ignored the sudden urge to drop to her knees and say a dozen *I'm sorry's* to the Big Feminist Upstairs. Instead, she put on her best smile. "It's just that I thought we could play a game of Scrabble. You like Scrabble."

"Scrabble is boring, dear. I'm through with boring. I want heart-pounding, blood-pumping excitement. I want to go all weak in the knees when a man looks at me. I want to have a real"—her voice lowered to a whisper—"*orgasm.* With a man."

More power to you. That's what Jacqueline should have said. What she'd said to countless women the world over. Every female, regardless of race, creed, color, or socioeconomic status was entitled to a good orgasm. It was every woman's basic right.

Every woman except the one who baked cookies for your second-grade Christmas party, and made a Joan of Arc costume for your first school play, and fed you milk shakes every time you got your braces tightened, and argued on your behalf when you got suspended for picketing school officials when they refused to let you join the varsity football team (not that you wanted to play football, but it was the principle at issue).

"Let's play Scrabble," Jacqueline pressed, trying to tamp down her sudden panic. Scrabble was safe. Familiar.

"Sorry, dear. I have a few letters to answer."

"These?" Jacqueline held up the monstrous stack that had been sitting in the mailbox when she'd come home from the studio a few hours ago. It had been less than a week since Eve's impromptu wedding and Ruella's decision to stay for an undetermined length of time, and already the woman was getting mail.

"Is that all?" Her mother looked disappointed.

"There are over fifty letters here, Mother."

"I got one hundred and eight yesterday. I'll definitely have to broaden my territory and try a different singles site. Or maybe I'll sign up for one of those dinner party dating deals—Eight at Eight—or something like that. The more men I meet, the better my chances of finding my perfect match. Oh, Donovan," she called out as she plucked the rubber-banded stack of letters from Jacqueline's hand and walked past her toward the living room. "Did you tape my favorite show?"

He glanced up. "Taken care of, Ruella, and I must say you look really fetching tonight."

Ruella blushed and sank into an armchair while Donovan swung his legs to the floor and pushed to his feet. He walked over to the VCR/DVD unit that sat on the dark cherrywood entertainment center just to the left of the television.

Jacqueline felt a measure of relief for the first time in days as she watched Donovan press the REWIND button and ready the tape to play. Her gaze shifted to her mother, who settled into the soft leather, an eager light in her eyes. Here was the woman who made it a point never to miss any event in her only daughter's life.

Jacqueline smiled. "Donovan doesn't have to go to so much trouble to tape my show for you. I can bring home a fresh copy from the studio. I would have if I had known how anxious you were to watch today's episode."

"Not your show, dear." Ruella motioned Jacqueline to be quiet as Donovan returned to the sofa, a remote control in each hand. A careful aim and a few clicks, and the television screen fired to life.

The minute Jacqueline heard the familiar theme song,

she knew something was very wrong. A few frantic heart-beats later, an announcer's voice confirmed it.

"If it's a man you need, don't be blue, Cherry Chandler's here with a wealth of advice for you!"

The air rushed from her lungs and her heart jumped into her throat. "You taped *Cherry Chandler?*" she finally managed, her voice little more than a croak. "Since when do you watch Cherry Chandler?"

"Since I decided to have my very first—"

"Don't say it. Please don't say it."

Excitement lit Ruella's gaze. "Tonight is 'Come-and-Get-Me Hair' night. Cherry's going to talk about proven hairstyles that men find irresistible." She touched her gray bun. "I've been thinking about getting mine cut."

"You're going to cut your hair?" Jacqueline tried to swallow past the lump in her throat. "For a *man?*"

"In the interest of finding a man, dear. Then again, maybe I'll get it permed. Or maybe I'll color it and then do some of those highlights that have become all the rage."

"I think you would look good with color and high-lights," Donovan said.

"Really?" Ruella smiled. "I just might do it if Cherry thinks it's a good idea. I'm sure it will take off years and give me a softer edge." Her gaze shifted to Jacqueline, who was still too stunned to talk. "You don't need to color, dear, but you might think about doing some of those low lights to add depth."

"I think low lights would be great on you, honey." Donovan eyed her with a look that usually made her toes tingle.

It would have, if she hadn't been this close to having a nervous breakdown. *Cherry Chandler* and *"Come-and-Get-Me Hair"* and *Jacqueline's mother?*

"They would definitely spice up that pale hair of yours," Ruella said. "You could do brown or maybe red. Why, Cherry said on 'Color Yourself a Man Magnet' that men absolutely love red."

"I don't care what men love," Jacqueline blurted out as the realization of the situation finally hit her. *Cherry and her mother. Her mother and Cherry.* "I'm not coloring my hair for a man."

"What if I asked you to?" Donovan pushed to his feet and stepped toward her. "Not that I would. But if I did, would you do it for me?"

"Of course not. Why don't you color your hair for me?"

"I thought you liked my hair."

"I do, when it's not attached to the brain that thought it was a good idea to tape Cherry Chandler, of all people."

"I did it because your mother asked me to, and I care enough about your mother to overlook my own personal preferences to do something just because it means the world to her. Because it makes her happy. And I think you would look good in red hair."

"I'm not coloring my hair for a man."

"I'm not just any man. I'm your man, and you're my woman."

She was *not* hearing this.

"I am not your woman. I am my own woman. An individual. A separate entity."

"Who happens to share the same space with me." He closed the distance between them and stared down at her. "And three beautiful daughters. And thirty-six years of memories."

She knew that look in his eyes. She'd seen it way too often over the past several weeks, and it didn't bode well.

"We share so much already, honey, which brings me to my next point." Donovan captured her hand in his before she could run the other way. "I wanted to do this in a more proper fashion, but you've been avoiding me lately. So I'm just going to say it."

"Okay, okay," she blurted out. "I'll open a joint checking account."

Surprise flickered in his eyes before fading into a determined light. "It's not about the checking account."

"You can have the monogrammed towels with your initials." She tried to pull her hand free.

"Will you—"

"I'll get the damned low lights." She pulled and twisted, but he wouldn't let go.

"—marry me?" he finished.

"I . . ." *Can't* jumped to the tip of her tongue, but for some reason, she couldn't seem to spit it the rest of the way out. Not with Donovan looking at her so intently and Cherry Chandler chattering in the background about short versus long hair and the floor tilting this way and that.

"I . . ." She swallowed. He leaned closer, his hand tightening around hers, his massive frame taking up all her space. "I—I think I need to lie down."

Chapter 13

"Mom, what are you doing here?" Eve blurted out when she opened her front door to find her mother standing on her doorstep.

"I need to lie down."

"O-kay. Is there some reason you drove all the way across town to do it?" Eve was getting a bad feeling about this, particularly when she noted the large black leather suitcase sitting near her mother's feet.

"Your grandmother is looking for the perfect sex partner. Not that I have anything against a mature, independent woman looking for great sex. But she's taken out a singles ad in a strange city and . . ." Jacqueline shook her head. "She's your *grandmother,* for heaven's sake. And then there's your father. That man is even crazier than my mother. He wants to . . ." Her body started to shake violently as if she were trying to ward off an incredible evil. "I can't even say it."

"He wants to marry you?"

She shivered again. "Just hearing it makes my skin

crawl. Can you believe he asked me to . . . That he wants us to get . . . Can you *believe* it?"

"After thirty-six years?" Eve shrugged and tried to ignore the suitcase. "It makes sense."

"Only to a warped, twisted, disturbed, *married* mind." *In other words, you.*

"I can't see why you're so surprised."

"I'm not surprised. I'm outraged. He knows good and well that enslaving myself to anyone is not an option. So why he's persisting in pushing me, I have no clue. On top of that, your grandmother is actually encouraging it. She even cried when he . . . when he asked . . ."

"When he asked you to marry him?"

"Exactly."

"I'm sure it was touching."

"It was outrageous. Your father has obviously gone off the deep end and taken your grandmother with him. Not that it's their fault. It's society, I tell you, what with those backwards, cretin-ish Himanists ruling the television with their *Monday Night Football* and *Thursday Night Smackdown* and all the other stuff in between. Then there's Cherry Chandler, who's spreading her vicious propaganda in the name of ratings. She's warped both of their minds, and no amount of reasoning on my part can help them."

"But you're going to try, right?" She cast a hopeful gaze on her mother.

"Of course I am. I'm going to formulate a reasonable course of action to prove to them both how silly they're being, which is why I'm here. I simply can't think straight with the constant nagging and— You really should try to tone down the makeup, dear. Anyhow, with so much harping on the same old, same old, I'm this close to throwing myself onto the nearest freeway."

"I know the feeling."

"In the meantime—"

"You're going back home to tough it out in the propagandist trenches with the two people you love most in the world?" Please, please, *please.*

Her mother picked up the suitcase, straightened her shoulders, and marched past Eve into the small hallway. "I'm emancipating myself from the insanity and moving in with you until I come up with a plan. Cherry can't get away with this. Why, she's been ruining my life since we roomed together at Harvard. Always influencing our instructors to get her way and promote her backwards belief in a perfect man and a perfect relationship. Do you know that she took my internship at Masters and Johnson with that load of baloney? Professor Mathews and his cronies might have bought that bunk—what do you expect? They're men. But I don't. If only I could figure out a way to debunk her. I will, but it's going to take time. Meanwhile, you and I can get to really know and appreciate each other."

Eve meant to breathe. But the minute the words registered, everything seemed to stop. Her heart paused. Her lungs froze. Her tongue stuck to the roof of her mouth.

Hello? You saw the suitcase?

She had, but Eve hadn't wanted to think . . . It couldn't mean . . . *No!*

"Eve? You don't look so good. You look pale, despite all that makeup." Jacqueline peered closer. "What's wrong?"

"I . . ." Eve forced herself to take in a breath. Her lungs

constricted before spitting the air back out and demand-
ing more, and more. "I think I'm the one who needs to lie
down." Or fall down. Yep, she was definitely this close to
keeling right over. "You can't . . . I mean, I'm *married*,
Mom."

Her mother looked as if she wanted to say *Don't
remind me*. Instead, she seemed to force a smile. "I realize
that, dear, but Linc will be gone so much of the time with
his racing and everything, won't he? So it's not like
you two are joined at the hip and there's no room for
me. Besides, I'm your mother." Jacqueline set her suitcase off to the side and peeled off her beige blazer. "It'll
be fun. It's been forever since we've spent any real time
together."

The statement sent a rush of panic through Eve that
quickly swamped the dread. Her gaze darted past her
mother to the small hallway that led to the closed door
where Linc had disappeared not more than fifteen minutes ago. There were still drops of water on the hardwood
floor where he'd walked from the bathroom to the guest
bedroom.

She'd been sitting on the sofa with her computer when
she'd heard the footsteps and glanced up in time to see
him pass the living room doorway wearing nothing but a
fluffy white towel and a grin.

The picture he'd made, all hard, tanned muscle drip-
dropping past her, had been enough to kick-start her heart
and make her seriously contemplate a full running tackle.
But then he'd disappeared, the guest bedroom door had
closed with a solid *thunk*, and she'd been safe.

"Don't bother to show me the way," her mother told
her. "I know right where the spare bedroom is."

"On second thought," Eve blurted out as her mother stepped forward. "Forget lying down. I really think I need to throw up."

But Eve didn't have time to toss her cookies. Her mother was this close to blowing her Happily Married cover.

So she grabbed the woman by the elbow and spun her around toward the kitchen.

"What are you doing?"

"You look thirsty, Ma."

"I had a cup of coffee on the way over—black with extra sugar. I thought the caffeine might make me feel better, more alert, so as to better figure out a way to fix that Cherry and save my family, but now I just feel jittery. I need to relax and get settled in. A good night's sleep will clear my head and give me the right perspective. I tell you, that woman should have never been put on the air in the first place. She's a danger to our society."

"Great," Eve said as if her mother hadn't uttered a word. "I'll make you a cup of tea." She flipped on the overhead fixture. Light flooded the black and white kitchen.

"I told you," her mother said as Eve steered her toward the stainless-steel, glass-topped table, "I'm not thirsty."

"It's a proven fact that brain power is fueled by a healthy constitution. You need to flush your body regularly with lots of fluids. I've got green tea. It'll do the trick."

"I don't want any green tea."

"Diet Coke."

"I don't do artificial sweeteners."

"Regular Coke."

"I don't do carbonated beverages."

"Orange juice."

"Too much acid."

"Apple juice."

"Too much sugar."

"Beer."

"Too much testosterone." Jacqueline dug in her heels and tried to shrug off Eve's grip on her elbow. "I really just need some time to myself."

"Look, Ma, you have to stay in the kitchen."

"Whatever for?"

"Good question."

"What?"

"I mean, that's a good question. I would ask the same thing if I were you and my daughter was acting a little strange." At her mother's pointed look she added, "Stranger than usual."

"Eve." Her mother pinned her with a gaze she remembered all too well from her childhood. It was the same look she'd given her when she'd demanded to know who had drawn a mustache and beard on the jacket picture of her first book. "Why are you forcing me into your kitchen?"

"Because . . ." Eve's mind raced. She needed an excuse that smacked of marital bliss. "Because I . . ." Something that said love and commitment. "Because Linc and I . . ." Something that screamed marital enslavement and female oppression. "Because Linc and I are christening all the rooms of the apartment to celebrate our union as man and wife. Since doing the whole missionary thing seven times would get a little boring, we decided to, um, spice things up."

"That's nice, dear," her mother finally said, after a long, shocked pause.

At least Eve thought it was shock, but her mother seemed unshockable these days, so she couldn't be sure.

"The christening part I mean," her mother went on, "not the union as man and wife. But I don't understand what that has to do with the guest room? If the room's a little out of order because you've been in there, I'll simply straighten up."

"It's not out of order. It's a dungeon," she blurted out. A dungeon? "Yeah, it's a fully-stocked, well-equipped chamber of torture."

"Excuse me?"

"Linc straps me down and has his way with me."

"He straps you down?" Her mother looked visibly pale. "*He* straps *you* down? That's humiliating and degrading and totally oppressive."

"I know." Eve forced her best smile before she did something really stupid like burst into tears. "It really turns me on."

Her mother's gaze narrowed. "You haven't been watching Cherry Chandler have you?"

"As a matter of fact—"

"Never mind." She waved her daughter silent. "I don't want to know. I think I need to sit down."

"Great." She propelled her mother into the kitchen chair that faced away from the door leading to the hallway. "You chill while I get things tidied up and have Linc put away his whip. And his handcuffs," she added for good measure before rushing down the hallway and bursting into the guest room.

She pushed the door shut behind her and turned.

"We've got big . . ." *Trouble* stalled on the tip of her tongue when she spotted him sprawled on the bed, a book in his hands. "You're reading."

"I *was* reading. Now I'm wondering what the hell you're doing in here."

"You're reading Nelson DeMille."

"And?"

"And you don't look like the DeMille type."

"What type do I look like?"

"The type who reads cereal boxes and those cheesey ads they put on the restroom stall walls. Not well-written, meaty fiction."

He winked. "I guess I was bored. You've just got dogs on your bathroom wall." He referred to the wallpaper she'd purchased at the local SPCA charity drive. All of the proceeds had gone to benefit the animal shelter where she'd found Killer all those years ago. "Is something up?"

"Up?" She didn't mean for her gaze to drop, but suddenly her eyes seemed to have a mind of their own. They fixed on his lap, which was hidden by the sheet. "I mean, yeah, something's up, all right. You have to sleep with me tonight."

"I thought we agreed not to do that again."

"I don't mean *sleep* as in sex. I mean *sleep* as in you have to crash in my room. My mother's here."

"Here?"

"*Here.* She left my father because he asked her to marry him and now she wants to stay here." Panic bolted through her and her heart pounded. "I can't believe this. She's here. Right *now.* Right *here.*" She shook her head. "It's not supposed to happen like this. She's supposed to stay away. That was the point of us getting married in the first place."

"Calm down. We can deal with this." He threw back the covers to reveal a pair of white boxer shorts. Tossing his legs over the side of the bed, he pushed to his feet. The boxers pulled tight across his derriere as he leaned over and retrieved his jeans, which were heaped on the floor.

Okay, the last thing she needed to think about was his tight tush when her world was this close to falling apart.

Bye-bye, concentration.

Adios, documentary.

Hasta la vista, commercial success.

"Take a deep breath," Linc said, coming up to her. He trailed a strong hand down her back and massaged between her shoulder blades for several long seconds. "Why don't you just tell her to leave?"

"I can't come out and tell her that."

"Why not?"

"Because . . . Because I just can't." It was one thing to push Jacqueline Farrel away with a lot of black mascara and a few fake tattoos, and quite another to just blurt out the truth. After all, the woman *had* given birth to her. She deserved some respect. "She's my mother."

Warm fingertips cupped her chin. He forced her gaze to his. "It's going to be okay." He stared deep into her eyes and for the next few moments, she actually believed him. "Your mother hates the thought of you happily married to a male chauvinist, right?"

"She hates the thought of me married to anyone. The chauvinist part is just icing on the cake."

"Then we'll serve her up a great big slice and let our actions speak louder than words. Just follow my lead."

Five minutes later, Eve stood at the kitchen counter wearing one of Linc's oversized NASCAR T-shirts that fell to midthigh, and slathered peanut butter onto a slice of bread.

"Hurry it up," Linc said. He sat at the kitchen table wearing a pair of old, washed-out orange board shorts and a frayed lime green T-shirt that read BEAUTY IS IN THE EYE OF THE BEER HOLDER. "I'm starving, dumpling."

"Yes, sir." Eve ignored the urge to slap Linc upside the head with the sandwich for the *dumpling* reference. She *was* Jacqueline's daughter, however much she hated to admit it. She concentrated on humming "The Wedding March" and busied herself reaching for the grape jelly.

"So, Mom," Linc said as he stretched out in his chair and hooked his feet at the ankles. "The little woman tells me you're a big TV star."

Eve caught her mother's reaction out of the corner of her eye. The woman stiffened and her mouth drew into a tight line. "I host a late-night talk show."

"The one with all those top-ten lists?"

"No," her mother said, her brows drawing together. "That's David Letterman."

"Right." Linc pointed a finger as he leaned forward and rested his forearms on the table. "You're the one with all the political viewpoints."

"No," Jacqueline ground out, "that's Bill Maher."

"Right. Oh, yeah, you did that 'My Mistress Is a Transexual' episode, didn't you?"

"That's Jerry Springer, and he's on during the day. They only rerun him at night." Jacqueline sat stiffly in her chair, her hands folded in her lap. With tight lips she said, "My show is called *Get Sexed Up!*"

"Oh." Linc made a big show of nodding as he slouched back in his chair and folded his arms.

He looked handsome and clueless, and it was all Eve could do not to bust out laughing.

"Don't tell me you haven't heard of it?" Jacqueline asked.

Linc shrugged. "I watch mostly ESPN or the Outdoor channel." He gave her a hopeful grin. "Any chance you'll be doing something related to fishing sometime soon?"

Jacqueline's frown deepened. "My show is all about the empowerment of women, Lincoln."

"Right." He nodded and gave her a knowing look. "So you don't know how to fish."

She scowled. "It's not a case of whether or not I know *how*. I choose *not* to fish. That's the key, don't you see? It's my choice. My right as a woman to do the things I like rather than what society expects of me. Besides, I don't have much time for hobbies these days. I have more important things to do."

He cocked an eyebrow at her. "Hunting?"

Her frown deepened. "Educating today's women on their basic rights as the dominant species."

"So you don't know how to hunt, either." He glanced over his shoulder and drummed his fingers on the table-top. "Honey? I'm *really* hungry here."

"Coming right up," Eve sang out as she retrieved a plate from the cabinet, arranged the sandwich on top, and headed for the fridge. Her gaze zeroed in on the Sweet Leaf Tea before moving on to the carton of milk, a can of soda, orange juice . . . *aha*.

She unearthed the can of Bubba Beer sitting at the back of her fridge. While she didn't drink the stuff her-self, she always kept some on hand in case her mother dropped by.

"Here you are, sweetheart," she said as she set the plate and beer in front of Linc. She tried to ingore the heat that rushed through her when Linc's large hand slapped her playfully on her bottom. "Mom, are you sure I can't get you anything?"

"No, no, dear." Her mother tugged at her collar as if she was doing her best to stay calm and conscious. "I'm really tired. If you don't mind, I would rather call it a night."

"Wait!" Eve held up her hand when Linc started to take a bite of the peanut butter and jelly. She grabbed a knife, leaned in front of him, and proceeded to cut the sandwich into four corners before slicing off the crusts. "There." She gave him a huge smile. "Now it's just the way you like it."

"On second thought," Jacqueline said, a horrified look in her eyes, "I think I'll go to a hotel."

Chapter 14

"Mom just left. She's on her way to a hotel," Eve told her father the minute his "Hello?" drifted over the line. She stood at the kitchen counter and slathered peanut butter onto another slice of bread. Linc was still sitting nearby at the kitchen table. "She wanted to stay here, but she changed her mind."

"Or you changed it for her?" Donovan asked, laughter in his voice.

"I might have helped a little." She topped the peanut butter with a second slice of bread and sliced the sandwich into two halves. "Actually, Linc and I together were the deciding factor."

"That's unfortunate. I was hoping your mother might be softening toward the idea of marriage." She heard him murmur, "She's okay. She's going to a hotel," to her grandmother before his voice came over the line again. "She's as stubborn as ever, it seems."

"Why don't you call her?" While Eve understood her father's stand on the marriage issue, they were still her parents, for heaven's sake. She wanted them together.

"I will do no such thing. Your mother needs to learn her lesson—namely that a man can only take so much. I've been patient. I've respected her views on love and matrimony. I've even refrained from watching any and all organized professional sports that don't include women."

"That's pretty much every professional sport."

"Exactly. I've given up a great deal for your mother. It's her turn to sacrifice for me."

"So you're not going to apologize and beg her forgiveness?"

"For wanting the woman I love to publicly acknowledge that she returns my feelings? I'm sorry, sweetheart. I know this is going to be tough on you and your sisters, but I'm taking a stand. I'm not asking your mother to come home. Actually, I think the time apart might do us good."

"Come again?"

"Your mother has convinced herself that she doesn't need me. I believe otherwise. If I'm right, this separation will likely show her how much she misses me and can't live without me. If not—"

"Don't say it, Daddy." Eve walked the two feet to retrieve a diet soda from the refrigerator. "Mom loves you. You know that."

"How do I know that? By the way she refers to me on her show as the man who gives her her orgasms, or when she's man-bashing me because I leave my socks in the living room?"

"Okay, so she's not overly affectionate." Eve pulled out a soda, popped the tab, and headed back to the counter for her sandwich. She could feel Linc's gaze, and every nerve in her body went on alert. "That doesn't mean she doesn't love you," she managed, despite the sudden pounding of her heart.

"I guess we'll soon see, won't we?"

"He's not going to call her, is he?" Linc came up to her as she slid the receiver into place.

"He says it's her decision, not his." She tried to gather her control and slow her rapidly beating heart.

"Maybe he's right." His deep voice stirred the hair on the back of her neck.

"He is right," she told him as she reached for her sandwich. "But that doesn't make me feel any better. They're my folks." She turned to face him, the sandwich between them.

"It'll work out." He towered in front of her and peered at her with vivid, concerned blue eyes. His nearness was disconcerting. At the same time, she felt oddly comforted. "They've been together a long time," he went on. "That has to count for something."

Eve nodded. "You're probably right. She'll come around. I just don't think it's going to happen any time soon. My mother can be pretty stubborn." Eve grinned. "Thanks so much for helping me tonight."

He winked. "You're the one who sent her running for the hills with the whole sandwich-cutting thing."

"True, but I couldn't have done it without you. The way you played dumb about her talk show was priceless. She definitely hates you."

"I can't say that I blame her."

She took a bite of her sandwich and arched an eyebrow at him. "I didn't think chauvinists had a conscience," she said after she swallowed her mouthful.

His gaze riveted on her lips for a long moment before he shrugged. "Yeah, well, you don't know everything."

She knew one thing. He wasn't half as chauvinistic as she'd originally thought. Sure, he was loud and proud and very, very male, particularly when he stared at her as if he wanted to take a bite out of her the way he was doing right now. But he also had a heart.

Her mind rushed back to the night she'd met his parents, and the look on Linc's face when he'd told her about his grandfather's funeral. The guilt. The regret. Not for himself, but for his father, who was stuck living a lie.

Not that the discovery made a bit of difference. It just made talking to him more tolerable. Nice, even.

"Maybe I missed my true calling," he told her as he plucked the sandwich half from her hand. His fingers grazed hers and heat tingled along her nerve endings. "I'm a pretty good actor."

She nodded and watched him take a bite. His jaw worked around the mouthful and need tightened low in her belly. "You're not at all what I thought you were," she finally managed. Her gaze lifted and collided with his. "You're actually *nice*."

His grin faded and his eyes took on a smoldering light. "If you knew what I was thinking right now, you wouldn't think so."

"What are you thinking?"

"About how much I really want to kiss you."

Okay, so he wasn't nice. He was psychic because all she could think of with him staring so intently at her was how much she *wanted* him to kiss her.

"I'm really thirsty," she blurted out, turning toward the counter to retrieve her diet soda. She reached for the can and was about to lift it to her lips when his arms slid around her waist. He dropped the sandwich half onto the counter and his deep voice vibrated in her ear.

"It's a good thing that your mother left. Otherwise, we'd be stuck in the same room all night."

Eve wanted to shrug away, but he was so strong and warm and *close.* Her brain launched into a chemical production frenzy. Her adrenaline level spiked into the danger zone. Pheromones erupted, bumping and buzzing into one another like june bugs fighting for space at a streetlight.

Been there, done that, a voice whispered. *And he-llo? You promised not to do it again.*

"Lots of people share the same sleeping space without having sex," Eve murmured as she set the can back on the counter with trembling fingers.

"True."

"So it wouldn't have been all that difficult." *Right.* "We could have just pretended there was a wall between us."

"A thick one." His warmth seeped through her clothes and upped her body temperature.

"A wall so thick that we couldn't see one another," she added, her voice suddenly husky.

"See no evil." His muscles bunched and tightened as he pulled her back against the hard wall of his chest.

"We couldn't hear one another." Eve licked her lips and tried to ignore the feel of his erection hard against her bottom.

"Speak no evil."

"We couldn't smell one another." Her nostrils flared in response to the delicious scent of raw male and fresh soap.

"Smell no evil."

"We're adults, after all." If only she didn't feel like a teenager during her first make-out session—scared and excited at the same time.

"Mature," his deep voice rumbled in her ear.

"We know sex isn't a good idea."

"A terrible idea." Warm lips nuzzled her neck.

"You're not even close to my type." *Sure.* He'd turned out to be a lot closer than she cared to admit. He was smart, thoughtful, caring, nice.

Temporary.

He was still temporary. A waste of time. A distraction. One she couldn't afford at this point in her life.

"You don't look a thing like Johnny Depp or Benicio Del Toro," she whispered, eager to find something to kill the strange warmth curling through her.

"And you don't look a thing like Miss Hawaiian Tropic, though you do have a pretty banging body."

"I don't like Sweet Leaf Tea."

"And I don't like Sugar Babies."

"I'm not even close to wanting you," she said, turning in his arms.

"Me, either, sunshine." He stared down at her, his eyes blue and blazing.

She licked her lips. "You're going to kiss me, aren't you?"

"I'm definitely going to kiss you." And then he did.

His tongue slipped past her lips, tangling with hers, sucking and stroking and stealing her breath. She slid her hands up his chest, feeling the powerful muscles beneath her palms. His body's warmth seeped through the cotton of his T-shirt to scorch her as fiercely as his mouth.

It started out fast and furious, but then slowed to a

thorough discovery that left her weak and trembling when he finally pulled away.

Regret washed through her, followed by a wave of panic because she wasn't supposed to be kissing him in the first place, much less regret the fact that he'd stopped kissing her.

What was she thinking?

She wasn't. That was the problem. Eve was too busy feeling to think, when it should have been the other way around. She was supposed to think. To focus. To work.

"I should really get to bed. I've got an early day." And then she ducked under his arm and retreated to her bedroom as fast as her legs could carry her.

"How in the world Donovan could even consider marriage, when he knows good and well how I feel about the subject? It just proves that he is completely oblivious to who I really am," Jacqueline said a half hour later to the only sane person, it seemed, left in the free world. She eyed the young waitress—no wedding band in sight—who'd wheeled in the room service cart. "To think I actually agreed to monogrammed towels, of all things. Then again, he's not totally at fault. He's a victim of our society and its subjugation of females in general."

"Um, sure thing." The waitress held out the tab for Jacqueline's signature. "Will there be anything else, ma'am?"

"That'll be all"—Jacqueline glanced at the woman's name tag—"Celeste." She smiled at the girl. "My, but that's a nice name."

"Thank you." Celeste turned and opened the door to leave. "Just ring seven if you need anything—"

"You know," Jacqueline cut in as she rounded the cart,

"I could use some extra ketchup." She eyed the small condiment cup sitting next to the platter of jumbo fried shrimp she'd ordered. "If you would be a love and bring me more, I would be extremely grateful. And it would give us a chance to talk a little more."

"Uh, yeah, sure. I'll, um, be right back."

Once the door had closed, Jacqueline slid off her low-heeled beige pumps and settled herself at the small table in the outer room of the suite at L.A.'s posh Four Seasons Hotel. Her gaze shifted to her cell phone sitting on top of her briefcase.

Her fingers clenched and she steeled herself against the urge to pick up the phone and call home. She wasn't calling Donovan or her mother. If they were concerned, as they well should be, they would soon be calling her.

As if her thoughts had willed it, the cell phone gave a shrill ring. She smiled and picked up the phone.

And then she frowned when she saw the caller ID.

"Where are you?" Barbara demanded when Jacqueline pressed the TALK button. "I've been calling you for the past hour."

"My phone only just rang." She knew that because she'd been listening for it since she'd left Eve's apartment. She'd even checked it twice to make sure it was actually working.

"Not your cell. Your home number. I called twice and no one answered. I thought you were in bed, but then Donovan finally picked up—I think I woke him. He said he didn't know where you were."

"He was *asleep*?"

"Yes, which brings me to my next question: Why aren't you home in bed with him?"

"Because I'm not sleeping with a clueless, inconsiderate, pushy, deceitful *man*."

Silence ticked by before Barbara finally said, "He asked you to marry him, didn't he?"

"Did he say that?"

"He didn't have to. You said pushy and inconsiderate. That, on top of his sudden move from Texas to L.A. just to spend more time with you says it all."

"I swear he's living in an alternate universe."

"Or maybe he's just in love with you."

"Have you been conspiring with Eve?"

"I don't have to. Donovan has to be in love with you. Let's face it, Jacqueline, you're brilliant, but you're not the easiest person to get along with."

"Why, I . . ." Okay, so Barbara was right. Jacqueline *was* brilliant, which made her confident in her opinions, firm in her beliefs, and somewhat rigid at times. "That's still no cause to ask me to . . ." The word stalled on the tip of her tongue and she swallowed. "I can't even say it."

"It's only natural," Barbara told her. "And popular. Everybody's doing it these days."

"Not me. *Never* me. Donovan should know that, but he's obviously indifferent to my needs."

"Speaking of needs, I need you at the studio an hour early tomorrow. The weekly production meeting has been bumped up on account of one of the assistant producers is attending a bridal luncheon and she can't be late. Can you make it?"

"One of *my* assistant producers?" Jacqueline shook her head. "Has *anyone* been listening to me all these years?"

"Great, I'll see you at eight sharp."

"Then again, it's no wonder, what with all of the exposure Cherry Chandler has been getting lately. Why, *Webster's* should cross-reference her with the word *antichrist*. Do you know that she actually did a show on hair?" Jacqueline started, only to hear a click on the other end.

Jacqueline had the sudden urge to cry as she pressed the OFF button and set her phone next to the room service tray.

Tears?

The sheer notion sent a wave of determination through her and she stiffened. She was a woman of principle and she was *not* going to cry. Nor was she going to call Skye or Xandra or even her assistant, Alexis, to alert them to the fact that the world was fast taking a nosedive straight to Himanist hell. And she most certainly wasn't going to lie awake all night and wait for Donovan to drag his lazy butt out of bed and call.

She was going to eat her dinner and then she was going to get some sleep herself. Two could certainly play at this game.

He'd kissed her. Of all the stupid things . . .

Linc stared up at the ceiling and tried to understand what had happened between them.

A kiss. A deep, thorough, delicious kiss.

Christ, he hadn't meant to kiss her. But she'd been smiling at him and she'd looked so soft wearing his T-shirt and he'd had this sudden urge to reassure her about her parents.

Dammit to hell.

The only urge he should be feeling right now was the driving desire to win this week in Tennessee. He was leaving first thing in the morning for Bristol Motor Speedway. Then it was sponsor commitments and a charity fund-raiser with the local Red Cross on Wednesday. He would have all of two days—Thursday and Friday—to practice before the qualifier on Saturday, and then Sunday's race.

He'd placed fourth last week. While it hadn't killed his point standing, he knew he could do better. He would have done better if he hadn't spent so much time in the days preceding the race thinking about Eve and the way she'd looked in those pink boxer shorts standing in his kitchen. And the way she'd looked at him when he'd told her about his grandfather and his father—her eyes so full of understanding and concern.

He didn't need either from her. He didn't *need* a damned thing except to keep his mind on business.

He turned onto his side and punched his pillow and closed his eyes. He was going to sleep and he wasn't going to think about her. Or wonder if she was thinking about him. And he sure as hell wasn't going to knock on her door and find out for himself.

Eve clutched the edge of the sheet, her knuckles white, as she stared at her bedroom ceiling. Her nerves still buzzed. Her legs trembled. Her heart beat a frantic rhythm.

And all because of a kiss.

One measly, tired kiss.

If only.

She closed her eyes and concentrated on taking deep, even breaths. *Think cool thoughts,* she told herself. *Boring thoughts. Cool and boring.*

You're drinking an ice-cold glass of tea. Sweet Leaf Tea. You're watching Linc turn the track for the two-hundredth time.

Her heart kicked up a notch.

Okay, forget Sweet Leaf Tea and Linc. You've got a diet soda and you're watching some anonymous someone turn the track for the trillionth time in Virginia. You take a drink, but it's just not quenching your thirst because it's hot outside and you're sweating.

A wave of heat flushed her cheeks and her lips parted to take in some extra oxygen.

Nix hot. It's cold. Fast-forward to October. You're at the track in the Poconos and you're watching an anonymous someone. You're freezing. Shivering.

The thought stirred a memory of the kiss and the way his hand had pressed at the base of her spine and her body had trembled in response.

She tried to shake away the vision, but it was no use. It stuck in her head, making her body ache with desire for the next several minutes as she prayed for sleep to come.

Fat chance. She wasn't going to get any rest while thinking about Linc and his kiss, and wanting even more.

An orgasm. That's what she needed. And so she did what she'd done many times over the past few years since instituting her No Meaningless Sex policy. She trailed her fingers south.

Oddly enough, it didn't feel quite the same this time. Her hands weren't calloused, her skin raspy, or her touch quite as purposeful as . . .

She frowned and stepped up the action, moving lower to the tender flesh between her legs. She closed her eyes and tried to picture Vin Diesel—hey, the guy could work a pair of Ray•Bans like nobody else—but the image just wouldn't come. Instead, she saw Linc looming over her, driving into her, and this time his moves were perfect. She came quickly, clamping down on her bottom lip to contain the scream and the screech and . . . *Ahhh.*

Delicious sensation gripped her for a few blessed moments and she slumped back, welcoming the satisfaction sure to follow. A feeling that wasn't nearly as intense as usual. She still felt edgy. Nervous. Needy.

Crazy.

She ignored the strange emptiness that lingered deep inside and focused on the positive: the clenching and unclenching between her legs, the trembling of her body, the numbness in her toes . . . *Yum.*

Linc stood at Eve's door and listened to the frantic breathing coming from the other side. He closed his eyes and leaned his forehead against the cool wood, Eve's scream echoing in his head. A different scream from the one she'd let loose when he'd been inside her that first time. This one had been the real thing. Slightly muffled, of course, but still recognizable.

Son of a bitch, she *had* faked it.

He listened for more noise—soft footsteps as she walked to the bathroom, or the creak of the window as she climbed out on the fire escape to call one of her sisters. Nothing. Because she'd probably rolled over, cuddled up with her pillow, and fallen into a relaxed sleep for some after-sex dreaming, just as the video had described.

Meanwhile, Linc wasn't anywhere near dreaming. He was hard and hot from their one kiss, and damned upset. Christ, he'd never had a woman fake it before.

Or had he?

He spent the next few hours pacing the guest room, going over as many past encounters as memory would permit before coming up with a unanimous No Faking. Except for that trophy girl he'd hooked up with a few years back who'd had a little too much wine to drink and so she hadn't been able to climax during the actual act. But he'd finished her off with a little rubbing and she'd been good to go.

He definitely had an impressive track record until now. Until Eve.

It was her. That's what he wanted to think. But he couldn't get over the muffled scream that had drifted from her bedroom. She was obviously capable of climaxing. She just hadn't climaxed with him.

Because he'd been too quick on the draw? Because he hadn't moved fast enough? Or slow enough? Or deep enough?

He tried to dismiss the questions, but they haunted him the rest of the night and into the next morning as Linc caught a plane for Tennessee and the next race.

Chapter 15

Late Friday afternoon, after finishing his practice laps at Bristol Motor Speedway, Linc headed through the motor park to his RV. The walk took longer than expected, thanks to several eager fans who wanted autographs, a familiar reporter from ESPN who wanted comments about the weekend's upcoming race, and his brake man, who wanted to talk about the specific adjustments Linc had requested before tomorrow's qualifier.

By the time he reached the solace of the bus, his heart was pounding with excitement and thirst clawed at his throat. He closed the door behind him, shutting out the typical chaos that filled the racetrack on Fridays—everything from outside barbecues to wandering photographers—pulled off his racing gloves, and headed for the fridge. A few seconds later, after downing half a bottle of Sweet Leaf Tea, he turned toward the table and eyed the brown-paper-wrapped box that sat near a stack of publicity shots. Other than a FedEx overnight label, there was no telltale logo on the wrapper. Not that he needed one.

He knew beyond a doubt it was the order he'd placed last night on the Sugar & Spice Sinema Web site.

Fishing his pocketknife out of his jeans, he popped the blade and sliced open the edges of the box. He'd been married to Eve over three weeks now, and last night had been the first time he'd visited her company's Web site.

He shouldn't have done so. He should have had his mind focused on Bristol and winning his race. But he was finding it harder and harder to concentrate. The more he knew about her, the more he wanted to know. The kiss between them after her mother had shown up had upped his frustration level. And the real orgasm he'd overheard had pushed him over the edge.

He wanted to see her when she had one. He wanted to be the one responsible for it. And that meant turning Eve on so much that she didn't feel the need to fake it.

Why?

The question pushed into his mind, and he quickly answered: Ego. His pride. Both were at stake.

The mounting desire inside him certainly had nothing to do with the fact that he was starting to like Eve Farrel.

The last thing, the very last thing Linc had time for was a relationship that went beyond sex.

But just sex . . . Where it had seemed like a distraction before, it now seemed the only way to ease his frustration and get him back on track.

And so he had to push Eve over the edge and give her the biggest and the best orgasm of her entire life. The problem was, his usual moves hadn't been enough the first time and so he wasn't so sure what to do next.

But he hadn't made it all the way to the Nextel Cup

series by being easily discouraged. He just had to buckle down and evaluate his options.

And so he'd visited her Web site.

There had been over forty-three titles, available on either video or DVD, to choose from. An impressive collection of work that had sparked a newfound respect for Eve and her career choice. Especially since he knew she was the driving force—writer, director, and producer—behind the entire How-To Sex series.

While he'd viewed the one DVD at her house, he hadn't realized the creativity behind the entire series. Forget the typical *put it here and do it there and work it just like this* instructional videos. Each one followed a specific couple, the now-familiar Jack and Candace, through their quest for the ultimate sexual fulfillment. Each episode had an actual story, complete with conflict and resolution, from Jack's overcoming premature ejaculation (*Putting on the Brakes*) to Candace's being invited to a swingers' party (*If and When to Bring in Reinforcements*). Even more, the characters were warm and funny and they seemed like real people. So much so that it made you want to see the next episode just to find out what happened to them.

Jack and Candace had him hooked from the get-go, thanks to the sample video clips on the Web site, and so it had taken over three hours to narrow his choice down to one specific DVD.

He pulled the DVD from its wrapper and stared down at the latest Sugar & Spice title—*Six Steps to Sexcess: How to Spice Up a Ho-Hum Sex Life.* After ten years together, Jack and Candace had fallen into a sexual rut and so they were going to try a six-step solution to jump-start their sex life.

Fake orgasms definitely qualified as ho-hum.

Linc slid the DVD into the player and retrieved the remote control. He'd just kicked back on the bed and pulled a pillow across his chest when a knock sounded on the door.

Before he could call out "Go away," the door swung open—he'd been in such a hurry to unwrap the DVD that he'd forgotten to lock it—and a woman climbed in.

The race team's publicist, Danielle Savoy, was intimidating enough over the phone with her deep voice and *don't interrupt* attitude. In person, however, she was downright scary, which was why Linc had done his damnedest to avoid her since tying the knot with Eve.

It wasn't so much the way Danielle looked in her brown skirt, matching blazer, and roach-killer heels that made her so frightening. It was the way she looked at you, as if you'd done something wrong. Clint had said she'd been a school principal in a former life before turning her love for Sunday NASCAR and its drivers into a full-time job. She was serious and meticulous. Perfect for relaxed, good ole boy Clint, who would rather work on his car designs than worry over the team's image.

"I've got a bone to pick with you, young man." She wasn't a day over forty-five, but she referred to every guy on the team as *young man,* or *mister* or, if she was really pissed, the dreaded *buster.*

"What's shaking, Danielle?"

"My hands, that's what." She touched a hand to her throat and ran a finger around her neckline. "They're trembling thanks to my rising blood pressure. Listen here, buster—"

Uh-oh.

"You've singlehandedly made me a nervous wreck. What were you thinking?"

"I'm going to take a wild guess and say that you're upset about my marriage."

"Give the man a prize!" She clapped before spearing him with a gaze. "Do you know what this is going to do to your image?"

"Make me a totally unacceptable mayoral candidate?"

"I'm talking about your racing image. I couldn't give a fig what you do in your own time. Since the news, your popularity has taken a major nosedive. Forget the Sexy Singles endorsement we had planned next week. They don't want you. And that commercial for Diet Coke? Forget it."

He arched an eyebrow at her. "Married people don't drink Diet Coke?"

"*Women* drink Diet Coke, and it's been statistically proven that their demographic prefers to see a sexy, good-looking, *single* man guzzling the product."

"I look the same as I did six weeks ago when they first approached us about it."

"But you aren't the same. Forget the whole bad-boy bachelor thing we had going." She touched her temples. "Christ, now I'm getting a headache on top of everything. Next, I'll be ordering Rogaine from the Home Shopping Club because my hair is falling out by the handful, thanks to all this unnecessary stress. Do you know I haven't slept in days?"

"You're getting bent out of shape over nothing."

"Nothing? Do you know that music publicists purposely hide this type of thing from the press because they know it can devastate someone's career?"

"I'm not a rock star. I'm a driver. All that really matters is winning the Nextel Cup. Everyone loves a winner."

"But you haven't won the Cup yet, which makes you a wannabe, which means we need all the help we can get."

"We're not really married."

"Popularity increases merchandise sales, which boost a fledgling driver's— What did you say?"

"The marriage is a fake. I needed a little insurance to keep me from winning the mayoral race, and Eve needed to get her mother off her back. Come November, it's over. Which means you don't have to permanently write me off the Sexy Singles thing. Just do damage control in the meantime. It'll all be over soon."

While the news did make Danielle stop calling him buster, she still had a worried frown on her face when she left.

Linc locked the RV door behind her, determined to spend the next few hours completely uninterrupted. Hell, he knew he should be trying to catch some z's, but falling asleep was about as likely as someone approaching him about being on the next *Bachelor*. In other words, it wasn't going to happen.

He hadn't had a good night's sleep since he'd arrived at the track. He'd never realized how loud Cal snored. He'd actually found himself missing the faint wheezing sound that Eve made when she slept. And the way she smelled like sugar and vanilla when she emerged from the shower.

Linc settled back down on the bed and pulled the pillow to his chest. His nostrils flared and the memory of the sweet lingering scent filled his head. He closed his eyes for a long moment and pictured her.

Her lips slightly parted, her eyes glazed with passion,

*her breaths coming in short pants. He plunged deeper
and groaned and the sound galvanized her into action.
She closed her eyes and started to moan . . .*

His eyes snapped open and he slapped the pillow aside.
Grabbing the remote, he punched the PLAY button. He
watched Jack and Candace follow step one for sexcess—
imaginative sex that encouraged breathing life into your
fantasies. The rest of the six steps were

2. Spontaneous sex—surprise is a great aphrodisiac.
3. Flexible sex—new positions equal new sensations.
4. Controlled sex—isolate and assault the senses.
5. Taboo sex—forbidden can be fun.
6. Elemental sex—get naughty with nature.

Linc watched the first step again and again until he for-
mulated a plan of attack. He normally headed home late
Sunday night, but this week's race was scheduled a few
hours later than usual and so he intended to stay over at
the track and head back to L.A. early Monday morning;
he needed a full night's rest if he intended to be at his best.
Eve should be at her office, which would give him the day
to set the stage for Monday night.

"Victory Lane, here she comes."

Monday started out like every other Monday for Eve—
hectic. She woke up late, thanks to a night spent tossing
and turning and thinking about Linc. And the fact that he
was coming home today. And their most recent kiss. And
the possibility that their first sexual encounter wasn't an
omen of things to come.

While she'd sworn off sex with him because she'd

needed to focus on her project, *not* having sex with him was proving even more of a distraction. There was no denying they had incredible chemistry.

Maybe they should just do it again. If it turned out not so great, then her lust would surely fade and she could get back to business. If it turned out to be incredible, then she would know firsthand, her curiosity satisfied, and so she could stop fantasizing about it.

"Are you okay?" Trina asked later that morning during the weekly planning meeting. They were expanding the key points for each of their twelve documentary episodes, and Eve had just passed around an outline of her ideas to the main players at Sugar & Spice Sinema: Trina; Dom, the lead cameraman; Portia, the casting coordinator; and DeeDee, the administrative guru.

They all stared back at Eve, concern in their eyes.

"What?" Eve asked, shaking away the image of Linc and redirecting her attention to the people seated around the conference table.

"You don't look so hot," Trina said.

"That can't be." She was definitely hot.

For Linc, that is.

"Are you getting enough vitamins?" Portia asked as she sipped a Dannon Banana Smoothie. "Nutrition is key to success."

"I'm fine, really."

"We've barely started the project." Dom tapped his pencil on his notepad and readjusted his black wire-rimmed glasses. "You can't go stressing out on us now."

"That's right." DeeDee paused to chew her nicotine gum before adding, "If you stress, we'll all stress, and it'll be total anarchy."

"I'm not stressing. I'm just a little preoccupied. I want this documentary to go according to plan, and speaking of plans"—Eve turned to the outline and tried to ignore Trina's knowing gaze—"I've detailed the specifics for each episode, along with a timeline that we'll follow throughout the entire project . . ." She spent the next thirty minutes explaining her outline and successfully shifting everyone's attention to the matter at hand.

Everyone, that is, except Trina.

"You're not a good liar," the woman said when they finally broke for lunch and everyone cleared out of the room, giving them some privacy. "My guess is something's rotten in paradise."

"There's no paradise. It's not a real marriage. We're just roommates working toward a common goal."

"Maybe that's the problem. Maybe you should be more than roommates. You're hot for him, aren't you?" Trina studied her for a long moment before declaring, "Yep, you're hot for him. And frustrated. That's why you're acting so spaced out. You need to get laid."

"I do not need any such thing."

"Trust me. If you don't vent the frustration, you'll regret it later."

"I thought the idea of me having sex with Linc bothered you and killed your fantasy."

"It did, but now I'm having erotic thoughts about Donald Trump again. And the bagel guy down on the third floor, who's really poor, but extremely cute."

Eve grinned. "You're hopeless."

"And you're horny." Trina winked. "Do something about it. Just go home and jump Linc before he has a chance to say hello."

"Don't you have a lunch date or something?"

Trina glanced at her watch. "Actually, I do have plans."

"Filet mignon over at Deville's?" she said, reminding Trina of her favorite restaurant.

The woman wiggled her eyebrows. "Blueberry bagels in the storage closet down on three."

Jump Linc?

The notion haunted Eve the rest of the day as she interviewed voices for the narrator of *Generation seX*, dealt with a botched delivery from a local props company— they delivered a twin bed rather than the super-duper king-sized she'd ordered—and fielded her usual amount of phone calls.

She couldn't just jump him. Not when she'd made such a big deal about them not sleeping together. At the same time, she'd never been one to ignore an impulse.

Especially one so strong.

Okay, so she was jumping him the minute she walked in the door.

That was the plan, but when she walked into her living room, her intentions faded in a wave of shock.

She glanced around and her eyes widened: Her living room had been transformed to look like the inside of a barn. Her red velvet sofa and chair had been pushed back, and hay now covered the floor, complete with several large bales situated here and there. A pitchfork stood in the corner next to an old milk can and a bucket of horseshoes. A trough full of oats sat near the far wall. A saddle draped a large sawhorse just to her right.

Her floor lamp was gone. The only light in the room came from dozens of candles that were situated throughout in old-fashioned mason jars. The sharp smell of freshly cut hay and new leather tickled her nostrils. Kid Rock's "Cowboy" vibrated from her surround-sound speakers.

Linc stood in the middle of it all, a smile on his face and a twinkle in his blue eyes. He looked as if he'd stepped out of a CMT video, from his white straw Resistol hat to his faded brown cowboy boots. He wore a white T-shirt that read COWBOYS DO IT BETTER and tight, faded jeans that fit his muscular thighs like a second skin.

He stepped toward her and she surprised them both by backing up a step. Eve had never been one to shy away from anything, but he wasn't some bad boy, and this wasn't going to be a one-night stand. She knew him now. She lived with him.

"What are you doing?" she blurted out, her sudden rush of nerves getting the best of her.

"About to live out one of my favorite fantasies." He took another step forward.

She took another step back. "But this is *my* fantasy."

"I was hoping you'd say that." He reached out and caught her before she could bolt for the door.

"No, I mean my fantasy, as in *my* fantasy. The one I used to demonstrate imaginative sex in my *Six Steps to Sexcess: How to Spice Up a Ho-Hum . . .*" He knew.

The truth struck just as he pulled her close.

"Tonight it's *our* fantasy, sunshine." And then he kissed her.

His lips covered hers, his tongue pushing past them to plunge into the warm recess of her mouth. The assault was so sudden, so consuming, that she couldn't resist.

Resist?

Excitement swamped any lingering doubts and she slid her tongue into his mouth and tasted him—a mix of Sweet Leaf Tea and wildness that stirred her hunger and made her want more. She slid her hands around his neck and threaded her fingers through the hair at the nape of his neck to pull him closer. He backed her up the few inches to the wall, his body flush with hers. His thick erection pulsed against the cradle of her thighs. The hard wall of his chest pressed into her soft breasts.

She sucked in a breath as his fingers found their way under the hem of her Gucci T-shirt. Calloused skin rasped across her stomach and sensation tingled up her spine. He tore his lips from hers to kiss a path down her neck. When he reached her neckline, he paused just long enough to push her T-shirt up over her breasts, unclasp her bra, and catch a nipple between his teeth.

Pleasure pierced her and made her gasp. He tongued the hard nub for a few delicious moments before sucking her deep into the wet warmth of his mouth. The motion, so deep and intense, stirred a wave of heat between her legs that spread upward. Each breath became more difficult than the last until finally she was panting.

He released her breast to lick his way across and catch her other nipple between his lips. He licked her over and over, his soft tongue a contrast to the hard edge of his teeth.

Her thighs trembled and she slumped against the wall, her hands splaying on either side to keep from sliding to the wall.

He kept licking her, torturing her nipple and the inside of her knee and . . . *The inside of her knee?*

Her eyes popped open to see Linc bent over at her breast. Killer, tail wagging frantically, was doing her best to hone in on the action.

"It's time for her to go out," she breathed. "She always goes out at seven."

"It's not seven yet. She can wait."

"Then what's wrong—" She started to glance at the dog, but Linc murmured, "Relax." His breath rushed against her nipple and electricity sizzled up her spine.

He shooed the dog away. Killer, tail still wagging, left the living room and went into the front hallway near the door.

Linc gave Eve a rough kiss, then picked her up and carried her over to a soft, thick blanket spread out on the floor. Kneeling down beside her, he peeled off first one of her thigh-high boots, then the other. His fingertips grazed her bare skin and she actually trembled. Desire speared her and she sat up.

She pulled her T-shirt over her head, along with her unhooked bra, and flung them both to the side. Then she grasped the waistband of her skirt and pushed it down, along with her thong, until she'd shed every article of clothing.

He undressed just as quickly, pausing only to pull a condom from his pocket and slide it onto his hard, thick length, before joining her on the blanket.

Wearing nothing but his cowboy hat, he settled himself between her thighs, looking every bit the man out of her most erotic fantasy. That's where she'd come up with the whole cowboy scenario in the first place: from her own thoughts. But nothing she'd dreamed of had ever felt this good.

He slid his hands under her bottom and tilted her up and then he plunged deep, deep inside. He held himself still for a few moments, his gaze locked with hers, before sliding back out and starting all over again. With each thrust, he pushed her higher. Closer. Until she knew beyond a doubt that this time it was going to happen of its own accord. A few more thrusts . . . A little deeper. A little harder. A little faster. Yes, this was it.

From far, far away, she thought she heard a knock on the front door and Killer's frantic barking. But the sensation was too overwhelming for her to pay too much attention.

She was almost there. Almost . . . Almost . . .

"Miss Eve?" Mr. Wilkie's voice pierced the haze of pleasure that surrounded her. "I'm here to take Killer for her evening walk."

Linc froze midthrust and Eve clamped her eyes shut.

"Just a sec," Linc called out. "We're, um, in the middle of something in the living room."

"Hey, there, girl," Mr. Wilkie said to Killer, who'd rushed to meet him at the door. "You folks just go on about your business," he said, obviously oblivious to what he'd interrupted. "I'll just grab Killer's leash and we'll be off." Metal clinked as he retrieved the leash from its hook near the door. Hinges creaked and the door *thunked* shut.

"That was close," Linc said, relief flooding his face.

Eve blew out an exasperated breath. "You have no idea."

Her words seemed to dawn on him as he looked first victorious, then angry, then disappointed.

A surge of warmth went through her. He'd gone to so

much trouble to give her a real orgasm. Not to mention, he deserved huge kudos for noticing the difference in the first place. Ninety-nine point nine percent of all men wouldn't recognize a fake orgasm if their lives depended on it. They didn't want to see the truth because that might mean they weren't capable of satisfying their partner. Most men preferred living in ignorant bliss.

But not Linc.

"I'm still close." The words were out before she could stop them. "Just move a little." He withdrew an inch and pushed back inside and she sucked in a breath. "Keep doing that."

She stared up into his eyes as he started to move again and tried to will herself back to the edge. If she could just tune in to him and the way that he made her feel then maybe . . .

But ten minutes later, she was still tense. She could hear Killer barking downstairs, and something about the way the animal had tried to get her attention earlier just didn't sit right.

Just close your eyes and do it, a voice whispered. But she'd promised herself no more faking. At the same time, it wasn't fair to keep him pumping away and holding off on his own orgasm when it just wasn't going to happen.

A few more thrusts and she closed her eyes. She opened her mouth and moaned. Once, twice. And then she was screaming.

He groaned, a loud, strangled sound that didn't quite fit with any of the sounds he'd made before. He collapsed on top of her for a few moments before pulling away.

She caught a glimpse of him, still hard and erect, as he reached for his clothes, and she knew his groan of victory had been just as fake as hers.

"Nice try," she told him. "A little more high-pitched than the last time, but still close. Really close."

He grinned and gave her a knowing wink. "What can I say? I learned from the best."

Chapter 16

She'd faked it again.

The knowledge played over in his head the rest of the night as he lay next to Eve in her bed for the first time since their wedding night. She snored softly, her expression passive and relaxed.

As if she'd really and truly had an orgasm.

She hadn't, but she'd been close. Linc had felt it. He still throbbed from the feel of her clenching and unclenching around him. Even more, he'd seen it in her eyes because they'd been wide open and locked with his.

Up until Mr. Wilkie had arrived to walk the dog, that is. Talk about a mood killer. Things had gone downhill fast, for both of them. He understood his own inhibitions. He'd grown up thinking of sex as a taboo subject, only to be undertaken behind closed doors and with the lights out. But Eve's childhood had been totally different. She'd been taught that sex was a pleasure and a right, not strictly a means of procreation. On top of that, she made her living teaching people how to have fulfilling sex. She was the last person he would have expected to be unnerved by being interrupted. She'd done an entire video on catering to the inner exhibitionist, for Christ's sake. She shouldn't have had a problem with someone being out in the front hallway—Mr. Wilkie hadn't a clue as to what Eve and Linc had been doing.

He could still see the sheer mortification on Eve's face and the terror in her gaze. For those few seconds, she'd actually looked vulnerable. Like a kid caught with her hand in the cookie jar. Shy, even.

Forget shy. That was definitely pushing it. But she did have her limits, and he'd just learned one of them. And damned if he didn't want to push her even farther and see if she had others.

In the interest of good sex, of course.

For the first time in his life, Linc was this close to living for himself. Nobody pushing him. No responsibility hanging over his head. He'd waited a long time to get to the point in his life where he didn't have to worry over anyone or feel responsible for them or put their feelings above his own.

So he wasn't going to mess things up by getting emotionally involved with anyone, especially a tough-talking, sexy as all get-out feminist who had a weak spot for dogs and a deep loyalty to her family, and the prettiest, greenest eyes he'd seen in a long, *long* time.

Physically, however, he was primed and ready.

So much so that he hauled himself out of bed later that night and into a cold shower. The first step of the *Sexcess* video had gotten him that much closer to giving her a real orgasm. He wasn't going to deviate now, no matter how much he wanted to roll over and plunge into her soft, warm body. Number two on the video was spontaneous sex, and so he couldn't very well make a move now. While he might catch her off guard by waking her up, she wouldn't be as surprised as if he waited. They were in bed together, after all. Undoubtedly, she anticipated having sex with him again tonight, which pretty much killed the spontaneity.

And so Linc wasn't going to launch another all-out offensive for the time being. As for a few tactical maneuvers . . . Well, the video *had* advised to keep her engine revved between encounters.

He hadn't touched her all night.

The realization followed Eve as she crawled out of bed the next morning—an empty bed, mind you—and busied herself with getting ready for work. The smell of eggs and sausage filled her head. She could hear Linc moving around in her kitchen, and she wasn't sure what bothered her the most—the fact that he hadn't made a move on her all night, or the fact that he was humming.

Humming, of all things. When she was this close to spontaneously combusting from all the sexual frustration boiling inside her.

"Good morning." He grinned when Eve finally trudged into the kitchen, her pre-coffee frown firmly in place.

"That's a matter of opinion." She bypassed where he sat at her kitchen table. He wore a T-shirt and jeans, his hair still damp from the shower. A steaming plate of breakfast sat in front of him.

She headed for the cabinet and her mug. She drank in the smell of coffee brewing and let it clear the cobwebs from her brain before taking a long drink. The liquid burned its way down her throat and revved her heartbeat.

"Here you go, Killer," Linc said, plucking a sausage from his plate and wagging it at the dog.

Killer growled and Eve actually felt a little less grumpy. At least her dog was starting to seem like her old grumpy self.

"Your mother called," Linc told Eve after he took a bite of scrambled eggs. "She said she would like to have lunch with you. I told her you couldn't make it because we're doing Thai."

"I hate Thai."

"She said as much."

"And what did you say?"

"That you love it now because I love it." He took another bite of eggs and her stomach grumbled.

For him, not the eggs.

Eve tamped down the sensation and asked, "And what did she say?"

"That I've brainwashed you." At her arched eyebrow, he added, "I told her that I didn't have to brainwash you because you were a willing victim, and then I called her Mom and told her she was welcome to join us."

"I thought you were flying out at lunchtime."

"Actually, I'm flying out in about an hour." He glanced at his watch. "I'm meeting Clint at Martinsville Speedway in Virginia later today to go over Sunday's race. I just said that for your mother—shock value."

"That's evil," she said as she put her cup in the sink and turned back to him. She grinned. "I like it."

"So do I," he said as he pushed his chair back from the table, stood, and closed the distance between them. He leaned into her, the motion arching her back against the counter. He reached around her to set his coffee cup in the sink and let his arm linger for a long moment.

"Pure evil," he murmured as he stared down at her.

"What?"

"Your shirt."

She glanced down and noted the tank top she wore. It was black with the words PURE EVIL in vivid red. The clingy material molded to her braless nipples, which hardened beneath the sudden scrutiny.

"I . . ." She licked her suddenly dry lips. "They're a band. I saw them down on East Hollywood last year."

"I'll have to check them out." Fire burned in his gaze, and she knew the *them* he referred to had nothing to do with rock music.

His gaze lingered on her chest a few more moments before shifting to her mouth. He leaned down. His breath fanned her bottom lip and she swallowed. She closed her eyes, fully expecting to feel his lips on hers, nibbling and sucking and . . .

Nothing.

Her eyes snapped open to find him staring down at her, a grin on his handsome face.

Disappointment rushed through her, along with a heavy dose of frustration. She stiffened. "It's not nice to make promises you don't intend to keep."

"Oh, I intend to keep this one."

"When?"

"That's for me to know and you to find out."

"This is boring as hell," Trina announced after previewing the final notes for *Generation seX*. It was late Friday afternoon, four days since Linc had left for Martinsville, Virginia, and Eve had just finalized the working script. They sat in Eve's fifth-floor office. Eve perched on her oversized leather chair behind her chrome and glass desk, while Trina lounged in a plush red velour chair on the opposite side.

"Which segment?" Eve asked.

"Every segment." Trina closed the folder holding Eve's outline and placed it on the desk. "We're talking a collective boring."

Tell me about it. "It's informative."

"So is the Weather Channel. You wouldn't catch me watching *that* for three hours straight. Why don't you spice it up or something?"

"Because the network doesn't want spice." Eve grabbed the folder and opened it in front of her. "They want a serious, thought-provoking look at the evolution of sex from one generation to the next."

"There's nothing serious or thought-provoking about sex. And if there is, you're definitely with the wrong partner."

"You're supposed to be enthusiastic about this. This project is going to give us some real exposure."

"I'm happy with the exposure we're getting right now. Jack and Candace are a cash cow."

"The cow's getting old." Eve sighed. "And Jack and Candace, while successful, aren't going to give us upward mobility."

Trina arched an eyebrow and leaned back in her chair. "Not serious or thought-provoking enough?"

"When you're filming a documentary, there are certain criteria you have to meet. It's not about getting laughs or making the audience feel good or coaxing a smile. It's about presenting information." At Trina's grimace, Eve added, "Look, I didn't make the rules."

"No, but when did you start playing by them?"

"Don't you ever just get tired of the same old, same old?" Eve asked as she placed her elbows on her desk and stared past Trina at the wall of windows that overlooked downtown L.A.

"Sometimes, but then I visit Dr. Shapiro and we reshape something"—Trina pushed out her chest for emphasis— "and I'm back to my usual optimistic self."

Eve grinned and tucked a strand of hair behind her ear. "I'm serious. I like what I do and it's fine for now, but I don't want to be a sixty-year-old woman producing the adventures of Jack and Candace's grandchildren. I want to grow as a producer. I want to reach a major network, and this documentary will help get me there." She tapped the folder in front of her. "I'll make great connections and, soon enough, I'll be in a position to actually pitch a solid idea of my own. Something fun and interesting."

"Why not cut right to the chase and pitch it now?"

"Because I don't have a strong enough foothold yet, and I wouldn't want HBO to pull this project and hand it over to JustforFolks." JustforFolks, a production company that had been in the running against Sugar & Spice Sinema to make the *Generation seX* documentary, would have landed it if not for Jacqueline Farrel's notoriety as a sex guru and the fact that she lent credibility to Eve. "They produce infomercials, for heaven's sake." She closed the folder and turned to tuck it into her briefcase. "What does selling real estate have to do with sex?"

"Well, I've had sex while looking at real estate before. In fact, I actually did it with my Realtor when he showed me this great little condo near Rodeo Drive."

"That's great, but we'll save that for *My So-Called*

Slutty Life." Trina frowned and Eve added, "I beat out JustforFolks because I have experience in this department. I'm a professional, and I'm going to give them a professional product. So tell me, personal tastes aside, does it look professional?"

"Extremely."

"Good, because I'm already behind on my schedule."

"That wouldn't have anything to do with one hot-looking NASCAR driver, now would it?"

Yes. "No. This has just turned out to be more involved than I imagined." She straightened her desk to avoid looking Trina in the eyes. "I can still make the deadline and I will; I just need to step up the pace a little."

Eve had never hesitated to talk about men with Trina before, but for some reason she didn't feel the usual urge to spill all the details of her latest conquest.

Maybe because it wasn't much of a conquest.

Yet.

With the subject of Linc effectively avoided, Eve turned her attention to the ad mock-ups that Trina handed her.

It was Friday.

The day before Saturday.

Which was the day before the day Eve would actually see Linc again. And touch him. And kiss him. And . . .

Her heartbeat accelerated and she drew in a shaky breath. She had a hunch what he had planned next—step two of her six steps to sexcess video. While the notion hadn't hit her at first, the more she'd thought about his effort in bringing her cowboy fantasy to life, the more she'd come to the conclusion that he intended to follow the video. Which would mean he was gearing up for spontaneous sex.

She drew in another shaky breath.

She'd come so close on Sunday, and she had no doubt she would go all the way the next time. Which meant, of course, that she could get him out of her system once and for all, which was the entire point. Then it would be hello, focus and good-bye to crazy, lustful, Linc-inspired daydreams.

One Big O and Eve's life would be back to normal.

Nothing was going according to plan.

She painted her nails and accidentally spilled her bright red polish on her living room carpet. She ran out of eyeliner mideye and found herself using a black Sharpie she found in the kitchen drawer. Her coffeemaker wouldn't heat and she had to borrow some instant from Mr. Wilkie when he came to pick up Killer for their midday walk. At the time, Killer wouldn't budge from the closet. No matter how much Eve pushed and pulled at the animal, she didn't want to move. Even worse, when she did move, Eve discovered that she'd had an accident on the carpet. She couldn't help but worry since Killer *never* had accidents, not since she'd been a puppy. Nor did the animal like to miss her walk. Then again, she'd been eating more lately. Maybe she was getting lazy and fat in her old age. She *was* eleven. On top of the dog situation, Eve's cable dropped out when she sat down to watch Sunday's NASCAR race.

The screen rolled and pitched while Eve tried to follow Linc as he raced the road track at Martinsville Speedway. It was the first time she'd actually sat down to watch a full-length race, but she'd been anxious to see him. Talk about rotten luck. The only thing she managed was the

occasional glimpse as he raced the track right behind
Jaycee Anderson in her hot pink Fit & Frisky car. Until
the last ten minutes, that is. Then the screen flickered
and the picture cleared. Eve fixed her attention on Linc
just as the Viagra car lunged past him and sent him spin-
ning toward the rail.

"Are you okay?" A frantic-looking Eve asked as she
hauled open the door.

It was one in the morning and Linc hadn't even had a
chance to knock. She'd obviously been waiting for him.

A burst of warmth went through Linc and he barely
ignored the urge to haul her into his arms and bury his
face in her sweet-smelling neck. "Hello to you, too." He
moved past her and set his duffel bag inside the doorway.
"I'm a little bruised up, but I'm okay. My car, on the other
hand, is in pretty bad shape." He couldn't help his grin as
reality hit him. "You watched my race."

"Of course I watched." As if she'd just realized what
she said, she tried to look nonchalant. "Not that I meant
to, but there was nothing else on." Concern lit her eyes
again as she frowned. "I can't believe that damned Viagra.
He cut you off just like that, and then he raced past Jaycee
and won."

"That's the name of the game, sunshine."

"That's not what you told that reporter," Eve said as
she followed him down the hall. She proceeded to remind
Linc of the choice four-letter words he'd used that the network had had to bleep out. He'd gotten his ass chewed
by Danielle for that, along with a lecture about how such
language could slit his throat when it came to the Bible
Belt fans.

"I was pissed, all right, but more at myself for letting him get the jump on me. Now, I'm more tired than anything else." After the race, he'd had to go over the video footage and give a play-by-play of everything he remembered to the NASCAR officials and his sponsor. And then he'd had to go over the damage done to the car with Clint and the car chief. He'd barely allowed the paramedics five minutes to give him a quick once-over to make sure he was all right.

In Eve's bedroom, he shed his clothes and crawled under the sheets. Eve undressed and crawled in on the opposite side.

She looked so soft with her hair mussed and her face free of most of the makeup she usually wore, and suddenly he wasn't half as tired as he was eager to be inside her again. He tamped down on the urge, gave her a rough kiss on her full lips, and rolled over.

"What are you doing?"

"Going to sleep."

"But you can't sleep. I mean, I know you had a really close call and all, but you're okay. You are okay, right?"

"I'm okay, and I'm exhausted. Sweet dreams."

"Maybe for you," she grumbled as she rolled the other way.

Linc closed his eyes. He *was* really tired. Not only from the day's events, but from sleeping in the RV for the past three nights. Cal snored so loud that he'd found himself lying awake each night long after he should have been sound asleep. He'd never noticed Cal's snoring until he'd spent those few days sharing the RV with Eve. She hadn't snored, but she'd made this faint wheeze with every deep breath that had driven him as crazy as the woman herself. He actually missed the sound. And the smell of her, all warm vanilla and sweet sugar.

He drew in a deep breath and the familiar scent filled his nostrils. The mattress dipped as Eve turned over and scooted closer to him. He felt the soft press of her lips on his temple, and his heart stopped for a long moment. Her arm snaked around him and he smiled, and it was the last thing he remembered before falling asleep.

Eve's initial opinion about Linc had been right: he really *was* an egotistical, chauvinistic jerk.

It was early May, over five weeks since the cowboy fantasy in her living room, and Linc hadn't so much as made a move toward her.

She'd obviously been wrong to think that he in any way, shape, or form resembled a thoughtful, sensitive intellectual like her Mr. Kaboom. No way would such a man leave her hanging this long. She was nervous and on edge, and no amount of masturbating could begin to ease the frustration.

Because she didn't want just an orgasm. She wanted one from Linc. She needed it. She tried to ignore the anticipation that built each week. A feeling that went into overdrive when she saw him race on the television. One glimpse and her insides started to ache and her heart started to pound and she actually found herself watching longer each week, until she was sitting through the entire race, pre- and post-coverage to boot. She'd watched him place fifth in the Texas 500 and come in third at Talladega Superspeedway in Alabama, and finish a close second at California Speedway—a race she'd witnessed firsthand because the track was only forty-five minutes from L.A. She'd been hopeful that the close proximity of that race would enable him to spend more time with her, but he'd been as busy as ever and had spent the days preceding the race in his RV near the track.

She'd had half a mind to move into the RV with him for the week, but then he'd made some excuse as to why she couldn't and so she'd stayed at her apartment. Alone. Lonely.

The week after Linc's tangle with the Viagra car, Eve had expected some action. She'd anticipated it. But he'd been too worried—his car still wasn't performing up to par and he was in danger of losing his top three standing, which meant losing points, which meant no shot at the Cup, which meant zero interest in anything that didn't involve an engine. The next week, she'd faced more excuses and so on.

She told herself he was simply following the video, trying to catch her off guard. But surely he would have made a move by now. Unless . . . Unless he just wasn't attracted to her anymore.

But that didn't explain the way he constantly looked at her when he thought she wasn't looking, the way he undressed her with his eyes, and touched her whenever she happened by, or the way he cuddled up next to her in the dead of night and she felt the hard press of his arousal against her bottom.

He had to be turned on, right?

She pondered the question for the umpteenth time as she sat at her kitchen table Tuesday night, her laptop in front of her. She was supposed to be going over the edits for the first segment of her documentary—she had to have them done first thing in the morning in order to finish the final cut and move on to the next. Concentrate, she told herself.

But it just wasn't happening.

She practically ran to the door when she heard the knock, grateful for the diversion.

"Why don't I join you to walk the dogs," she started, convinced it was Mr. Wilkie. A burst of panic went through her when she found her mother standing on her doorstep.

"We need to talk, dear."

"Trust me, Mom. We don't. I'm happy in my life and nothing you can say will change that. So, see? We don't need to talk."

"Okay, I need to talk." She walked past Eve and headed for the kitchen. "Your father hasn't called me."

"Call him."

"I can't call him," her mother said as she sat down at the kitchen table. "He's the one who's wrong here. He should call me, but he hasn't."

"Maybe he's busy." Eve sat opposite her mother and tried to tamp down the sudden uneasiness.

"He's on sabbatical." Jacqueline eyed Eve's half-eaten peanut butter sandwich. "Is that the crunchy kind?" At Eve's nod, she added, "Crunchy peanut butter is my favorite."

"It's all I had." Eve pushed the plate toward her. "You're welcome to it. I really don't like crunchy. Smooth is so much better."

Jacqueline took a bite of the sandwich and looked thoughtful. "What could he possibly be busy with?" she finally asked.

"He's volunteering at the local community college."

"He is?"

Eve nodded. "Two days a week. At least that's what he said when I talked to him last week."

Jacqueline's hopeful expression faded into one of skepticism. "He's so busy with volunteering that he can't at least pick up the phone? Then again, your father is very dedicated. He's probably putting in a ton of extra time preparing for his volunteer hours. To help alleviate those long, tedious hours of boredom and loneliness. Trust me, I know."

Eve eyed her mother and noted the dark circles under the woman's eyes. "You miss Dad, don't you?"

"Ridiculous," she scoffed, despite Eve's knowing look. "And I don't *know* know. I meant it figuratively because I'm a sensitive person. Unlike your father, who obviously doesn't give a care one way or the other about my health and well-being . . ." Her voice faded as the shrill ring of the doorbell sounded.

Eve bolted to her feet and hauled open the door to find her father standing on the threshold. She grinned. "Mom's in the kitchen."

"I'm not here for your mother."

"Is that your father?" Jacqueline asked as she came up behind Eve. "Why, it is. I almost didn't recognize you. It's been so long."

"Obviously, not long enough," her father said, pinning Jacqueline with a challenging look for several long seconds before he turned to Eve. "It's your sister. She's having the babies."

After a four-hour flight and a long cab ride, Eve arrived at Humana Hospital in the Dallas Metroplex area with her mother, father, and grandmother. She was exhausted, nervous, and this close to slitting her wrists after an endless plane ride where she'd been forced to sit between her parents while her gram lucked out and got a seat on the next row.

Her mother had huffed and snorted, and her father had rambled on as if Jacqueline didn't exist. Eve had read every page of the airline's shopping magazine and done her best to keep from screaming.

"Is she okay?" Eve asked Xandra when she found her younger sister standing with her husband, Beau, outside the double doors that led to the labor and delivery room. The waiting room to the left overflowed with people, most of whom she recognized from Skye's wedding.

"She's fine, but she's scared," Xandra said. "We were the first to get here." Xandra and Beau lived in Houston, which was a forty-five-minute plane ride from Dallas. "We got here a few hours ago. It took Clint longer since he was in North Carolina."

"Lowe's Motor Speedway," Eve said, remembering the race highlights she'd seen touting the upcoming Coca-Cola 600. "Linc's there. I tried to call him." He was a member of their family now, for however brief a period of time, and so she'd felt it her obligation to keep him posted on what was happening. It certainly wasn't because she was nervous and anxious and she'd wanted to hear his voice. "But he didn't pick up his cell and so I left him a message."

Xandra looked surprised before her expression faded into a knowing light. "Clint arrived about an hour ago," Xandra went on. "I was with her until then. The last I heard, she was seven centimeters dilated. She changed her mind about doing natural childbirth and asked for the epidural, but it's too late." She took a sip of her Sprite, her hand shaking. "I never realized how painful having a baby could be. I mean, I knew, but I've never seen it firsthand."

"It's okay, babe." Beau rubbed the small of Xandra's back and kissed her temple in a gesture that made Eve smile. "You'll be okay."

The minute his words registered, Eve's expression went from happy to shocked. "You're not . . ." The smile quickly returned. "Ohmigod, you *are*."

"You can't tell anyone. We just found out, and we don't want to tell anyone just yet. This is Skye's day, and I want all of the attention on her and the babies."

"My lips are sealed. So are you okay?"

"I'm dying for a bag of Doritos, but otherwise, I'm fine."

"I'll be right back." Beau gave her a possessive look and a lingering kiss on the lips before heading for the vending machines.

"You should let the nurse know you're here," Xandra told her. "Skye will want to see you. So where are Mom and Dad and Gram?"

"Gram is retouching her lipstick in the ladies' room in case she runs into any hotties here, and Mom and Dad are downstairs arguing over who is going to pay the cab-driver. He wants to do it, but she's insisting on paying herself."

"Arguing? They never argue."

"They never argue because Dad gives in. He's not giving in anymore." At that moment, their parents' familiar voices drifted from down the hallway.

". . . need you to pay for me, you overbearing, egotistical *man*."

"You wouldn't know overbearing or egotistical if it jumped up and bit you on the ass."

Eve turned just as her father and mother approached.

Her gram followed them, her lips slicked with a bright peach lipstick that matched her dress.

Donovan kissed Xandra on the cheek and slid his other arm around Eve. "Pardon my language, girls."

"It's okay, Daddy." Xandra gave him a hug.

"It most certainly isn't okay," Jacqueline huffed. "It's offensive and totally inappropriate and I can't believe—"

"Farrel family?" A nurse's voice disrupted her mother's rant and they all turned to see the nurse holding open the double doors. "Mrs. MacAllister wants you all front and center right now."

Eve and her family followed the nurse into her sister's delivery room.

"Should we be in here with her?" Eve asked the nurse.

"She wants you here." She glanced at the six of them. "All of you." The nurse hurried to assist the other nurse preparing the tiny incubators off to the side that waited for the new arrivals.

Eve approached the bed where Skye was hunched over, her face a tired, exhausted mask as she blew out a series of breaths. She kissed her sister's cheek. "How are you doing?"

"I'm"—*hee, hee, hee*—"so glad"—*hee, hee, hee*—"you're finally"—*hee, hee, hee*—"here—*yowwwwwww!*"

"Baby one is crowning," the doctor announced as he dropped down onto a round stool and pulled himself into position for the main event. "Get ready, people. We're having a baby!"

The next twenty minutes passed in a noisy blur that didn't slow down until both fat, pink baby boys—five and six pounds respectively—were wrapped in the matching blankets Eve had quilted and placed in their mother's arms.

Then a calm settled over everyone as all eyes focused on the two new arrivals. Eve gave each of the boys a kiss on the forehead and a quick, "I'm Auntie Eve and if you ever need anything, you come to me." Then she stepped back and let everyone else make their introductions.

Eve stood near the doorway while her grandmother snapped pictures of the happy couple.

Make that *couples*.

It seemed her parents had temporarily forgotten their fight. They stood to Skye's right and smiled down at their grandchildren. Likewise, Beau stood with his arm around Xandra, who had tears running down her face. Clint hugged Skye and for the first time in her life, Eve truly felt like the outsider she'd always pretended to be.

Alone. Lonely.

And then she heard the door swing open and felt a strong, soothing touch on her shoulder.

Chapter 17

I got here as soon as I could," Linc said, slightly out of breath as if he'd been running. He wore board shorts, a politically incorrect yellow T-shirt that read SAVE A HORSE, RIDE A COWBOY, and flip-flops. A worried expression creased his handsome face and stirred a warmth in her chest. "Clint and I were in the middle of a practice run on the car when the news came," he went on. "He took off, but I had to wait and give the adjustments to the crew chief before I could leave. I didn't try to call you back because I knew you had to have your phone off on the plane. Looks like I'm too late."

She smiled, took his hand, and twined her fingers with his. "Actually, you're just in time."

He looked at her and surprise flickered in his gaze, as if he were seeing her for the first time. But then he turned back toward Skye and the babies, and Eve was left to wonder if she'd only imagined the look.

They spent the next fifteen minutes *ooh*ing and *ahh*ing over the new arrivals before the nurse ordered everyone to leave so that Skye could get some sleep.

"That sounds like a good idea for everyone," Donovan Martin said. "But first we need to get your grandmother something to eat."

"Now, now, I'm fine," Ruella Farrel said as she cooed at one of the sleeping boys. "Great-Grammie Farrel is just as fine as ever, now isn't she, sweet pea?"

"Maybe so, but we're hitting the IHOP next door."

"That's right," Jacqueline said as she came up next to Ruella. "You have to eat, Mother."

"I could use something to eat, too," Xandra said. She gave Beau a knowing smile and he nodded.

"I'm really not hungry, Dad," Eve told her parents. "You guys go on ahead."

"We'll go on over to the Doubletree a few blocks from here and get a couple of rooms," Linc told her father, who nodded his approval.

Eve hugged Skye and said good-bye and then let Linc lead her toward the nearest exit.

"They looked really happy," she said during the cab ride to the hotel. "I don't think I've ever seen Skye so emotional."

"She just had two babies." Linc glanced sideways at Eve, the same strange expression on his face that he'd worn when he'd first seen her. "It's a momentous occasion."

"I wonder how it feels."

"I never would have pegged you for the mother type."

"Because I look totally inappropriate?" She bristled.

"Actually, because you work so damned much. Being a mother takes a lot of time."

"Oh." So much for being offended. "Sure, I work hard now. I'm trying to jump-start things with my career, which means complete focus. But that doesn't mean I plan to do it forever."

"Are you saying you want to be a mother?"

"Someday. When the right man comes along."

"Ah, the right man, again. This thoughtful, sensitive, intellectual Mr. Kaboom."

"He'll come along in the next ten years or so, and I'll live happily ever after for the next fifty years after that."

"I think that's the plan with most everyone."

"Not with us," she pointed out.

"We married for convenience." Linc gave her another odd look before shaking his head. "There's no love between us."

It was true. So why did Eve feel a sudden sadness at hearing him say it?

She didn't. She was emotional because of the twins, end of story. She most certainly wasn't this close to throwing herself into Linc's arms because of *him* or the fact that she actually *liked* him. He'd just shown up at the right time and she was feeling needy and . . . Enough said.

At the hotel, Linc registered and paid for four rooms—one for Xandra and Beau, one for Eve's mother and grandmother, one for her dad, and one for Eve. It seemed Linc wouldn't be staying over. With Clint busy with Skye and the babies for the next few days, the extra duties fell to him, so he needed to catch the first flight back to North Carolina.

Eve tried to stifle the sudden disappointment as he walked her toward the elevator. She'd been hoping that they might finally get to step two, but it looked as if it really wasn't going to happen.

Fine by her. If he didn't want to, he didn't want to. It wasn't like she *needed* to do it, or anything like that. It was her choice, and she could just as easily choose not to.

At least that's what she told herself as she punched the UP button and waited.

A few seconds ticked by and she felt him eyeing her again. She turned on him. "What? Did I suddenly sprout horns? Because you keep staring at me, and it's really getting on my nerves."

"You're not wearing any makeup."

"I wasn't expecting visitors when Mom and Dad showed up and I didn't have time to put any on." She indicated the UC-Berkeley T-shirt she wore and the slouchy jeans she'd snatched out of her closet. "To be honest, it was the last thing on my mind. What's the big deal? You've seen me without makeup before."

"Not completely. You've always had something on. Eyeshadow. Lipstick. Mascara. *Something.*"

"So?" she said when he lapsed into silence, his gaze still on her face.

"So, you've got three freckles on your nose." The tip of his finger caressed the spot. "I never knew you had freckles. They're sort of . . . cute."

Eve had been called many things in her life, but "cute" had never been one of them. Puppies were cute. Winnie the Pooh was cute. Mature, exciting, wild women who made sex a top priority in their lives were not cute, and so she shouldn't feel the least bit flattered by his words.

But her heart did a double thump and her mouth went dry.

"There's something I've been meaning to do since I

got here," he said, as he followed her onto the elevator and the doors slid shut.

"And what would that—" Before she could finish the question, he kissed her.

His lips were wet and hungry, his tongue greedy as he devoured her for a fast, furious moment that left her heart pounding and her head dizzy.

The elevator jerked to a halt as he punched the STOP button and stalled them between floors.

He backed her up against the wall and pinned her in place. He pushed up her T-shirt, flicked her bra open, and bared both breasts.

"I guess we're doing step two," she breathed a heartbeat before he dipped his head and drew her nipple into his mouth. He sucked her so hard that she felt the pull between her legs.

She shuddered as he released her to drag his hot, wet mouth to her other nipple and catch it with his teeth. She lifted her hands and threaded them through his hair as he flicked her with his tongue, over and over. She squirmed until he opened his lips and suckled her again.

Heat spiraled through her body and pleasure gripped her for several heart-stopping moments. But it wasn't enough. She'd waited too long for this and her body was too needy.

With frantic fingers, she grappled at his shirt, pulling and tugging until she found her way underneath. Warm, hair-dusted skin met her fingertips and she shivered. Muscles rippled beneath her eager touch as she trailed her hands over his chest and down to the waistband of his shorts.

She unbuttoned him with several frantic tugs. He sprang hot and huge into her hands and she held him for a breathless moment.

He leaned his forehead against hers, his eyes closed, as if trying to get a grip on what he was feeling.

She felt him throb against her palms, his erection twitching in anticipation, and then she stroked him. Her fingers slid back and forth, tracing the bulging head, the hard, smooth length. She cupped his testicles and massaged them, and he groaned.

He leaned up and stared down at her, his gaze dark and hooded and hungry. He reached for her jeans, freed the buttons, and shoved them down until she stepped free. Her panties followed until she wore nothing.

He turned her and placed her hands on the wall. His arms came around her and he cupped her sex, dragging a finger over her wet folds in a smooth, sweet rhythm that made her catch her bottom lip. He paused only to slide on a condom before touching her again.

She had the fleeting thought that she was buck naked on an elevator for the first time in her life. A fact that should have stirred an illicit thrill because Eve prided herself on doing the wild and unusual, but she felt nothing save the need clawing at her belly. Her senses were focused solely on the man who surrounded her, his hands on her hips. Behind her, his arousal throbbed, pressing against her buttocks, hot and desperate for entry.

His palm met the wall next to hers and his other arm slid around her, anchoring her for a full upward thrust until he was buried to the hilt. He didn't move for a long moment. He just stood there as her body throbbed around his.

She barely heard the ring of the emergency phone through the haze of pleasure that surrounded her. He withdrew then, only to plunge back in. She strained against him, moving her hips and meeting his thrust with a sense of urgency that had little to do with the constant ringing and everything to do with the need building inside her. A fierce, encompassing feeling unlike anything she'd ever experienced before with anyone else.

Because of *him.*

He turned her on physically with his hands and his mouth and the raw magnetism of his body. But it went even deeper than that. He stirred her emotionally with the possessive way he'd slid his arm around her at the hospital just when she'd needed him most, and the way he seemed genuinely concerned about her sister, and the way he'd noticed her freckles. And liked them.

She *liked* him.

The truth rooted in her brain as he thrust harder and deeper and she went higher. Fear gripped her, but it wasn't the fear of *not* having an orgasm. Suddenly, she was terrified to climax. Because if she did, and it turned out to be spectacular, then she was bound to want to do it again. And again. And again.

Eve Farrel didn't do *again.* Not with a man like Linc— a man who'd made it perfectly clear that he didn't have time for a relationship.

She didn't have time, either. Not now. Not yet.

No!

She closed her eyes and started to moan for everything she was worth. When she reached an earsplitting crescendo, he slid deep inside her and held himself.

She blew out a deep breath and tried to think of anything and everything other than the feeling of fullness between her legs. Because if he moved one more time, she was a definite goner. Her toes already tingled. And her thighs were shaking. And her nipples pulsed. Just one more thrust and she would plunge all the way over . . .

Rrring!

She fixated on the sound and started to count. One ring. Two rings. Three rings.

Seconds ticked by and he finally withdrew.

"Yeah?" Linc growled as he snatched up the phone on the twelfth ring.

Eve took the opportunity to snatch up her clothes and start yanking them back on, careful to keep her gaze diverted from his.

"Sorry," he went on, "but my wife was feeling dizzy and I had to stop the elevator and give her a few minutes to catch her bearings." He listened for a few minutes. "Sorry if we caused any inconvenience. She's fine now."

Right. Eve was anything but fine. She was a fake and a fraud and she was totally freaked out.

From the corner of her eye, she saw him pull up his underwear and shorts. He yanked his T-shirt down and punched the ON button. With a loud screech, the elevator started moving again.

Holy Mother Upstairs, she really and truly *liked* him. And that put a whole new perspective on things.

She wasn't supposed to fall into *like* with him. She wasn't ready for that in her life just yet. She had too much going on. She couldn't focus on her project if she was busy liking some man.

And what if she liked him and he didn't like her? Or what if she liked him too much and he only liked her a little? Or what if she liked him totally and completely, despite the fact that he was completely unlikable?

It happened. Trina, an intelligent, happening kind of woman, had fallen for her share of bums. Xandra had fallen for a total user and loser prior to meeting Beau. Even Skye had been a bum magnet before she'd met Clint. In her search for rock-solid commitment, she'd only managed to hook up with buff, macho, temporary types who'd all taken a hike before she could say the word *relationship*, much less develop one.

To Linc's credit, he wasn't the total chauvinist he'd made himself out to be. But he wasn't 100 percent her Mr. Kaboom, either. He was all about temporary. About *not* having a relationship.

His behavior proved it. He said nothing as he walked her to the hotel room, as if he hadn't even noticed that she'd faked it. As if he didn't care.

"I'll see you next week after the Coca-Cola race."

"Are you coming in on Sunday night or Monday morning?" Ugh, was that hope in her voice?

"I'm not coming in at all. You're coming to me. The fund-raiser in Adams, remember?"

"That's right."

"You can pick up your ticket at the airport. Your flight leaves from LAX at seven A.M. Monday morning. Sleep tight." Then he kissed her on her nose, right on top of the three freckles, and left to catch his plane back to the race-track.

The minute the door closed, Eve hit the bathroom and spent the next hour in a very cold shower. She did her best to talk herself out of liking Linc Adams, but it didn't work. By the time she stepped out, she was no closer to solving her new problem. She only knew she wasn't about to make it worse by having sex with him again.

From here on out, she was flying solo, even if it wasn't half as much fun as the real thing.

"What is up with you?" Cal, Linc's crew chief, came up to him as he climbed out of the car and pulled off his helmet after a disappointing practice at Lowe's Motor Speedway.

"Nothing," Linc growled as he downed a bottle of ice water while his crew went to work fine-tuning the car.

"Nothing?" Cal shook his head. "Bernie was on the horn talking you through that last turn and you ignored him." Bernie was Linc's spotter, and the boss of tactical maneuvers when Linc was on the track.

"I heard him; I just thought it was better to take that turn on the inside." In truth, he'd been gripping the steering wheel, his gaze on the stretch of track in front of him and his mind on Eve and her fake orgasm.

Fake?

He still couldn't believe it. The timing couldn't have been more perfect. She'd looked first surprised, then turned on, just as the video had said. And she'd been into it. He'd felt it in the way she'd trembled beneath his hands and how wet she'd been. Christ, it had been all he could do to control himself. He'd wanted her for so long that he'd been ready to explode in the first moment of penetration. But he'd paced himself, determined to bring her with him all the way. She'd been right there . . . Right friggin' *there . . .*

". . . what the headset is for. If you're not going to listen to the point man, there's no reason to have one."

"I made a bad call." Linc wiped a hand over his face. "It won't happen again."

Amen to that. He was through busting his ass to please

Eve Farrel. Forget the damned video. The next move would be hers, and if she didn't make one . . .

He didn't want to think about it.

He pulled on his helmet and climbed back in the car for more laps.

"Listen to the point man," Cal said.

Linc nodded and climbed back into the car. He gunned the engine and steered back into position.

If she truly had been turned on and she'd faked it for whatever reason, then she would be back for more. An attraction as fierce as theirs was too powerful to resist. If she wasn't turned on and was just a damned fine actress, then she would keep her distance.

Either way, the ball was in her court. Linc wasn't making any more moves except the ones on the track.

He pressed the gas and opened up the engine and in a matter of seconds he was running wide open.

Jacqueline was *not* going home, not unless Donovan asked her to. Which she fully expected him to do as they walked off the plane together in L.A.

Other than their initial bickering, they hadn't said one cross word to each other since Skye had given birth to the babies. Obviously sharing such a special moment with their oldest daughter had helped him see the error of his ways. He'd been pleasant ever since. Sensitive. Understanding. He'd even let her pay for breakfast that morning without so much as an attempt to take over the situation and pay himself.

He was back to his old self.

Jacqueline eyed the woman who walked just ahead of her. Even her mother was acting normal. Greatgrandmotherly with her constant picture-taking and her incessant chatter about how beautiful the babies were.

There'd been no talk about Cherry Chandler or orgasms or hot-to-trot seniors.

It seemed as if things were returning to normal.

Jacqueline smiled as she slid into the backseat of a waiting cab next to her mother. Donovan helped the driver with their luggage and gave instructions before joining them.

He was going to say something any minute now, she told herself as they navigated the freeways and headed into downtown. It was just a matter of time.

"Over there," he declared, pointing to the left.

Her smile disappeared as the driver pulled into the circular driveway in front of the Four Seasons Hotel.

"What are we doing?" Jacqueline asked as the cab came to a stop.

"This is your hotel, isn't it?" Donovan cast a sideways glance at her.

"Yes, but—" She caught her bottom lip to still its sudden trembling.

"But what, darling?" His knowing gaze drilled into hers.

"Nothing." She swallowed and steeled herself against the urge to press herself into his arms, his strength.

Just as the urge struck, she battled against it because the last thing Jacqueline Farrel needed was a man's strength. She had her own, and plenty of it.

"I just thought you might go home first, that's all," she told him, "which would eliminate an argument as to who is going to pay. I would be the last out, so I would pay."

"Well, now I'm the last out, so I'm paying." Before she could say anything, Donovan climbed out and held the door open for her. The driver had already retrieved her luggage from the trunk and slid back into the front seat.

"Good-bye, dear." Ruella gave a warm smile and a quick wave before turning her attention to the driver. "How much time until we get to Hanford Street? Because I've got a date this afternoon."

Jacqueline felt the first twinges of a throbbing headache coming on. So much for a return to the peaceful family they'd once been.

A bellboy rushed to attention to take the bags as Donovan waved a ten-dollar bill.

"I can tip my own bellboy, thank you very much," Jacqueline said as she turned toward the father of her children and opened her purse. "And I'll give you my share of the cab fare."

"I don't want your money." He stared at her as if to say, *I want something completely different, and you know exactly what it is.*

She stiffened. "I can pay my own way, and what you want is none of my concern."

He frowned. "I'm starting to realize that." He climbed back into the cab.

Jacqueline started to turn toward the hotel entrance, but his voice stopped her.

"Obviously things aren't going to work out between us. Maybe we should try testing the waters."

Her heart stalled. "Excuse me?"

"Maybe we should see other people." His gaze caught and held hers. "It's not like we're married or anything, right?"

"Right," she managed, despite the sudden tightening in her throat. "We most certainly are *not* married. Or *any-*

thing," she added, and then she turned and walked into the hotel before she totally embarrassed herself.

By yelling and screaming and crying.

Or worse, by rushing back into his arms and kissing him for all she was worth.

She knew he wasn't serious. Donovan loved her. It was so obvious. He was merely trying to push her. To manipulate her. To weaken her.

She *knew* it. Unfortunately the knowledge did little to ease the tightness in her chest as she walked into the hotel, took the elevator up to her room, and went back to life without her Holy Commitment Man.

Chapter 18

Linc Adams is the man,
There's no doubt about that.
He's got a heart for people,
And his look is totally phat!

So what do you think?" Betsy slid into her seat at the large round banquet table at the Stonebridge Mansion just outside Adams, Georgia, the host site of Linc's campaign fund-raiser.

Betsy handed Eve a blue campaign button imprinted with silver glitter type. "Grandmother thought I should have called Linc 'a real hep cat,'" Betsy went on, "but *nobody* says that."

"I think *phat* says it perfectly," Eve told the teenager.

"You would." Grandmother Adams forked a bite of white fluffy cake with a tiny blue A VOTE FOR LINC IS A VOTE FOR ADAMS pennant sticking out of the center. "I just love the fox-trot," she said as she dabbed at her mouth. She smiled and swayed side to side as she adjusted her bifocals and stared in the general vicinity of the dance floor. "Your grandfather didn't like to dance, but I could cut a mean rug in my day. First place at the annual Adams Dance-Off five years running."

"You wouldn't catch me doing the fox-trot, especially in front of anyone," Betsy said around a mouthful of cherry Bubble Yum. She wore a bland navy skirt and a simple white shell. A small strand of pearls hung around her neck. She looked like a younger version of her mother, who sat on the opposite side of the table. Only her glitter-tipped nails and the portable CD player sitting on the table next to her plate gave any indication that she might not be as conservative as she looked. "That dance is *so* over, isn't that right, Eve?"

"Way before our generation." Grandmother Adams cut Eve a frown. She gave the woman her best smile.

Betsy blew a bubble. *Pop.* "This is *so* boring. I'm missing the *MTV Video Music Awards.*"

"It's a rerun," Linc's mother, Susanna, said as she glanced at her daughter, "and sit up straight, dear. You're slouching."

"I'm not slouching, and so what if it's a rerun? I didn't see the whole thing the first time because you had that stuffy dinner at the house with that old man who smokes those awful cigars."

"That old man is Republican Senator Marshall from Florida and you'd do well to remember that. Why, I could name every senator—and party affiliation—by the time I was your age. I have always loved politics."

"But I don't." Betsy frowned. "I like music. And speaking of music, can't the DJ play something besides all this big band stuff? It really bites."

"It's lively and upbeat and wholesome and lends just the right tone to this campaign." She spared a frown for Eve. "Heaven knows we need all the help we can get."

Eve took a sip from her crystal water glass. "I've told you, Susanna, that I would be happy to donate the proceeds from the next thousand copies sold of my latest video if you'll just give Sugar & Spice a mention on one of Linc's campaign buttons."

"I think I'm getting a migraine," Susanna said. "Hello, dear," she said to Linc, seemingly grateful for the distraction when he slid into the seat next to Eve.

His thigh brushed hers. Eve relished the rush of heat through her body for a long moment before she stiffened and forced herself to the far edge of her chair. She'd made up her mind over the past week since the elevator incident—no sex. Nada. Zilch.

Of course, it had been fairly easy so far, since he'd been in North Carolina and she'd been in L.A. Today had been the real test, which was why she'd brought Killer along for moral support.

That, and the fact that the dog had been snapping and fussing lately when Eve left for work. While Killer snapped and fussed at strangers—with the exception of Linc—she didn't do it to Eve. Eve had come to the conclusion that her dog's odd behavior was a form of acting out because she felt put off by Linc's sudden presence in their lives. After all, she and Killer had been a duo for over ten years. Eve had vowed to spend more time with the animal and so she'd brought her along to Adams.

Luckily, Linc had been busy helping Craig beef up his speech for some American Legion dinner and so Eve had spent most of the day making herself very visible around town. She'd worn a leopard-print spandex dress and handed out more flyers for her latest video, along with sexual how-to advice to anyone who would listen. Then she'd returned to Linc's, locked herself in one of the spare rooms with a grouchy Killer, and got ready for the party. The ride over had been silent and filled with tension, as if Linc were trying to resist her as much as she was trying to resist him.

Forget trying. She was succeeding. For the past forty-five minutes she'd presented a calm, cool, controlled front thanks to inner strength and unflagging courage and the three glasses of wine she'd consumed thus far.

"I didn't get a chance to tell you before," Linc said as he turned his full attention on her for the first time since they'd left his house, "you look really great." His gaze lingered on the cleavage visible just above her fitted black bodysuit. Heat swamped her and she had the sudden urge to slide off the short jacket that completed her outfit. But her bodysuit had cap sleeves and her arms would be bare. Bare arms brushing up against the coarse material of Linc's tuxedo was not conducive to accomplishing her goal: to remain completely unaffected by his presence. "Eve looks great"—he turned back to his mother, who sat across the table—"doesn't she, Mom?"

"I don't know if *great* is the right word"—Susanna adjusted the napkin on her lap and nibbled a small bite of her cake—"but she certainly looks . . . *interesting*."

"Why, that's exactly the look I was going for, Mother Adams." She glanced down at her shiny black bodysuit. The waistline had a built-in corset that plumped her breasts and pushed them out and up. She wore black boots and her short black leather jacket speckled with rhinestones. "Interesting and intimidating. Sort of a cross between a Spanish bullfighter and Catwoman."

"Catwoman is so totally cool." Betsy pushed aside her own untouched dessert plate and blew another bubble. *Pop.* "I don't know about a bullfighter, but that jacket looks just like one I saw Little Kim wear on MTV."

"Actually, it *is* a Little Kim jacket. I got it on Hollywood Boulevard at this really great shop, along with some fishnet stockings and a pair of neon-blue vinyl boots."

"I knew that was a Little Kim design. I wish I could get a Little Kim jacket." *Pop.*

"I can't even imagine what type of store you would go to for something like that. Certainly not Saks," Susanna said.

"They're sold at specialty shops," Eve told her.

"Eve knows all about shopping. She loves spending money on clothes," Linc added, sliding his arm around her shoulder and giving her an affectionate squeeze. "And shoes."

"And firearms," Eve added, taking a long gulp of her wine to help with the sudden rush of heat from Linc's closeness. She knew she wasn't being a team player at the moment, but she couldn't help herself. She was desperate and he was close.

"Do tell?" His mother took a sip of her water and cleared her throat. "Um, Linc, darling"—she fixed her gaze on her son—"maybe we can just keep that bit of information to ourselves. Your father is pushing a new piece of gun-control legislation at the next Senate meeting. I'm sure he would be happy to tell you all about it." She turned toward the man who was standing near the next table talking with another guest. "Jackson, come on over and have your dinner. You and Governor Walsh can talk shop later."

Jackson Adams, an older, more severe version of his son, sat down next to his wife. For the first time, Eve noted the lines around his eyes and the dark blue of his irises. There were no gold flickers like those in his son's eyes. No sparkle. His looked more bland, lifeless.

"I was just telling Linc about your new piece of handgun legislation. Tell him about it."

"I thought you were tired of me talking shop."

"As if you could ever stop."

Eve could have sworn she saw a flicker of anger in his gaze, but then it faded and his gaze went back to their usual placid blue.

"Well"—he forked a mouthful of chicken Kiev and chewed—"it's designed to lengthen the waiting period between purchase and acquisition. I'm also working on a legislative piece geared toward firearm manufacturers that would force them to add an extra identifying code to each individual gun . . ." The explanation continued in the same monotonous tone as Eve finished off her glass of wine and did her best to concentrate on her dessert.

"I know this is fascinating," Linc whispered after several bites, his lips warm and stirring against her ear, "but duty calls."

"Babies to kiss?" She arched an eyebrow.

"A few eager supporters to dissuade." He eyed a man standing near the shrimp buffet. "Malcolm Langtree has offered a ridiculous amount of money and I need to give him a reason to change his mind."

"Don't tell me—you're going to tell him that I'm a lewd pornographer and offer him an autographed copy of Jack and Candace's *Six Steps to Sexcess*?"

"I'm afraid even that wouldn't dissuade Malcolm. He's

Republican. I could be Jack the Ripper and if I'm running with his party's endorsement, he'd be the first to buy me a new scalpel. I'm going to have to pull out the big guns."

"You're going to tell him I'm a Democrat?"

He grinned and pushed to his feet.

Thankfully.

Unfortunately, with Linc across the room, Eve didn't have anything to worry over, which meant her full attention shifted to Jackson Adams and his description of a bill or something or other.

". . . responsibility of citizens like yourself to do something about the crime in our state. That's why it's imperative that voters race to the polls come election day—"

"Speaking of racing," Eve cut in, desperate for a change of pace before her eyes crossed and she drank another glass of wine, "what about that Coca-Cola 600?"

"What about it?" His father gave Eve a blank look as he grabbed his fork and cut into his large piece of cake.

"The Coca-Cola 600," she repeated. "As in NASCAR. Linc just raced it yesterday. He came in third, but he's still leading the series in points."

"You know that, Jackson," Susanna told her husband. She took another small bite of her own dessert. "It was all over the sports section this morning."

"Ah, yes," he said after swallowing his mouthful. "He had a good showing."

"A good *showing*? He was in the fifteenth spot halfway through the race thanks to a carburetor leak. But he came back and just passed those other guys like it was nothing. It was incredible." His father didn't so much as blink as he ate another forkful of cake. "The greatest comeback of the year."

"I didn't think you were a NASCAR fan," Linc's mother said. "Then again, you're obviously a fan of the opposite sex and NASCAR is predominantly male."

"I'm not a fan of the opposite sex. I'm a Linc Adams fan." She would have worried over the implication of what she'd just said if she hadn't been too busy being stunned by the blank look on his parents' faces. And a little outraged. They were his family, for heaven's sake. Even her mother, who totally disapproved of the Jack and Candace series—for her *how-to* meant step-by-step instruction, no plot allowed—owned every tape in the series. And she'd been at the adult video awards last year when Eve had walked off with Best-selling Video of the Year for Jack and Candace's *Panting, Screaming, and After-Sex Dreaming.* She'd even clapped.

"I bet neither of you has ever been to a NASCAR race."

"We're very busy people. We have commitments. Jackson is a state senator, and I'm the wife of a state senator. We don't have time to flit about the country every Sunday. We serve this great state and the people who live here."

"How do you suppose Linc is going to juggle his racing and the mayor's position if he wins?"

His mother smiled and set her fork down. "*When* he wins, I suppose he'll have to race less. Maybe do it every other weekend if he has time."

"It doesn't work that way, Mother," Betsy pointed out. "I told you he loses points if he misses a race. He has to be at all of them." She shook her head. "She never hears anything."

"I hear everything," Linc's mother told Betsy.

"But do you listen?" Eve asked pointedly. "Maybe Linc likes racing more than he likes politics."

"I'm sure he does. I enjoy golf, but you don't see me shirking my responsibilities to go putting around the green. Hobbies are fine, but there's a time and a place for them. Why, my father loved to fish. So did your father, remember that, Jackson? But they did it when they had time."

"Which wasn't very often"—Jackson waved his fork—"I remember many a Saturday when we were supposed to go down to Lake Sheridan, but something or the other would come up." Eve saw something flicker in his gaze. The same something she'd seen in Linc's eyes when he'd told her about all the football games he'd missed. And all the friends he'd never had time for. And all the fishing trips that had fallen by the wayside. But then it disappeared and Eve was left to wonder if she'd seen it at all. "He was a busy man and it couldn't be helped. Duty calls."

"It's time for Linc to get his priorities straight," Susanna said as she pulled the napkin from her lap and folded it. "He will once he wins this election and sees how time-consuming his position is going to be. Speaking of positions, Jackson, did you talk to the sheriff about those extra funds for the jail? He says he'll gladly give Linc his full endorsement if you give him your word that Linc will approve their budget adjustments . . ."

And she thought her own mother was close-minded when it came to listening to someone else's opinion. Linc's mother could definitely give Jacqueline a run for her money in that category.

Eve kept her mouth shut and spent the next hour listening to Linc's mother and father go back and forth about various issues. The only reprieve was when Betsy slid her a sheet of paper with her latest rap.

I loved you so much and I thought it would last,
But I liked things slow and your hands were too fast.
Then you lied and cheated, so time to hit the road,
I thought you were a babe, but you're a horny toad.

"What's this?" Eve whispered.

"My best friend Angela's sister's friend's boyfriend messed around on her and she wants to break up with him. But she didn't want to just write him a letter or call. They're both so lame. So I said I would write her a rap. Cool, huh?"

"Definitely the way to go if you're breaking up."

The conversation continued and Eve sipped more wine, but even the halfway decent chardonnay did little to ease her boredom. And so she didn't resist when Linc returned to the table, reached for her hand, and pulled her from her seat. She did wobble a little, however.

"How much did you have to drink?"

"One glass. Give or take three or four."

He shook his head and tightened his grip on her hand.

"Where are we going?" she asked as he led her through the maze of tables.

"To have some fun."

Her heart skipped at the notion. Linc and fun could only mean one thing, and she'd already vowed no more sex. Then again, she could always head back to the table and listen to his father.

"Walk faster," she told him.

But instead of pulling her toward the nearest storage closet, or even the bathroom to try step three from the *Sexcess* DVD, he rounded a table and headed for the dance floor.

"No." She dug in her heels as he tried to tug her onto the floor.

"Why not?"

"I don't fox-trot."

"Neither do I."

As if on cue, the big band song came to an end.

The disc jockey, a middle-aged man wearing a tuxedo and a really bad toupee, flipped on his microphone. "This next one is a special request by the man of the hour himself," he said, almost apologetically.

Five seconds later, Eve understood why.

Forget the smooth sound of Sinatra. Instead, an acoustic guitar and a whining fiddle poured from the speakers, launching a popular country tune.

"Come on," he told her.

"No," she tugged against his hand. "I don't do Tim McGraw."

"I can't discourage this entire town by myself and you haven't exactly been a team player tonight. Just dance with me. This one dance."

"I can't two-step," she finally admitted. "Not that I would do it even if I knew how. These boots were made for walking, not sliding." She indicated the three-inch stilettos.

"We're not going to two-step." He pulled her out to the center of the dance floor and into his arms. "We're going to swing a little."

"Swing— Whoa!" Before Eve knew what had happened, he'd twirled her and sent her whirling in the opposite direction.

Thanks to the wine and the impractical boots, she was dead certain she was about to eat the floor. But his fingers tightened around hers and just as she teetered to the side, he pulled her back to him, turned her under his arm, and the wild ride started all over again as Tim sang about missing the good old days and "back when." By the time the song faded to a close, she could hardly breathe.

Even worse, she couldn't stop smiling.

"Not bad." He grinned and drew her closer as Patsy Cline's "Crazy" drifted from the speakers. "But now comes the real challenge."

"And here I thought you were testing my coordination."

"I was and you passed." To emphasize, he twirled her, slower this time, before pulling her back into his arms. "But I wonder how you'll hold up with a little closer contact."

"I think I can hold my own."

"Want to know what I think?" Before she could reply, he leaned down and whispered, "I think you're scared right now."

"Why would I be scared?"

"That's what I'm trying to figure out. I'm a harmless enough guy."

If only.

Linc Adams was the opposite of harmless. He was addictive. The way he grinned when he smiled at her. The way his fingertips stroked the small of her back. The way he kept glancing at her nose as if hoping to get a glimpse of the damned freckles she'd spent her entire life trying to cover up.

"What makes you think I'm scared of you?"

"You're trembling right now and looking at me as if you're ready to run the other way. Which doesn't make a bit of sense because I know you want me." His deep voice slid into her ears and her body couldn't help but respond.

Her nipples tightened and an ache started between her legs. She couldn't help herself. She leaned into him, molding herself to his hard frame despite the couples that surrounded them. The music faded until she heard only the pounding of her own heart and his deep voice.

"I just don't get you."

"Maybe that's the point."

He frowned. "If you're really not attracted to me, just come out and say it. I'm tired of all the games."

She didn't mean to kiss him, but with him staring down at her, into her, with that strange light in his gaze, as if he liked her back, she didn't stand a chance.

She slid her arms around his neck, leaned up and pressed her lips to his. Her tongue swept his bottom lip and dipped inside, stroking and tasting and coaxing him to kiss her back.

He didn't. His arms were around her waist, holding her close, but they didn't pull her closer. And while he was open to her exploration, he wasn't exactly an active participant. A bad feeling worked its way up her spine.

Bad?

It was good that he wasn't kissing her back. What *wasn't* good was the fact that she couldn't seem to keep her hands off him.

"I didn't just do that," she breathed as she pulled away.

She had to get out of here.

She left him standing on the dance floor, staring after her. She rushed into the safety of the ladies' room and slumped against the sink. Her heart pounded and her ears buzzed.

What was wrong with her? She'd *kissed* him of all things. *She'd* kissed *him.*

Because you like him.

She ignored the voice and turned on the faucet. Cool liquid rushed over her fingers. She splashed her face, desperate to relieve her hot cheeks. It didn't help. To make matters worse, the room started to spin.

She worked her way into the nearest stall and sank down onto the toilet seat. There. She needed to sit and regroup. If she could just shut out the sudden pounding in her temples . . .

Her head snapped up and she saw the stall door tremble from the force of the knocking on the other side.

"Eve?" It was Linc.

"Go away."

"Are you okay?"

"No. I'm weak and confused and disgusted, in no particular order." *Particular* didn't come out as clearly as she would have liked thanks to her suddenly thick tongue. "And I'm drunk," she croaked. The floor tilted and her stomach pitched and she found herself hugging the toilet in the next few seconds.

She wasn't sure how he did it, but the stall door opened and the next thing she knew, Linc was handing her a cold compress of paper towels. He helped wipe her face and then he swept her into his arms and took her home.

Back at his house, he tucked her into bed, kissed her

forehead, and killed the light. The door shut behind him and she found herself alone in his bedroom.

She wasn't sure if she was disappointed or relieved about the alone part. She only knew she didn't want to think too much about either. Instead, she closed her eyes, snuggled down into his pillow, and prayed for the pounding to stop.

Chapter 19

Through the haze of sleep, Eve felt the licking at her fingertips. The tickling sensation sent a rush of warmth through her and she smiled.

And then she frowned.

The last thing, the very last thing she wanted was to have Linc licking any part of her body.

Yeah, right.

Okay, so she wanted it—in the worst way—but she'd made up her mind to keep things completely platonic, which meant staying far, far away from Linc.

Distance was key. She'd thought she could hold it together and go through the motions, but her resolve was no match for Linc Adams and his raw sexuality.

Her eyes popped open as she snatched her hand away. "Don't—," she started, the objection dying when she found Killer looming over her, tongue wagging as if she were out of breath.

Relief swamped Eve as the dog, tail wagging furiously, lapped at her knuckles again.

Okay, there *was* a god and she was most definitely female. If Linc had been the one doing the licking and the begging, Eve shuddered to think what would have happened.

Ka-boom!

Okay, so *shuddering* wasn't the right word. *Shivering* more accurately described the strange sensation rippling through her body. The anticipation. The need.

She needed to get out of here.

Eve rolled out of bed, her gaze darting frantically for her clothes. The latex-looking catsuit lay in a heap near the foot of the bed. She snatched it up and managed to shove one leg inside when the bedroom door opened.

"You're up—"

"Stay back." She held up a hand as she struggled to pull up the bodysuit. "Just stay right there."

"What's wrong with you?"

"Nothing." *Everything.* Just one look and her heart had kicked up a notch. Goose bumps danced along her bare flesh followed by a wave of heat. Her toes tingled. "This is not happening to me."

"You don't look so good."

"You do." Laughter bubbled from her lips. "I feel like death warmed over and you still look good. And you smell good. And I'd be willing to bet you feel good. Not that I'm finding out. This is it. The end of the line. No more being nice to each other or touching or kissing." Last night rushed at her full force and the damned tummy tickles started. "No more."

"But you kissed me last night."

"I did a lot of things I regret last night." And she had the pounding temples to prove it. "I shouldn't have kissed you and I won't kiss you again— Stop," she burst out when he took a step toward her. "Don't even think about it."

"Let me get this straight. You kissed me but you didn't mean to, and now you're saying you don't want to kiss me again."

No. "Yes."

He ran a hand over his face. "I don't get you. One minute you're hot, the next you're cold. Is this a hormonal thing?"

Her anger bristled. "Look, maybe I just don't want you."

"I might believe that if you didn't get all googly-eyed when I touch you."

"I do not get googly-eyed," she said on behalf of hormonal women everywhere.

"You can't even see straight."

"You wish." She struggled to haul the top half of the bodysuit up and under the oversized T-shirt she wore. "You're just full of yourself like every other man out there and don't want to consider the possibility that you just don't do it for me. Maybe that's why I'"—she squirmed and tugged and . . . *there*—"don't want to fall into bed with you again. Maybe I realized I'm just not interested."

"Prove it," he countered, his gaze dark and challenging and oh so disturbing. "Look me straight in the eye and touch me."

"I will do no such thing." She hauled off the T-shirt and tossed it onto the bed. "I don't need to prove anything to anyone. The bottom line is—" Her sentence stumbled to a halt as she stepped in a puddle of reddish-brown water. "What the . . ." Her gaze shifted to Killer, who sat next to the water and panted, her mouth open, tongue lolling, as if she couldn't catch her breath.

"Killer?" She dropped to her knees, her gaze darting from the water to her beloved dog. "Ohmigod, what's wrong?"

"I told you before—she's pregnant."

"And I told you she can't be pregnant." She cradled the dog's head and studied the animal.

"She's pregnant and she's in labor."

"Says you. She can't be pregnant." She noted Killer's bright black eyes and the way her whiskers twitched. "She's eleven years old. Not to mention, to be pregnant, you have to have . . ." For the first time in her life, she couldn't bring herself to say the word. "She's *always* in the house."

"Except during her evening walk." Linc hunkered down next to Eve.

"But that's just around the block. There are no other dogs in the neighborhood except Mr. Wilkie's blue heeler, Lady and the Tramp."

"So which is it?" Linc's question drew Eve's attention. His deep blue gaze drilled into her. "Lady or the Tramp?"

"I don't know." She shook her head and turned her attention back to Killer. "I assumed it was Lady since that's the first part of the name, but I never really looked."

"So it could be the Tramp?"

"No. Yes. I guess." The dog panted, her mouth open, tongue lolling, and Eve remembered Skye's frantic breathing and the fierce labor pains. "Ohmigod, she's in labor. Oh, Killer." She stroked the dog's head. "It's okay, baby," she crooned while Linc went to retrieve a soft, fluffy blanket.

He set up a pallet in the adjoining bathroom and whistled for Killer. The dog followed him in, but she didn't settle down. She sat, still panting, her ears twitching and her tail wagging.

"What do we do?"

"We give her some peace and quiet and try to keep her calm."

"Calm? Yeah, calm." Eve's heart pounded ninety to nothing as she dropped to her knees in the bathroom doorway and stroked the dog's head. "There, there, girl."

"You don't have to sit with her."

"I can't just leave her." She settled next to the pallet. "Easy, girl. It's going to be okay. Just try to breath slow and— Wait," she blurted out when Linc pushed to his feet. "You're not leaving, are you?"

"I have to or I'll miss my plane."

"But you can't leave. She's having a baby."

"She's having puppies, and she'll be fine. Just keep an eye on her and let nature take its course."

"But shouldn't I do something? I've never had puppies before."

He grinned. "I should hope not."

"You know what I meant. Shouldn't I be doing something? Boiling water or something?"

"The only water she needs is to drink. Give her plenty of cool drinking water—that's what I did back when I was a kid and my dog had puppies—and that's about it."

"But what happens next?" Eve straightened the edge of Killer's pallet. "I mean, her water broke, which means she's in labor. Doesn't she have to push?"

"She'll do it when she's ready."

"Isn't she ready now? And when she does push, how many pushes to get a puppy? And how long between each puppy? Does she pop them out *bam, bam, bam*?"

"When my dog Sadie had her twelve puppies, it took about two hours for each one."

"Two hours *each*? As in twenty-four hours of pushing?"

"Come to think of it," he said, looking thoughtful, "it was twenty-six hours of pushing—she had thirteen initially. Speaking of which, you might watch to make sure she doesn't eat one of them."

Her stomach jumped. "You've got to be kidding!"

"When a dog has too many, particularly large breed dogs, they'll eat the runt because they don't have enough milk to feed them all."

"You're making that up."

"Just keep an eye on her and keep count," he said as he walked toward the dresser to retrieve his wallet and keys, "and I'll be back late tonight."

"But she's only half large breed," Eve said as she watched him through the open bathroom doorway. "Maybe the poodle side will cancel out the cannibalistic impulse— Wait," she blurted out again when he grabbed his duffel bag. "She's eleven and she's never had a litter before. What if something goes wrong? You can't just leave."

He could and he should, reason whispered to Eve. He had commitments and Killer *was* just a dog. Dogs had puppies all the time.

One of which they sometimes ate.

Her stomach pitched and rolled and she turned a desperate gaze on Linc.

He stared at her for a full five seconds before tossing his duffel bag to the bed and walking into the bathroom. "Move over."

Four hours later, Killer still hadn't had her first puppy and Eve had all but paced a hole in Linc's bedroom carpet.

"Something's wrong."

"Maybe." Linc sat on the edge of his bed and eyed the dog through the open bathroom doorway. Killer moved back and forth across the tile. She was restless and panting. "I'll be right back," he finally said as he pushed to his feet and started for the bedroom doorway.

"Where are you going?"

"To call the vet."

An hour later, Eve stood in treatment room number one at the Adams Animal Hospital and listened to Dr. Abe Peterson explain Killer's condition.

"Frankly, she's so old, her uterus just doesn't know what to do. We gave her some Pitocin to speed things up. It increased her contractions, but her body just isn't responding. We did an ultrasound and the puppies look fine. But with her in such distress right now, that might not be the case if we wait any longer."

"Which means?"

"We help her out and do a cesarean."

"They do C-sections on dogs?"

"Of course. We've given her some pain medication right now and as soon as you give the go-ahead, we'll get her to the operating room and prep her."

"How long?"

"An hour at the most. Then I'll want to observe her for an hour or so after that to make sure she's okay."

"And then?"

"If all goes well, she can go home."

"You're kidding?"

"She's a dog, Mrs. Adams. They're extremely resilient."

Eve was so worried that she didn't even correct him on the *missus* thing. "But she's going to be okay, right?"

"She's going to be fine. She's old, but healthy. You just go on home and let us take care of her and we'll call you soon with an update. And by the way, congratulations."

Eve took a deep breath as she let the news sink in. A C-section and puppies and two hours and *she's going to be fine*. Relief swamped her. "Congratulations?" she asked a few seconds later when the sentiment finally registered.

"On your marriage."

"You're congratulating me?" She glanced down and saw her flip-flops, gray running shorts, and white T-shirt she'd changed into in a hurry before they'd left for the vet. Her long, dark hair was pulled back in a haphazard ponytail. She wore only the faint smudges of last night's mascara beneath her eyes. So much for the hot, shocking sex diva. Not to mention, being an animal lover undoubtedly scored major points with a vet.

"Me and the missus have known Linc since he was a baby," the man went on. "He's a good boy. You're a lucky woman."

If only, Eve thought as the doctor left the room. From the get-go, it had been back-to-back disasters in her life as far as Linc Adams was concerned. First, she'd fallen into lust with him. Then she'd fallen into *like* with him.

Talk about *un*lucky. And stupid. And flat-out unexplainable.

She eyed him. He sat in a chair near the exam table, a woozy Killer in his arms. He nuzzled the animal and stroked her soft fur, and something tightened in her chest.

He was her Mr. Kaboom, all right. From his refrigerator stocked with Sweet Leaf Tea, to his law degree from Yale. He was nice and kind and sensitive enough to go to a huge amount of trouble to give her an orgasm. On top of that, he had enough heart to be genuinely concerned about her dog. And enough compassion to take care of Eve after she'd freaked out on him and tossed her cookies in the ladies' room. And enough courage to go after what he wanted most in life—a Nextel Cup Championship—despite the fact that he had to go it alone, with no encouragement from his own family.

She liked him and she wanted him, and suddenly she wasn't half as scared to have sex with him as she was *not* to have sex with him. To feel his arms around her and his lips on hers and his body filling hers. He wanted her and she wanted him. *Want.* It didn't have to go beyond the physical lust if she didn't let it. She could cut herself off from her emotions the way she'd done so many times in the past—every time—and enjoy herself, even if only for a little while.

That was the kicker. It wasn't the right time in her life. At the same time, the right time was ticking away.

She watched as Linc handed Killer over to the nurse before crossing the distance to her.

"What did Doc Peterson say?"

"That they're going to do a C-section and we should come back later."

"Got any idea what we should do until then?"

Eve smiled. "Actually, I do."

They drove back to Linc's house in silence. The car's air conditioner hummed full-force to ease the summer heat, but it wasn't enough to cool the fire that raged inside Eve. Sweat dampened her forehead. The SUV jumped and jolted over bumps. Her sensitive nipples rasped against her bra, her bottom rubbed against the soft leather seat. The ride was short, but enough to stir her senses and build the anticipation of what was to come.

Then again, the anticipation had started months ago when she'd first met Linc Adams and gazed into his deep blue eyes.

They made it into the house and as far as the living room before Eve turned on him.

She took a deep breath and whisked the T-shirt up and over her head. Anxious fingers worked at the clasp of her bra and freed her straining breasts. The scrap of lace landed at her feet. Her running shorts soon joined the heap until she stood in nothing but a leopard-print thong. She hooked her thumbs at the waistband, slid them down and stepped free.

She expected him to step forward and do something, but he stood motionless in the middle of the room, his gaze hooked on her. Watching. Waiting.

It was her move. She knew that. She'd faked it their very last time and so the ball was completely in her court. She gathered her courage and touched her tight, hard nipples.

Her breath caught at the first swirl of her fingertips.

She rubbed and stroked for several breathless moments as he stared at her, into her, his gaze dark and hot.

She moved her hands lower then, down the quivering skin of her stomach, to the dampness between her legs. The air seemed to stand still around her and she saw Linc's breath catch and his chest hitch.

She slid one fingertip along the soft, wet folds between her legs. Heat pulsed through her and a moan curled up her throat.

The sound seemed to galvanize him into action, and suddenly it seemed as if it wasn't enough to watch her. He stepped forward. Strong, muscular arms wrapped around her and drew her close. His mouth claimed hers in a deep, thorough kiss.

Large, purposeful hands slid down her back, cupped her bottom and urged her legs up on either side of him. Then he lifted her, cradled and kneaded her buttocks as she wrapped her legs around his waist. Her aching sex settled over the straining bulge in his board shorts.

She rubbed herself against him, creating a delicious friction that sent a sharp spike of desire through her. "I really want this," she murmured. "I really want you. *Now.*"

As anxious as Linc was to be inside the warm, willing woman in his arms, he wasn't going to risk another fake orgasm. Not this time. Not ever again.

He pressed his fingers into her soft, sweet ass and stilled her movements long enough to give her a slow, deep kiss. His heart pounded and seconds ticked by as he tasted and explored before he finally pulled away. He carried her to the bedroom and stretched her out on his bed. Bright sunshine pushed through the open curtains and filled the room with a warm light that bathed her flawless skin as she lay naked on his sheets.

He grasped his T-shirt and pulled it over his head, but he didn't take anything else off. Instead, he leaned down and kissed her again, even slower this time. His tongue swept her bottom lip and nibbled before dipping inside. He tasted and explored and stirred with more deep kisses as his hands trailed over her body, learning every curve, every indention. He cupped her breasts and plucked at her nipples until she whimpered and tugged frantically at the waistband of his shorts.

He covered her hand and stilled her movements. "Not yet. If I take these off, there's no way we'll be able to take this slow. And thorough. And I want both this time. I want you." He feathered his lips over hers. "Out of control," he murmured against her mouth. "Coming undone. *Coming,* period."

"So stop talking about it and get on with it."

He grinned and placed a soft kiss on the tip of her nose before nuzzling the side of her neck. He trailed his mouth down her fragrant skin and the slope of one beautiful breast. He licked at the ripe nipple before blowing on the tip and making her moan.

Her fingers threaded through his hair and held him to her as he drew her deep and sucked her long and hard. She tasted so sweet and it was all he could do not to explode right there in his pants. His erection throbbed and the blood rushed through his veins, but he held himself in check, determined to make it good for her.

He kissed a path down the warm skin of her belly to the sweet heat between her legs. He trailed his fingers over her slick folds and she gasped. He spread her legs until she was wide open. Then he cupped her bottom and tilted her for better access.

At the first flick of his tongue, she moved her hips, begging for more. He licked her softly, slowly at first, before touching her completely with his mouth. She started, a gasp parting her full lips as she bowed toward him. He tasted her, licking and drinking her sweet essence and soon her muscles relaxed and her legs spread wider. He feasted on her, his tongue rasping her tender flesh until she splayed her fingers in his hair and arched her hips.

She was close. She had all the signs of a woman on the cusp of orgasm—from her panting to the flush of her beautiful skin to the ripeness of her nipples and her tense muscles.

Close, but not quite there. Not yet. And not without him inside her.

Eve felt him pull away and her eyes fluttered open in time to see him shed his shorts and briefs. She couldn't help herself. She reached out and stroked his rock-hard length. He went stock-still and his eyes closed as he seemed to relish her touch for the next several moments before he caught her hand.

"If you don't stop, I'm going to explode."

She smiled. "That's the point." Before he could pull away, she leaned closer and took him with both hands. She stroked the long, solid piece of him until liquid beaded on the ripe head. Then she dipped down and tasted him.

Linc groaned and caught her head. Threading his fingers through her hair, he cradled her as she loved him with her tongue. It wasn't long before his chest heaved and his body went rigid and his grip on her tightened.

"Wait," he growled and she stopped. "Just wait."

As much as she wanted to keep tasting him, she wanted to feel him deep inside of her even more. Because she knew there would be no faking this time. Just pleasure. Sweet, fierce, consuming pleasure.

He pulled away and retrieved a condom from his nightstand. Rolling the latex on in a swift motion, he pressed her down into the mattress and settled between her legs. The head of his erection slid along her damp flesh and she shuddered. She lifted her hips and tried to pull him deeper, but he held back, building the tension a few more sharp seconds before he plunged inside.

He went still for several fast, furious heartbeats, his forehead resting against hers as he seemed to catch his breath.

"Wrap your legs around me, sunshine," he finally murmured, his voice husky and raw.

She did. The motion lifted her and he slid even deeper. The sensation of being stretched and filled by the sheer strength of him stole her breath for several long moments and made her heart pound that much faster.

When he started to move, she clutched at his shoulders. With each thrust, the pressure built, pushing her higher, until she didn't think she could take any more. She was close. So very close . . . And in another deep, dizzying thrust, suddenly she was there.

Heat washed over her, swamping her body and turning her inside out. She cried out, her nails digging into the hard muscles of his shoulders, her legs clamping tight as tremors swept through her.

Linc plunged into her again and again, drawing out the pleasure as he searched for his own. And then he found it. His groan filled her ears and she opened her eyes in time to see him poised above her, his body rigid, every muscle in his neck taut as he spilled himself inside her.

Without breaking their contact, he rolled over and cradled her on his chest.

"I'll get the phone for you," he murmured as she settled herself against him. "But I'm afraid there's no fire escape."

She lifted her head and stared up into his deep blue eyes. "I don't think I'd have the energy to climb out if you had one."

He smiled and she gave him a smile of her own. And a kiss. And then she nuzzled his neck and closed her eyes.

Chapter 20

Has your father said anything about me?" Jacqueline Farrel asked after showing up on Eve's doorstep late Friday evening. The same question she'd been asking every Friday night for the two months following Killer's C-section—resulting in three healthy puppies—and the best orgasm of Eve's life.

Eve retrieved a diet soda from the refrigerator and arched an eyebrow. "As in how much he misses you?"

Her mother shrugged and tried to look nonchalant as she set her briefcase on the kitchen table and sat down at the table. "That and when he intends to call to beg my forgiveness."

"No."

Correction—the best orgasm of Eve's life up to that particular moment. It seemed every subsequent orgasm put the previous to shame. Not that Linc himself was responsible. Sure, he was good and they had chemistry. But they also had the situation working for them. After the initial session in his apartment, they'd decided to finish the *Sexcess* six.

The following week when he'd arrived at her apartment after placing second at Michigan Speedway, they'd had a wonderful version of flexible sex where they'd tried a very difficult Kama Sutra position involving a stack of pillows. The position itself had failed, but they'd gotten so turned on trying to get into it, that even the missionary sex that followed had been fabulous.

The following week, after a win at Dover Downs International Speedway, they'd given controlled sex a try. Linc tied her to the bedposts and stirred each sense until she'd been a screaming mass of nerves. She did the same to him the following night and *bam* . . . Incredible.

The week after that they'd met in Adams after he'd placed in the top three for yet another race, for more campaign fund-raising and step five—taboo sex. They'd done things in his kitchen with whipped cream that she'd only read about in books. The week after that, they'd had elemental sex beneath the stars on the hood of Linc's first-ever car, an old Mustang that had been parked in a field in the back of Craig's body shop.

The week after that they'd been on their own, but the lack of a plan hadn't put a damper on things. It had been late in the evening after Sunday's race—Eve had put in an appearance as the dutiful NASCAR wife, which gave her the chance to see Clint and Skye and the loudest pair of baby boys in the free world. The track had already cleared off by the time Linc finished with all the picture-taking and fanfare of winning the Fourth of July Pepsi 400. Linc had coaxed Eve into the seat of his race car for a ride. Literally. With the roar of the engine in her ears, the wind rushing through the open windows, and Linc deep inside her, they'd barely gone five laps before hitting Victory

Lane. At least for her. He'd been excited, but controlled—he'd had to drive, after all—and so she'd made it up to him on the way back to the hotel. And again on the beach when they'd gone for a moonlit walk. And later that night on the hotel balcony. And—

"Maybe your father is having a midlife crisis." Her mother's comment drew her back to reality.

"Didn't he have one ten years ago when he dyed his hair and signed you two up to learn how to do the macarena?"

"Well, yes, he did. But I'm beginning to think that was just a precursor of things to come." Jacqueline peered at the container of Chinese noodles Eve had picked up for dinner. "Mmm, I love Chinese. Do you mind?"

"Knock yourself out. I really wanted Mexican," she said, eager to wipe the sudden look of camaraderie from her mother's eyes. "But the line was too long."

"Oh." Jacqueline retrieved a fork and took a bite. "That man is so stubborn," she went on after she'd eaten several forkfuls. "He just can't admit when he's wrong."

"Maybe you should call him. You know, be the bigger person."

Her mother seemed to think about that. "Well, I *am* the stronger sex. And, obviously, more mature and objective. I'm afraid it's our burden, dear, to always be the voice of reason." Jacqueline pulled out her cell phone, punched a button, and waited. "He's not home," she finally declared, a stunned expression on her face as if she couldn't believe what she'd just said. She clicked her cell phone shut and slid it into a pocket inside her briefcase. Her gaze went to her watch. "It's nine o'clock and he's not at the apartment. *My* apartment, mind you. And it's not his volunteer night at the college."

"What about Gram?"

"Your grandmother is undoubtedly out cruising the grocery store or a Laundromat or the Home Depot, or wherever else Cherry Chandler listed in yesterday's show entitled 'Male Meet Markets.' "

"You watch Cherry Chandler?"

"Only in the interest of Womanists everywhere. We have to know what absurdity we're up against. And believe you me, it's not pretty. Why, I practically gobbled an entire roll of Tums while Cherry went on and on about men and their love of tools and electronics and how women should capitalize on it when man-hunting. Imagine any woman hunting for a man! *They* should be hunting for us." She seemed to think better of her statement. "Not that I advocate men hunting for women. We are in no way the weaker prey to be devoured by the big, bad male. I simply meant that men are the ones who should be putting themselves out there. Can you imagine hanging out in the condom section at Wal-Mart just to pick up a man?"

"It does allow you to kill two birds with one stone."

Her mother shook her head and glanced at the clock again. "Your father's always home by nine on a Friday. He never misses the local news. He likes to be informed."

"Maybe he's just not picking up the phone. He could be asleep."

"That's probably it." She poured herself a cup of coffee and took a thoughtful sip. "You don't think your father meant what he said about us testing the waters?"

"*Dad* suggested testing the waters?"

"He mentioned something a while ago, but I'm sure it was just a bunch of nonsense. Your father isn't the type to do such a thing. Then again, he did say it and he's also not the type to lie." She shook her head. "He wouldn't."

Eve tamped down on her own anxiety. The thought of her father testing anything other than the knowledge of the students in his advanced anthropology class . . . She wasn't going there.

"I'm sure it was just a scare tactic," she told her mother, eager to ease her own mind rather than Jacqueline's.

"That's right." Her mother stiffened. "And it's not going to work. I could care less if he's home or not. Or if he's out with some weak-willed female from the college who probably laughs at his lame Amazon rain forest jokes. Your father has absolutely no sense of humor." Several seconds ticked by before she added, "Lameness aside, it *is* endearing at times." She stared blankly ahead, her eyes bright and worried.

Tears? No way. This was her mother. A rock of sexual knowledge and Womanist strength. She didn't cry. She ate condescending male chauvinists for breakfast, lunch, *and* dinner. She didn't break down. She couldn't.

Finally, *thankfully,* her mother blinked several times and shifted her attention to Eve. "So what are you doing tonight, dear?"

"Trina and I are watching videos." It was that or pine away for Linc, who was in Texas qualifying for yet another race.

"Oh. What are you two watching tonight?"

A Steven Seagal movie. That was an answer guaranteed to send her mother running back to her hotel. Alone. Lonely. *"The Terminator,"* Eve heard herself say.

Her mother smiled. "Isn't that the one where the woman is the only one to survive?"

"That's the one. She kicks the Terminator's ass and rolls off into the sunset to raise her unborn child." She was definitely going to regret this, but she couldn't seem to stop herself. "You want to watch with us? We've got kettle corn."

"Why, I haven't had kettle corn since your father took me to see *The Life and Times of Joan of Arc.*" At Eve's puzzled glance, her mother added, "That was back when we were at Harvard. It was part of an independent film festival at the campus theater." A faraway look gleamed in her eyes and a smile crooked her lips. A sad smile. "Kettle corn is my favorite."

It was Eve's, too, not that she intended to admit as much. Instead, she waved a bag of the microwave popcorn and wiggled her eyebrows. "You game?"

"If you're sure you don't mind."

"I'm sure." Her mother beamed and for the first time, Eve didn't feel the urge to run in the opposite direction.

Okay, so maybe she felt a tiny urge, but she didn't let it get the best of her. It was just a few hours, for heaven's sake. It wasn't as if they were going to buy matching outfits and start finishing each other's sentences. It was no big deal.

And it certainly wasn't a big deal that Eve actually enjoyed the next two hours sitting next to her mother, of all people.

She simply chalked it up to temporary insanity brought on by the enormous amount of great sex she was having with Linc Adams and the fact that she liked him for more than just sex. She liked watching him give it his all at the racetrack. And she liked seeing him win. And she liked having breakfast with him at the diner in Adams. And she liked waiting up for him on Sunday nights and inhaling the scent of wind and leather and wildness that always surrounded him after a race. And she liked snuggling up against his back in the middle of the night.

She liked his company.

But she didn't love it, and so it would be no problem to say good-bye. She'd given up brownies and Dr Pepper, and she'd had extremely strong feelings for both of those. But, ultimately, they'd been bad for her on a long-term basis, and so she'd gone cold turkey. She would do the same with Linc when the time came.

In the meantime . . . Eve ignored the strange tightening in her chest, scarfed down a mouthful of popcorn, and watched an eighteen-wheeler run down Arnold Schwarzenegger.

"I want you to publicly declare that your entire platform is nothing more than a load of propagandist bunk, designed to fund your dependency on lip gloss and cosmetic surgery," Jacqueline declared as she walked into Cherry Chandler's dressing room at the studio where she taped her so-called talk show.

"Come again?" The attractive blonde paused in painting on her lipstick and her gaze shifted to Jacqueline's reflection in the massive mirror. Cherry's eyes were as blue as Jacqueline remembered from their college days, and just as knowing.

"Or at least write a private e-mail to Donovan and my mother saying pretty much the same thing."

Cherry smoothed her lips together and capped her tube of M•A•C with French-manicured fingers. "Have you been chasing the moon pies with Yoo-Hoo again?"

"I haven't touched a moon pie since our senior year at Harvard. Not that it was my fault in the first place. Who knew so much sugar could actually cause hallucinations?"

Cherry smiled, her glossy pink lips parting to reveal straight, white teeth. "You thought you were Joan of Arc. You were this close to shaving off your hair and tying yourself to the flagpole. You would have if I hadn't been there to grab the razor."

"And you would have failed Testosterone versus Estrogen if I hadn't let you copy my lecture notes."

"That makes us even then."

"What about Reeducating the Darwinian Male? You would have failed that one for sure if I hadn't helped you write your term paper, which means you owe me and I'm here to collect." She ripped off a piece of paper and scribbled down two e-mail addresses. "Just say something to the effect that you're wrong, but you continue to advocate the whole sensitive mate thing because you're a materialistic, money-hungry, superficial ditz who prefers to use her feminine wiles rather than her brains to get ahead in an equally materialistic, money-hungry superficial society."

"I am not a ditz, and I'm not calling my life's work a bunch of propagandist bunk." She eyed Jacqueline, her gaze as assessing as it had been all those years ago. "What's all this really about? You don't agree with my views; I don't agree with yours. We've never seen eye-to-eye, but we've always agreed to disagree. Or at least keep our distance from each other to avoid any hair-pulling."

The statement stirred a memory and Jacqueline did her best not to smile. "You totally deserved that. You tried to set me up on a *date*."

"Dates are fun and you needed to have some fun. You were much too serious." She eyed Jacqueline's beige blazer and slacks. "I see things haven't changed much."

"I'm serious because I like being taken seriously by a society that expects sexologists to flit about wearing pink chiffon lounge pajamas."

"They were fuscia and comfortable, and I only wore them once when I did the fashion show segment 'Lasso Him with Lingerie,' which totally blew away your 'What Taking Out the Trash Really Means.'" The tension hung between them for several long moments before Cherry murmured, "Give. What's your real problem?"

"I'm facing utter catastrophe." Jacqueline sank down into a nearby chair. "Donovan wants to . . ." She shook her head. "Heavens, I can't even say it."

"He wants to . . . Have sex with you, buy you a condo in Maui, hang you upside down and flog you with red licorice— What?"

Jacqueline licked her lips and stiffened. "He wants to . . ." Another lick and she swallowed. "He wants to . . ." She lowered her voice and forced the words out. "He wants to *marry* me."

Cherry smiled. "The handsome, educated, sensitive father of your children wants to *marry* you? Imagine that." She shook her head. "Hello? He's always wanted to marry you. He stood outside our dorm window and sang 'Only You' by the Platters just to get you to have dinner with him. It was so romantic."

"It was silly, and the only reason I agreed to have dinner with him was to shut him up."

"And you ended up liking him."

"Once I got to know him and realized that he was an intelligent, ambitious graduate student who appreciated Joan Baez. We had a lot in common."

"He wanted to marry you before that, and if you didn't realize that, you're a lot ditzier than I am." Cherry stood and straightened her low-cut blouse before grabbing a small, cordless microphone from the table and clipping it just shy of her cleavage. "You are so self-centered, Jackie."

"I am not, and don't call me Jackie." Jacqueline slapped at an invisible piece of lint on her own jacket. "I hate that name."

"Yes, you are. You're so wrapped up in your own stupid fears that you totally overlook the happiness of the one person who actually sees you at your worst—and trust me, it isn't pretty—and still wants to be with you anyway. We should all be so lucky."

Jacqueline's head snapped up and her gaze collided with Cherry's. "You and Ron are having troubles?"

"Ron was my second husband." Cherry shook her head and turned back to survey herself in the mirror again. "Then there was Jack. Then Richard. I'm dating Steve now. Fourteen months, two days, and three hours. I swear, I've bent over backwards for that man—literally—and I still can't get him to propose."

"Miss Chandler?" A man ducked his head in the doorway, a pair of headphones around his neck. "We're ready on the set for you."

She turned a radiant smile on the man. "Give me just a minute, James." He nodded and she turned back to Jacqueline, her smile fading. "On top of that, I've got two ungrateful daughters hell-bent on publicly humiliating their loving, devoted mother by starting an Internet-based matchmaking service."

"Matchmaking?" Jacqueline shuddered. "That's horrible."

"It's not the matchmaking that's horrible. It's the nature of the matchmaking. Forget trying to find your soul mate, or at the very least a kind, decent man with a nice bank account who isn't afraid of commitment. Their service is totally anticommitment."

"How's that?"

"UltimateSexMatch.com." Cherry retrieved a tube of lipstick and smeared another coat of bright pink onto her pouty lips. "You think you have troubles? Try to imagine what it's like to have the fruit of your womb turning their backs on everything you've raised them to believe in." At Jacqueline's raised eyebrows, she shook her head. "Okay, so you know. But it's not like you taught your girls the truth when it comes to men."

"The truth? As in trading sex for taking out the trash?"

"It works."

"It's prostitution."

"You're overly dramatic."

"And you lack self-respect."

"You're still jealous because I got that internship at Masters and Johnson and you didn't."

"I am not jealous. Besides, you cheated. You flaunted your cleavage in exchange for a few extra points on your stupid thesis."

"At least I have cleavage to flaunt."

"You're as shallow as ever."

"And you're as anal. I can't imagine why a man like Donovan would even want to marry you."

"Because we're perfect for each other, that's why. We have great sex and we share all the same interests and we respect each other."

"Then why not marry him?"

"Because marriage, in and of itself, is an institution created by men to perpetuate their male-dominated society through the oppression and enslavement of women."

"Horseshit. That's what you want to believe because you watched your mother endure a load of physical and mental abuse from your father, and you're scared of finding yourself in the same situation. Hel-lo? Not all men are like your father."

"I most certainly know that."

"Do you? Because you don't act like it. Get some therapy, get over it, and get married."

"I shouldn't have to stand up and tell the world that Donovan is the perfect man for me by signing my life over to him on a piece of paper."

"It's not about telling the world. It's about telling him."

"Miss Chandler?" It was James again.

"I'm coming. Look, I'm sorry if you're having trouble, but I've got my own to contend with. Not to mention I totally believe in what I'm saying. You'll have to weasel out of this all by yourself because I've got a show to do."

"Various eye shadow colors proven to rev his libido?"

"Lip gloss flavors."

Jacqueline grimaced. "It figures."

Chapter 21

The next few months passed much too fast for Eve. She and Linc had exceptional sex, and shared numerous peanut butter sandwiches while talking about anything and everything. Meanwhile, the puppies grew and soon it was time to give them away. She presented one to her twin nephews, one to her pregnant sister, Xandra, and one to her father to keep him company while her mother persisted in being stubborn.

Before Eve knew it, she was leaving newly spayed Killer with Mr. Wilkie while she flew south to meet Linc in Homestead, Florida, for the second to the last race of the Nextel series—her last official appearance as his wife. It was the Saturday before election Tuesday. The plan was for Linc to secure his point standing by winning Sunday's race. Immediately following, they would drive to Adams and spend Monday and Tuesday making a last-ditch effort to dissuade voters. Eve had brought her most outlandish outfit—a short, short leopard-print spandex dress held together on either side by a row of safety pins that showed a tantalizing display of skin—to cinch the loss.

She didn't think of what would happen after Tuesday. Every time she tried, she got this sick feeling in the pit of her stomach, so she concentrated on the howling baby boy in her arms.

"I'm so sorry," Skye said above the wailing. She held a matching baby in her arms who was giving Eve's a run for his money with the crying. "They're a little colicky."

"A little?"

"Ssshhh," Skye pleaded, rocking the baby to and fro. "Mommy's here."

"That's not going to work, is it, little Clint?" Eve eyed her own howling devil. "Let's show 'em how it's done."

Eve propped the baby on her shoulder and started to rub the small of his back. He wiggled and cried, but soon the wail faded into an occasional sniffle.

"How did you do that?"

"That Red Cross babysitting course in seventh grade. While you were making cookies for all the boys back in junior high and high school"—Skye's weakness for chocolate chip cookies had her cultivating her baking skills at a very early age—"I was babysitting, remember?"

"Well, do it to Donny, will you?" She switched babies with Eve and cuddled the now quiet Clint Jr.

"What would your mommy do without Auntie Eve?" she asked the screaming boy before she propped him on her shoulder and started to rub. He'd obviously inherited his grandfather's stubbornness as well as his name. A little more rubbing and he finally settled down into a series of faint hiccups.

"You need a few of these for yourself," Skye told Eve as she settled little Clint into the backseat of a double stroller.

"Eventually."

"I was thinking more sooner than later." Skye eyed her. "You and Linc look really happy together."

"Me and Linc?" Eve faked her best laugh, but judging from the knowing look on Skye's face, it obviously wasn't convincing. "You know this marriage isn't for real."

"I know that, but I was sort of hoping . . . I mean, I know I was totally against it in the beginning, but I've changed my mind. I think you two make a nice couple."

"Linc and a Barbie doll make a nice couple. I'm not his type."

"You make him smile."

"Me and a six-pack of beer."

"You know that whole drinking, partying thing is just an act."

"I know." She busied herself putting baby Donny into the front part of the stroller. "And so is our marriage. We do not now, nor will we ever, make each other happy." That's what she said, but the truth was, she *was* happy. She was enjoying the moment because she knew it was going to end.

But knowing what was going to happen and actually having it happen were two very different things. She quickly found this out when a reporter cornered her on the way to the owner's box to watch the race.

"Is it true that your marriage to Linc Adams was just a publicity stunt?" Before Eve could answer, another reporter flanked her. And then another. Until she found herself surrounded, the bull's-eye of a shower of verbal bullets that had her nervous and trembling by the time Skye—wielding the double stroller—managed to gather a handful of security guards and push her way to Eve's rescue.

The moment Eve had tried not to think about for the past few months had finally arrived. Too soon, her mind screamed. But truthfully, she feared it was too late.

Because Eve Farrel didn't just like Linc Adams. She loved him.

Son of a bitch.

Linc dodged reporters and rushed through the pit area in search of Eve.

Son of a fuckin' bitch!

Danielle had been so anxious that she'd gotten her dates mixed up and had sent out the press release too early. *Early,* of all things. This morning, in fact, and now everyone from coast to coast knew the truth.

"So your marriage was nothing more than a publicity stunt?"

The question echoed in his head, along with a dozen others that had been tossed at him after he'd finished up his prerace meeting with Clint and the Big Tex execs. He'd opened the door to find himself blinded by a series of camera flashes. The questions had started, and they hadn't ended until Linc had finally pushed his way past everyone and left the garage in search of Eve.

It wasn't supposed to happen like this. Not now and not like this. The election wasn't until Tuesday and he hadn't had a chance to talk to her and work out their next move.

Talk about what, buddy? You spelled it all out in the beginning. Election. Divorce. End of story.

But things were different now. They were closer. They were . . . Committed? Hardly. They liked each other and had good sex, but neither really changed anything. It wasn't like they were going to stay married, for Christ's sake. He couldn't. He was *this* close to seeing his dream realized. He couldn't get sidetracked now. He had to focus on these last two races.

Besides, Eve didn't want a real marriage any more than he did.

Yet here he was thinking about her, worrying about her, racing around like a crazy man trying to find her just to see if she was okay.

"Drivers, report to the pit area," the announcer's voice boomed over the loudspeaker.

Linc slowed his steps as reality hit him. He had less than thirty minutes until the race. Thirty minutes to go over last details and psych himself up for the task at hand—third place or better if he wanted to stay in contention for the Cup. Third or better. That's all he could afford to think about right now. He'd had the best qualifying time yesterday so he sat in pole position today. *Third or better.* He could do it. He had to do it or the past months meant nothing.

"All team members to the pit area. All team members to the pit area." The announcer's voice blared over the speakers again.

Linc came to a complete stop, his hands on his knees as he leaned over and tried to catch his breath. Fear welled inside him and pulled him back to the funeral home, to that small room where his father had leaned over his grandfather's casket and whispered those words.

"I hope you're happy now, because I'm not."

His chest tightened and he gasped for a deep breath. He couldn't lose his way now. Not when he was so close to reaching the top, to erasing the one and only regret that haunted him night after night. He had the chance his father never had. He was young enough, good enough, to undo all the regret that ate at his insides. Linc could escape the legacy that had been handed down in the Adams family for the past few generations and he could be happy. Really and truly happy. For the first time in his life.

He turned and headed back to pit road.

It really *was* over.

Eve knew it the moment she entered the garage and spotted Linc standing near the car. He wore his racing uniform, the familiar red, white, and blue Big Tex emblem emblazoned on the chest. Dozens of patches from his other sponsors surrounded the main logo. He wore a ball cap with the same Big Tex logo, the brim partly shielding his blue-eyed gaze. He straightened and pushed the brim back just enough. His eyes locked with hers and . . . Over.

Her stomach hollowed out and she had the crazy urge to run the other way. That, or throw herself into his arms and hold on for dear life.

She swallowed and forced herself to take slow, measured steps.

"I'm sorry it went down like this," Linc said when she walked up to him.

"Sorry? What for? The reporters?" She forced a laugh. "Not a big deal."

"There wasn't supposed to be a press release yet. It was just supposed to be between you and me, not half the fucking country."

"It really is no big deal." Eve smiled. "I can use the press."

"You plugged your documentary?"

No. "Yes. That's what all this is for in the first place, right? To help us both stay focused on our business? So I kept the focus."

Linc nodded, his gaze narrowing, as if he didn't like hearing the words any more than she liked saying them.

"I just want you to know that it wasn't me," he told her. "I didn't say anything to the press. It was my publicist. I gave her the scoop months ago, and I guess she was counting the days and got overly anxious."

"I know the feeling."

His eyebrows drew together. "You were counting the days?"

"Absolutely." She'd been counting them with a heavy heart, hoping that time would slow and maybe . . .

Eve shook away the *maybe.* It was over and done with, end of story. "I just hope it doesn't hurt the election," she told him, as anxiety of a different nature rushed through her. "We've put in so much time and effort. I really think you have a great chance to lose." He couldn't win. Eve didn't think she could stand to see him angry or bitter or regretful. "You *have* to lose," she added. "I could make some sort of statement saying what a lying, conniving sleazoid you are, or maybe say how you stole money from me, or something really atrocious." Her gaze locked with his. "This can't have all been for nothing."

"I'll handle it," he told her, a surprised look on his face, as if he couldn't believe she cared one way or another.

But she did. Too much.

"I'll just hold a press conference," he went on. "Profess my devotion to you, and kill the rumor for the next few days. Look, I know we were going to put in an appearance in Adams, but it's not necessary. I'll just tell them you're feeling sick and you couldn't make it."

"Sounds good to me." Or it should have. The last thing she wanted was to keep going with the charade as planned. Not now that she'd realized the truth.

She loved him. Of all the crazy, rotten things that could have happened, she'd actually fallen in love with him.

"I really need to get out of here. I've got a ton of things left to do on the documentary."

"You're not staying for the race?"

"I wish I could." *Liar.* "But Trina called with some problems on the final film cut that require my immediate attention. She booked me on a flight back to L.A. If I leave now, I should just make it to the airport." She shrugged. "Duty calls."

"Yeah." He popped his hat back onto his head and glanced over his shoulder at the pit crew waiting for him. He signaled them to give him another minute. "So I guess this is good-bye."

"I guess so." She licked her lips and barely ignored the urge to press her lips to his. "Take care," she murmured instead. "And good luck today. I'm sure you'll do great. This is your year."

"Yeah, it is." It seemed as if he said the words more to convince himself than her. "I've worked hard for this."

"You deserve it." And then she turned and did what she'd done so many times in the past. Every time, in fact, with every man in her life.

Eve Farrel walked away.

Linc roared around the track, taking lap after lap at a record-breaking pace. He held third place for most of the race, despite the fact that the car was a little loose, the brake slipping around a few of the turns. He kept pushing, however, until he hit the last two laps and then he made his move. He swerved out of formation and punched the gas. The car reared to the left and damned near went into a spin, but Linc gripped the steering wheel and held it tight. He lived up to his name, shot into second and pushed for first.

Just a little more . . . Come on, come on . . . Faster, faster . . .

He punched it, bolted past Tony Stewart, and crossed the finish line. The flag went down and the race was over.

He hadn't just placed in the top three. He'd taken first place. That meant enough points to not only keep him in contention next week, but practically guarantee the damned Cup. All he needed was a tenth or better finish and he would win this year's series.

The truth echoed in his head as he swerved into Victory Lane and brought the car to a stop. He climbed out and into the arms of his excited team members. Clint caught him in a hug and the celebration started.

Tenth or better. All he had to do was show up next week, and he was a sure thing to walk away with the Cup. This was it! His year. His win. His dream.

He hauled off his helmet and stared up into the stands.

Skye smiled back at him, the twins overflowing her arms, and disappointment rushed through him.

Eve was gone.

He knew it.

He'd known it even before he'd looked, but he'd done so anyway. As if deep down he expected to see Eve, arms overflowing with her own babies. *His* babies.

The minute the idea struck, he pushed it back out. Babies? Oddly enough, the notion didn't scare him half as much as the thought that he would never see Eve sitting in those stands ever again. Never feel her in his arms. Never hear her voice. *Never.*

The thought haunted him over the next few days until Linc came to the startling realization that letting Eve go was his biggest regret in life.

And the only one he might not be able to fix.

"You can't be here," Eve blurted out when she opened the door the following Sunday morning to find Linc standing on her doorstep.

One of the numerous prerace shows blared from the television set in the living room.

". . . pick to walk away with today's race is up-and-comer Linc Adams. This would be Adams's first Nextel Cup and a well-deserved end to an impressive year . . ."

She blinked her eyes. He couldn't be here when he was supposed to be there and . . . She blinked again, but he didn't disappear. Her gaze slid from the worn jeans that hugged his thighs and lean waist, to the white cotton T-shirt that covered his broad chest, the words LOUD, PROUD, AND REDNECK printed in red, white, and blue letters across the front.

"You can't be here," she said again as the meaning behind his presence sank in. He was here. Now. For her.

Denial rushed through her and she shook her head. "You have to race in a few hours. In Atlanta. On the other side of the country!"

"I don't give a shit about the race." For the first time she noted the dark circles rimming his eyes. "I want a championship, but I want you more. I want to stay married."

He was *here* on her doorstep, miles away from his dream.

It could only mean . . .

"You blew your race and your point standing just to come here and tell me that you want to stay *married*?"

"Actually, I blew my race and my point standing to come here and tell you that I—"

"Don't say it!" This couldn't be happening. She was moving on with her life, consoling herself with the fact that she'd fallen for the right man, but at the wrong time.

It was too early. For both of them.

"I love you." The words were deep, gruff, heartfelt.

Eve shook her head, fighting the truth and the emotion in her heart. He couldn't *love* her, of all things. He wasn't supposed to love her. He didn't want to fall in love right now any more than she did.

"Don't do this, Linc." She blinked back the tears that suddenly threatened to overwhelm her. "Just go."

"Eve?" Strong, warm hands cradled her face as he searched her gaze. "Didn't you hear me? I was a jerk and I never should have let you walk away. I did and I'm sorry. I'm here right now to prove that. I love—"

"Don't!" Joy rushed through her, so fierce it stirred her fear and panic. She pushed his hands away and gave a furious shake of her head. "Don't make this any harder. It's over."

"It's not over. I love you and I know you love me."

"No, you don't. You don't know what I feel. You hardly know me." The tears spilled over. "You wouldn't know me at all if the situation had been different and you hadn't been desperate to lose your election. You wouldn't have given me the time of day, and I wouldn't have given you the time of day. We don't have time to build a relationship."

"We already have one. We're married."

"It's not real."

"Isn't it?" Fierce blue eyes drilled into hers. "Isn't marriage about being with the person you love? Well, I love you and I want to be with you. You're the most exasperating woman, but I want you anyway."

"Well, I don't want you." She forced the words out. She wouldn't let him throw his career away on account of her, because then he would only end up resenting her the way his father had resented his grandfather. "I'm filing for divorce. So you might as well turn around and get yourself back to the track before it's too late."

"Divorce?" He looked as if she'd smacked him across the face.

"That was the plan in the first place, wasn't it? We make it to November and then we split. So go." She shoved at his chest. "Now."

"Things change. I've changed."

"But I haven't. I'm the same person I was then, Linc. I dress the same and look the same and I want the same things. I can't just change my entire plan because you say you love me."

"How about because *you* love *me*?"

She shook her head "I still won't change it."

But in all honesty, she feared that she would. It would be so easy to give in to the emotion gripping her heart, to throw herself into his arms and forget all about her own hopes and dreams—everything but Linc and the way he made her feel—and beg him to stay. To miss his race.

Too easy.

"I'm not sacrificing my career. I've worked too hard to get to this point, and I want more. I want to go all the way to the top, and that won't happen unless I buckle under now. There's no room for you."

"You're right," he finally said after a long moment.

The words bothered her a lot more than they should have.

"It would never work between us because you won't let it work between us. You're scared."

"I'm not scared of you."

"Not of me, baby." His voice softened. "You're scared of yourself. You've spent your entire life trying to convince everyone you're the opposite of your mother. But truth be known, you're just like her."

She clung to the sudden anger his words stirred and ignored the truth churning in her gut. "I am not."

"You're afraid of commitment."

"I am *not*. Just because I have certain plans for my life doesn't mean I'm afraid to commit."

"That's exactly what it means. Your plans are for shit, just like your Mr. Kaboom is for shit. You'll never find a man who meets all your requirements, which is the point itself. You can pretend that you're open to marriage with the right man, but since he can't possibly come along, then you don't have to put your money where your mouth is." He shook his head. "Don't you know that it's not about *finding* the right guy? It's about taking a chance on him. Trusting him."

Before she could tell him he was even more delusional than her great-uncle Eustess, who stuck green beans in his nose and pretended to be a walrus, Linc leaned down, kissed her roughly on the lips, and then he walked away.

Eve stared at the closed door, her hands trembling and her heart pounding, and barely ignored the urge to go after him. She wouldn't because she wanted him to make the race in Atlanta. Even more, she *was* right. It would never work between them right now. They would each have to give up too much and, in turn, it would undoubtedly lead to resentment later on. She didn't want him to end up resenting her, and she didn't want to resent him. Letting him go was the right thing to do. So why did it suddenly feel so wrong?

Wiping frantically at a flood of hot tears, Eve steeled herself and turned toward her living room. She had to finish the final episode if she intended to stay on schedule and meet next month's deadline and she wasn't going to get any of it done standing around, crying her eyes out like some idiot. She had to get busy. To get back into her groove. To focus.

Unfortunately, the only thing Eve could seem to focus on the rest of the afternoon was the television and the season finale Napa 400, which Jaycee Anderson won in a record-breaking race that undoubtedly had Womanists the world over burning their bras in tribute. She didn't win the overall Cup because her point standing wasn't high enough, but it was a sweet victory nonetheless. The Nextel Cup went to the damned Viagra driver thanks to Linc

Adams and the fact that he'd forfeited everything just to come to L.A. and declare his feelings for Eve. He hadn't hopped a plane back to Atlanta to make the race.

Instead, he'd blown everything in the name of love.

Delusional? He was just plain crazy. The exhaust fumes had finally killed off the majority of his brain cells because he would surely regret it tomorrow.

Chapter 22

She was *not* like her mother.

Eve told herself that over the next several weeks as she stopped crying and started to get mad. Linc Adams had a hell of a nerve telling her she was just like her mother.

She was the polar opposite. She looked different and acted different and she was totally open and receptive to the entire concept of marriage and love and happily ever after.

So that's why you're sitting here on a Saturday night with your computer?

Her gaze shifted to the woman seated across the table from her. While Eve's father had been disappointed with her breakup, her mother had been thrilled and further justified in her firm stand against marriage. She'd started visiting more frequently to bond with her newly single daughter. Tonight, she'd shown up to talk and Eve had been too depressed to shock her into leaving. So they'd both wound up eating grilled cheese sandwiches before pulling out their laptops to work. Same brand, as a matter of fact. Same make and model. Same color—black rather than silver.

Eve forced her attention back to her own screen. She stared at the final cuts on the final boring segment of her documentary and the truth crystallized.

Linc was right. She *was* her mother. She might walk and talk and act differently thanks to a lifetime of training, but deep down, she was the same.

"Why, you're the spitting image of your mother."

On the inside, as well as the outside.

Deep down, she was just as stubborn and as headstrong, and just as terrified to let a man, even a man she loved, close to her.

So terrified, in fact, that she was going through the motions on her project just as her mother would have done—with a serious, thoughtful, boring take on what should have been a fun subject. She feared disappointing the network and killing her future in cable television. Even more, she feared trusting her own instincts. Better to play it safe than take a chance and risk having her dreams crushed.

Likewise, she'd let the only man she'd ever loved walk away from her without so much as a word edgewise. Better to let him walk away than risk a failed relationship.

A failed relationship would confirm her greatest fear— that the Holy Commitment Trinity provided the only recipe for long-term success. While she and Linc had great sex and mutual respect, they didn't have any shared interests. They were polar opposites, in fact, from their upbringings to their professions, to the way they squeezed a tube of toothpaste—Linc from the bottom up while Eve was strictly a middle-type of gal.

All or nothing.

But her mother had all three in her own relationship, and it still wasn't enough to ensure longevity.

Eve closed her eyes as the truth crystallized. The only real recipe for success was trust. Without it, even the Holy Commitment Trinity couldn't endure. Trust was the foundation that the three were built on, and love was the glue that held it all together. Her mother refused to trust her father, and so her own relationship had crumbled.

Her mind rushed back to the delivery room and the way Skye had stared into Clint's eyes and he'd reassured her that she could do it. She'd believed him because she trusted him. Just as Xandra trusted Beau.

But Eve refused to trust Linc, because trusting him meant giving him the power to hurt her.

Or make her incredibly happy.

It hadn't seemed like a risk worth taking. Better to keep her power and control her own happiness.

And how's that working for you?

It wasn't. She had the power to control her own happiness, but there was no happiness to control. She was terribly unhappy. And lonely.

And she was making the man she loved just as unhappy and just as lonely.

"Why, you're the spitting image of your mother."

She closed her laptop and eyed her mother. "You have to get over it, Mom."

"What's that, dear?" Her mother peered at her over the rims of her glasses.

"This thing with Grandpa. You can't keep blaming every man for what Grandpa did to Grandma."

Her mother took off her glasses and turned her full attention to her daughter. "I don't know what you're talking about."

"You're punishing Dad because Grandpa was mean to Grandma."

"I am doing no such thing to your father. I give him plenty of freedom and space."

"That's the punishment. Don't you miss Dad?"

"I'd rather not talk about your father."

"You miss him, but you'd rather miss out on being with him because you're afraid to get too close for fear you'll be stuck like Grandma. Meanwhile, you're punishing Dad. You're hurting him."

"That's nonsense."

"It's true. I know because I'm doing the same thing." She shook her head. "I kissed off Linc for the sake of my career. But it's really not my career that's at stake. It's my heart. All this time, I've convinced myself that I've been afraid to hurt him the way you hurt Dad, when the thing I've really been terrified of is getting hurt. Trusting Linc means giving him the power to hurt me." Her gaze met her mother's. "Or make me the happiest woman alive."

"You should make yourself happy first."

"Being with Linc makes me happy. Loving him makes me happy." She shook her head. "I've totally screwed up my whole life and lost the one thing important to me because I'm afraid to trust him."

On top of that, she was totally screwing her career because she refused to trust herself. She was this close to turning in a documentary that would put even the most boring person to sleep. It had no personality. No oomph. No Eve.

No more.

Her gaze shifted to the rap Betsy had handed her at the fund-raising dinner and an idea struck. At the moment, she wasn't sure how to go about fixing things with Linc. Or if it was even possible.

But she could be true to herself when it came to her project.

"I am *not* afraid to trust," Jacqueline finally declared after the lunch dishes had been cleared and the coffee served the next afternoon. She'd invited her mother to lunch at a small bistro on Rodeo Drive to talk some sense into her regarding the orgasm quest. Instead, she'd spent most of the time eating and thinking about what Eve had said to her. "And I most certainly am not *afraid* of marriage."

"Come again, dear?" Ruella paused, coffee cup in hand.

"I simply don't like marriage. Therefore, I choose not to get married. There's a big difference between being afraid and making a life choice. Why did you marry my father?"

"Because my parents insisted, you know that. I was pregnant and they didn't want the embarrasment."

"Exactly." Jacqueline took a long sip of her coffee. "You would never have married my father if you had had a choice in the matter."

"Actually," she said after a silent moment, "I would have."

"*What?*"

Ruella shrugged. "Marriage was my dream. Heavens, it was the dream of most girls my age. Sure, a few had aspirations of becoming teachers and nurses, but for the most part, those were unreachable expectations to someone like me. I had never been very good in school and so college wasn't even a consideration. Not to mention, my family didn't have much money. For me, it was all about having a family of my own. Your father seemed like a good enough person to do so with, otherwise, I never would have slept with him. So if he had asked me and I hadn't been pregnant, yes, I would have agreed without any coercion. I didn't realize what sort of man he was until it was too late."

"And then you were stuck because of a piece of paper." Jacqueline motioned to the waiter for a refill before meeting her mother's gaze.

Ruella's eyes glittered with a sad light. "I was stuck because I didn't have the courage to leave." She touched Jacqueline's hand. "I should have, but I simply couldn't."

"Out of fear for your life."

"Out of fear of being alone." She gave Jacqueline's hand a final pat before pulling away. "My parents wouldn't have taken me back into their home, so I would have been on my own, and I just didn't think I could do it. I was a coward. A weak, stupid coward." She closed her eyes for a long moment as she cradled her coffee cup. "But we all have to face our fears sooner or later," she said when she finally opened her eyes. "I refused to face mine, so the Powers That Be took the choice out of my hands. Your father died and suddenly, I was on my own." She smiled. "But you know what? It wasn't nearly as bad as what I had feared."

"What are you saying, Mother?"

"That you can't live your life being afraid. Donovan is a good man. A patient man. A loving man. He's not your father. Give him a chance. Give yourself a chance. Don't wait until it's too late and you're too old to make up for lost time."

"I take it the orgasm quest isn't going as planned?"

"I've had more excitement watching the National Chess Classic."

"Maybe you're trying too hard."

"And maybe I'm just too old."

"Nonsense. You're an exciting, vibrant woman. What's more, you're strong, Mother." Her gaze locked with Ruella's and she saw the doubt swimming in the older woman's eyes. "I know all the things that my father used to say to you, about you, but he was wrong, Mother. You're strong and brave and beautiful, and any man would be lucky to have the chance to give you an orgasm."

"You really think so?"

"I know so." At that moment, her cell phone rang. It was Alexis, undoubtedly eager to know why she wasn't at the studio. She stood and reached for her briefcase. "Speaking of orgasms, I've got a production meeting in fifteen minutes for tomorrow's show on the newest sex toys for women—we're featuring Xandra's company—so I have to run. I'll see you tonight."

"So you're going to stop all this nonsense and come back to the apartment?"

"Let's hope."

It wasn't going to happen.

The realization sank in as Ruella stared at Harvey Wallcrest, the latest in her orgasm search. He sat in the living room, his eyes closed, a snore flaring his nostrils. She'd left him to retrieve a platter of strawberries, chocolate sauce, and sugar-free whipped cream. He'd been cute and charming and she'd actually felt her pulse flutter when he'd kissed her hand.

But now he was sleeping.

"You're strong and brave and beautiful, and any man would be lucky to have the chance to give you an orgasm."

Jacqueline's words echoed in Ruella's ears and where she'd told herself as much the past few months, she'd never actually believed it until she'd heard her daughter say the words and truly mean them.

She eyed Harvey and frowned.

She knew she looked nice for her age. She'd highlighted her silvery hair and had it cut into a stylish bob that swayed when she walked. *And* she wore her new burnt orange pantsuit, complete with matching lipstick—a color guaranteed to light any man's fire.

Any man under the age of seventy-five.

It was Harvey. He was the dud.

Suddenly Ruella wasn't half as worried about having an orgasm with a man as she was about having a bad orgasm. Maybe fantasizing about wild, hot passionate sex wasn't all that bad a thing. Not at her age.

"Harvey." She tapped his shoulder. "Wake up."

"Are we doing it yet?"

"Not yet." *Not ever.*

The quest was over and Ruella Farrel was going home.

"Okay," came the familiar female voice when Donovan Martin picked up the telephone and said hello.

"Who is this?"

"The Queen of England. Who do you think it is?"

"Hello to you, too, Jacqueline. I would love to talk, but I'm going to a seminar at the University of California. It's a special presentation on redwood trees and the threat to their survival. Maybe we can chat later—"

"Didn't you hear me? I said okay. I'll do it."

"Do what?"

"You know what."

"It's been so long. I'm not so sure that I do."

"I'll . . ."

"Yes?"

"I'll . . . marry you," she finally finished. "There. You get your way."

"I'm not so sure I want my way. Being apart has helped me evaluate my position, and I think I like being single."

"What?"

"I've got the freedom to come and go as I please. I wouldn't want to jeopardize that by tying myself down to one person for the rest of my life."

"You're not funny."

"I'm not trying to be. It's about freedom, isn't it? You don't want to give up yours and so you don't want to marry me."

"It's not about freedom," she admitted. "It's about trust, and if you say I told you so, I'm going to hang up this phone and you can just go marry some redwood tree specialist."

"If I didn't know better, I would say you were jealous."

"I am not jealous. I am, however, extremely tired of all this." She fell silent and he knew the next words were hard for her. "I miss you, Donovan. And I love you. And I need you. And if you tell anyone, I'll hunt you down myself."

He laughed. "You won't have far to go. I'll pick you up in five minutes."

"Linc, you're the favorite to walk away with the Winston Cup this year, particularly now that you've won the Daytona 500. But you were in the same position last year, and you blew it on the last race three months ago in Atlanta. What's to say it won't happen again?"

Linc stood behind the podium at the press conference following the new season opener. He thought about smiling and giving the reporter some spiel about how he was too much man for one woman—the story Danielle had carefully devised over the past three months since November to boost his bad-boy image and reaffirm his bachelor status. Instead, he shrugged. "I had personal matters to deal with."

"Running for the mayor of Adams, Georgia?"

"That, and other things, and so it just wasn't meant to be last year."

"And this year?" the reporter pressed. "You lost the election, so you don't have to worry about doing double duty. It seems you could have a winning season if you give it your all."

"We'll have to wait and see."

"Any comment about the breakup of your marriage?" another reporter called out.

"Some things just don't work out as planned. It happens."

"So why haven't you filed for divorce?" another voice called out.

"I don't think that's any of your business."

"Is it because you still love her?" yet another voice called out.

"Again, that's none—," he started before his gaze found the source of the question.

An attractive blonde wearing a black leather miniskirt and a black Linc Adams T-shirt stood up. She wore a minimal amount of makeup, her full lips a soft pink. She had high cheekbones and a small nose with three freckles sprinkled across the top. Familiar green eyes gazed back at him.

"Do you?" she asked him again.

"As a matter of fact, I do."

Her eyes glimmered with what looked like joy before the emotion faded and her expression turned exasperated. "Then why don't you tell her?"

"I already did, but it didn't seem to make a difference. She didn't love me."

She looked sad for a moment before she stiffened. "Maybe she did, but she was too scared to tell you. Maybe you were right about her. Maybe she was afraid to commit."

"Was she?"

She licked her lips and it was all he could do not to climb over the podium and haul her into his arms. But he needed to know that this wasn't one of the wild and crazy dreams he'd had over the past few months. He needed to know that it was real.

That she was real.

His fingers balled into fists and he waited.

"Yes," she finally said. "Then."

"And now?"

"She's still scared. But she's more afraid of *not* committing."

"Why?"

"Because she loves you." She licked her lips again. "I love you."

The words sang through his head and he reached her in a few swift strides. He kissed her then, hard and hot and hungry at first. And then slow and sweet and thorough before he finally pulled away and stared down at her.

The room went crazy around them. People hooted and hollered. Cameras flashed and video cams rolled.

But Linc didn't care about any of it. His attention fixed on the woman in his arms. The woman smiling up at him. The woman who loved him as much as he loved her.

"You know, I think it might be a pretty good year, after all."

"Pretty good? I expect fantastic, buddy," Eve told him. "And I expect it for a hell of a lot longer than a year. Try the next sixty."

"Are you trying to scare me off?"

"Is it working?"

"No."

"Good. Because I'm serious. I'm not scared anymore of turning into my mother or being with you or making a total flop of a documentary. In fact, I'm not making documentaries, at all."

"They didn't like it?"

"They loved it, but it wasn't a documentary. I created a fictitious character who writes breakup cards. Sophie Martin, creator and poet behind Ode to a Toad Breakup cards. She's single and successful and a generation seXer. The series follows her through twelve different story lines all centered around sex and its changing role in her generation. It's informative without being preachy, and funny and sexy, and they loved it. So much, in fact, that they want to turn it into an actual series."

"That's great."

"Thanks to your sister. Her raps inspired the whole greeting card thing. Look, I know that greeting cards and sex and my try-anything-once attitude is so totally different from you and your driving and your whole conservative upbringing. And while I have decided to reexplore my blond roots and settle down some, I can't promise that I won't wear sexy clothes. Or get a tattoo. Or have something pierced. I might not be as wild and bold as I pretend to be for my mother, but I do like being different."

"I like you because you're different. I don't want you to change, Eve. I fell in love with you, and I'll keep loving you."

"Despite what your family may think?"

"They're my family and I love them, but I don't have to please them. I never will, and that's okay. The only person I want to please is you."

"Through sickness and health?"

"I do."

"Through bad hair days and good ones?"

"I do."

"Through good times and PMS hell?"

"I'll have to think about that one." She punched him and he smiled. "Through good times and PMS hell," he vowed, planting a kiss on the tip of her nose. "From this day forward. Till death do us part."

"I do," she murmured, and then she kissed him.

Epilogue

"If I could have everyone's attention," the disc jockey's voice boomed over the PA system set up in the far corner of the large observation deck at the Lake Sonoma Winery.

Banquet tables draped in crisp white linen filled the rest of the space that overlooked the beautiful countryside of Dry Creek Valley. A crescent moon hung in the clear sky, surrounded by twinkling stars. Candles floated in giant crystal bowls at the center of each table, giving the entire place a fairy-tale-like aura. It was the perfect place for a wedding.

A double wedding.

Ruella watched as Eve, clad in a floor-length, fitted white gown walked hand in hand with Linc toward the center of the dance floor. He wore a black tuxedo and a huge smile. A round of applause erupted for the attractive couple, followed by a quiet hush as everyone waited for Jacqueline and Donovan to give up their seats at a nearby table.

Ruella's gaze shifted to her daughter as she unfolded

herself from a chair. She wore her no-nonsense signature beige, her dress a floor-length satin shift with a matching blazer. It was simple. Too simple for a wedding, in Ruella's opinion. Even so, Jacqueline had never looked more beautiful. Where her dress lacked sparkle, her eyes more than made up for it.

Now, that is.

Before the ceremony, however, she'd been a nervous wreck. Thank heavens the event had been held at a winery. While Eve had chosen the winery for sentimental reasons— she'd first met Linc at nearby Sears Point Raceway— Jacqueline had agreed because of the wine. She'd been nervous enough about marrying Donovan, and so she'd jumped at the chance to have several thousand bottles of courage on hand. Just in case.

"Each of the happy couples will share their first dance as husband and wife," the disc jockey went on.

Jacqueline's smile dissolved and she disengaged herself from Donovan's arms and approached the music setup. She whispered a few quick words that wiped the smile from the disc jockey's face before turning and walking back toward her new husband.

"That is, each of the happy couples," the disc jockey hurried on, "will now share their first dance as two, um, equal, independent partners fully capable of making separate, independent choices." The young man paused, his gaze going to Jacqueline, who nodded and urged him on. "Despite," he continued, "the fact that they've signed their names to a legal document that often tries to hinder such choices."

Laughter echoed around the room and Ruella glanced toward a nearby banquet table where Skye, who wore a leopard-print bridesmaid dress, sat next to Clint. The one-year-old twins bounced on their laps and clapped excitedly. Across the table, Xandra, looking beautiful and vivacious despite the same outlandish dress, sat next to Beau, who cuddled his sleeping four-month-old daughter in his strong arms. A tiny crown of baby's breath sat on the infant girl's head.

Ruella's gaze shifted back to the dance floor and Eve and Linc, who smiled at each other. Nearby, Donovan stared deep into his wife's eyes, as if oblivious to the cameras and the hundred-and-fifty-plus guests that overflowed the observation deck. Ruella watched as her son-in-law touched his lips to Jacqueline's and warmth filled the old woman's heart.

It seemed as if her entire family had each found their own happy ending. Finally. Thankfully.

The knowledge helped to ease the sudden surge of regret that washed through her because she still often found herself wondering what it might be like to meet her own special someone. To feel her heart flutter and her palms sweat. A *what if* that never failed to sneak into her thoughts when she was just getting into *Wheel of Fortune,* or about to shout a loud *Bingo!* at Seniors' Night.

Not that she gave it *too* much thought. She'd found peace and contentment in her own life and that was enough.

Champagne sparkled from the glass in front of her and she reached for the bubbly. She'd just taken a sip when she heard the deep voice.

"May I?"

Her gaze shifted to the old man who stood behind the seat next to her. He was average height, his snow-white hair a dark contrast to the black suit jacket he wore with matching trousers. A crisp white shirt and a black bow tie completed the outfit. He had pale blue eyes partially hidden behind a pair of wire-framed glasses. The faint scent of Old Spice filled her nostrils.

He wasn't particularly attractive, but he certainly wasn't ugly, either. He was average. Ho-hum. But her stomach flipped anyway when he smiled at her and revealed a row of straight white teeth.

"Is this seat taken?" he asked when she simply stared up at him.

"I, um, no," she finally said when she realized that she'd been staring at him. "Help yourself. I'm Ruella Farrel . . . Jacqueline's mother."

"Eve's grandmother," he added. "I would have known you anywhere. She's the spitting image of you." He pulled back the chair and set his cake plate down on the table.

"The spitting image about fifty years ago."

"Nonsense. You don't look a day over twenty-nine."

"Now I know why you're wearing glasses."

He grinned. "I'm Wilbur Wilkie," he said as he slid into the seat next to her. "I live in Eve's apartment building." His arm brushed Ruella's and heat sizzled along her nerve endings as he leaned in closer, as if to whisper some torrid secret. "But I'm not just her neighbor. We're practically family."

"You're related to Linc?"

"My blue heeler was romantically involved with her labradoodle. Damned mess, it was. Seems Eve had no clue that my Lady and the Tramp was a male. Meanwhile, I had no clue that Killer hadn't been fixed. Why, they took to each other like flies to a fresh-baked apple pie."

"I see."

"Can't say as I blame them, what with spending all that time together. A man can get mighty lonely with nothing but *Wheel of Fortune* to keep him company in the evenings."

Ruella turned a surprised look on him. "You like *Wheel of Fortune*?"

"It's my favorite show." He flashed her another grin before reaching for his punch. His strong hands cradled the cup and a thrill danced up her spine.

Ruella stiffened. A thrill? Why, she was much too old for such a thing. She'd come to that conclusion months ago. Her gaze hooked on his mouth as he took a bite of his cake. He had really nice lips. Strong. Not too thick. Not too skinny. Inviting, even.

Awareness skittered through her and she drew a deep, shaky breath. All right, so she was old. She wasn't dead. Not yet.

"I, um." She cleared her throat as he turned those pale eyes on her. *Come on, old girl. You can do this.* "Are you by any chance married, Mr. Wilkie?"

"Widowed."

"Seeing someone?"

He grinned and caught her gaze. "Only you."

Ruella smiled. Why, she just might get her own happy ending, after all.

About the Author

Award-winning author Kimberly Raye lives deep in the heart of the Texas Hill Country with her very own cowboy, Curt, and their young children. She's an incurable romantic who loves Diet Dr Pepper, chocolate, Toby Keith, chocolate, alpha males, and chocolate. Kim loves to hear from readers. You can visit her on-line at *www.kimberlyraye.com* or *www.gotsexauthors.com,* or write to her c/o Warner Books, 1271 Avenue of the Americas, New York, NY 10020.